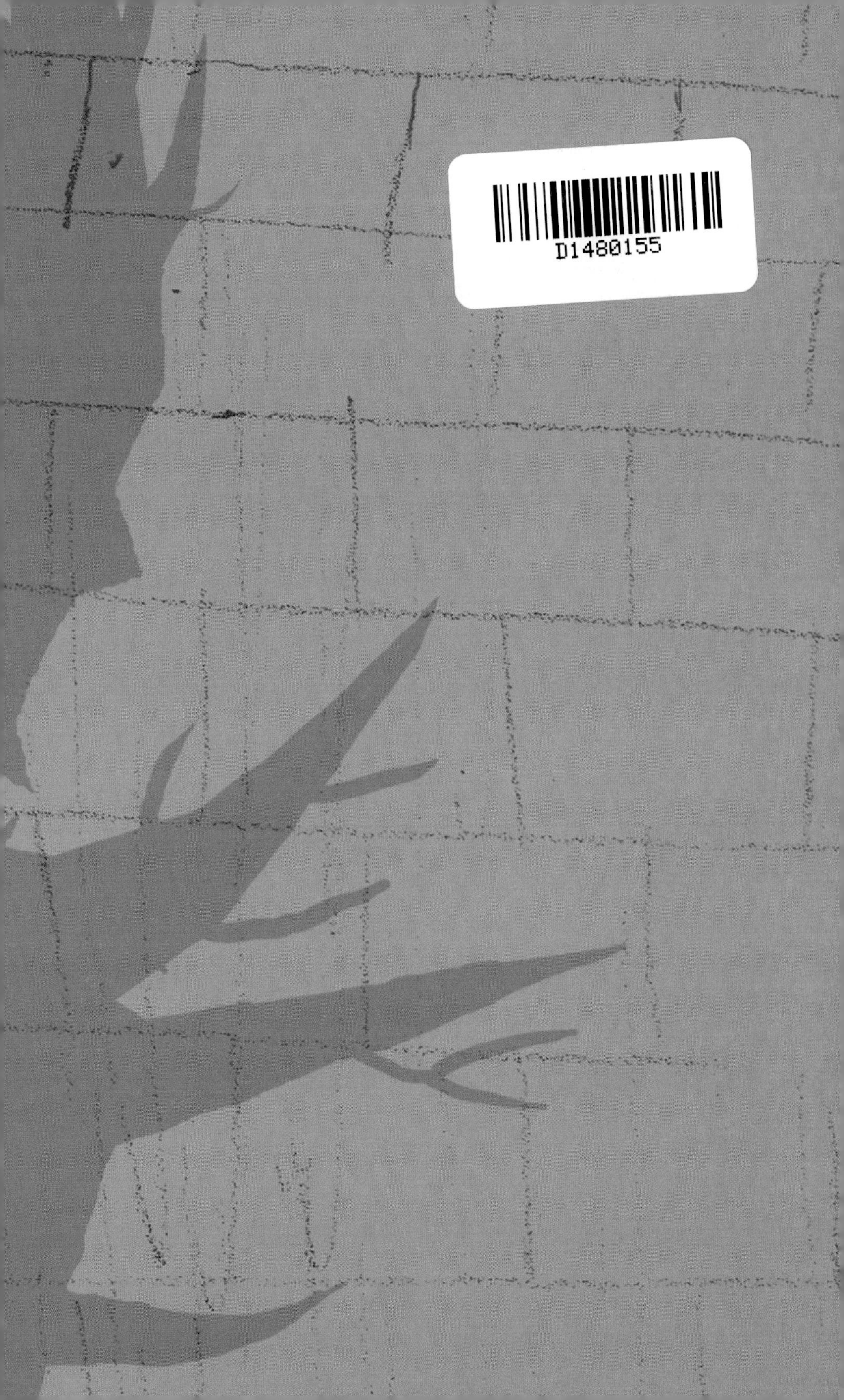

KARIM FRIHA

RISE OF THE ZELPHIRE

Book One: Of Bark and Sap

Written and Illustrated
by
Karim Friha

Translation by Jeremy Melloul
Localization, Layout, and Editing by Mike Kennedy

LION FORGE™ MAGNETIC™

ISBN: 978-1-942367-73-4

Library of Congress Control Number: 2018962939

Rise of the Zelphire, Volume 1, published 2019 by The Lion Forge, LLC.
Originally published in French under the following title: *Le Réveil du Zelphire*

10 9 8 7 6 5 4 3 2 1

Thank you
to Joann and Thierry for their trust, and
to Lena, my parents, and friends for their encouragement and precious help.

— Karim Friha

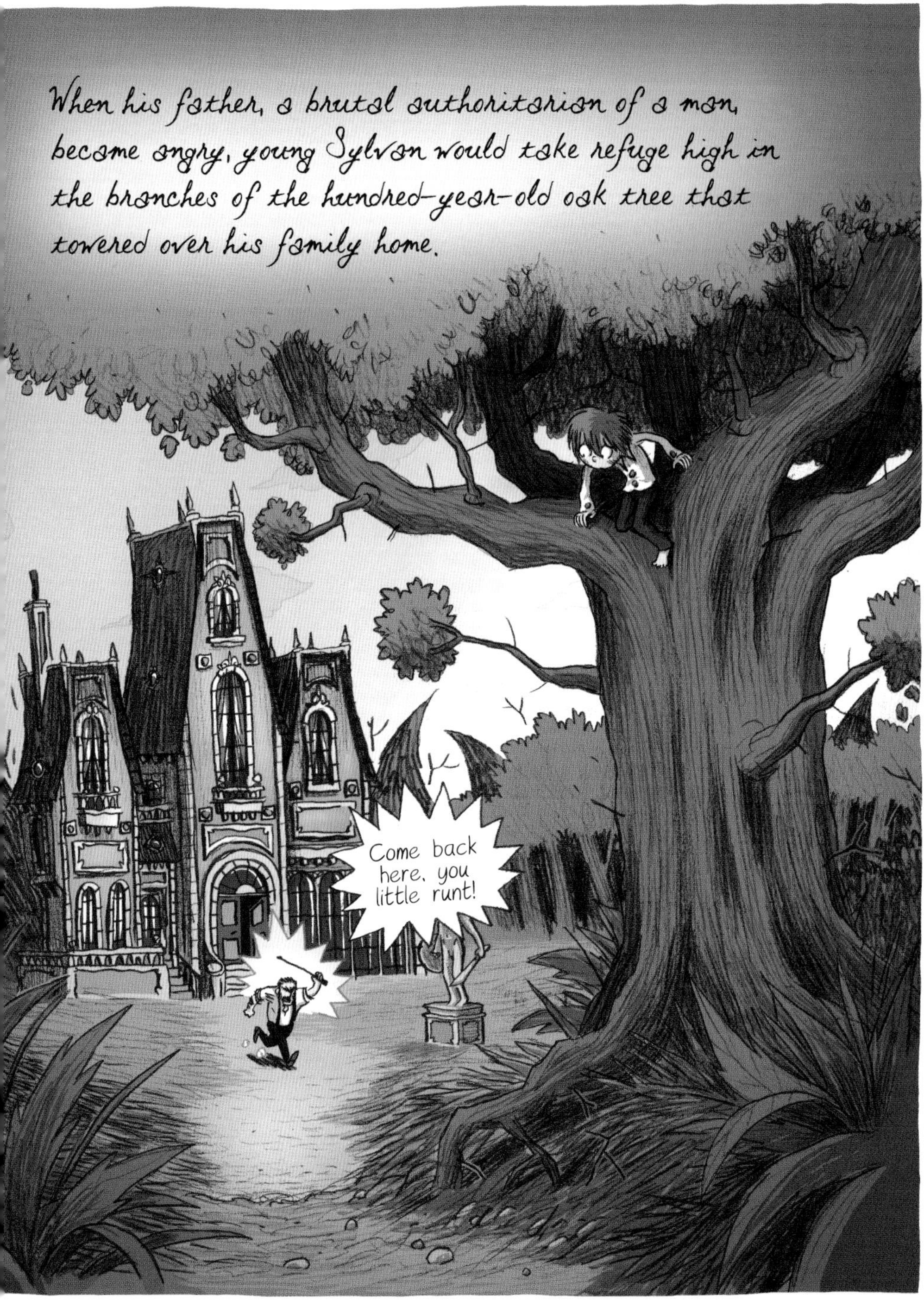
When his father, a brutal authoritarian of a man, became angry, young Sylvan would take refuge high in the branches of the hundred-year-old oak tree that towered over his family home.
Come back here, you little runt!

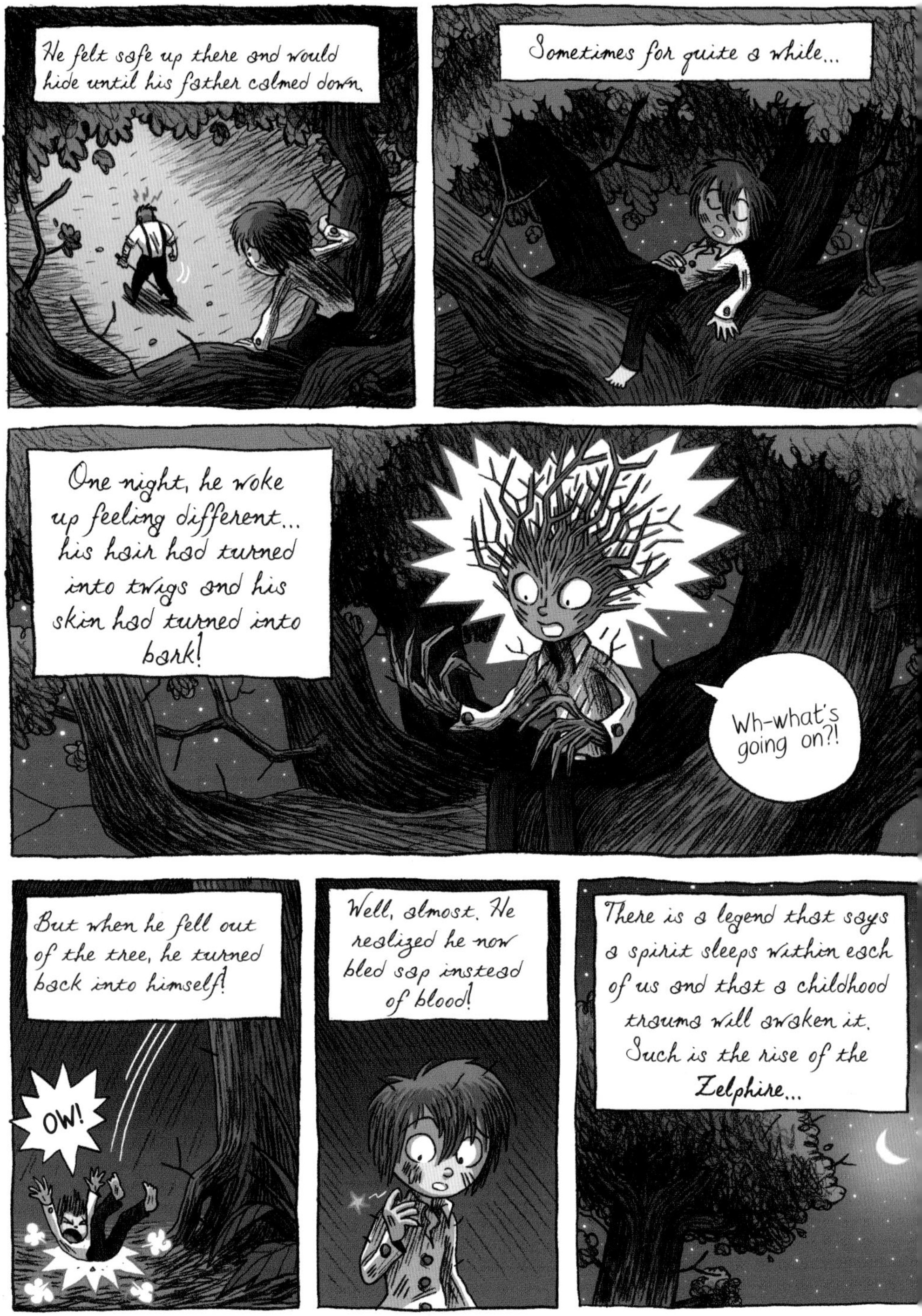
He felt safe up there and would hide until his father calmed down.
Sometimes for quite a while...
One night, he woke up feeling different... his hair had turned into twigs and his skin had turned into bark!
Wh-what's going on?!
But when he fell out of the tree, he turned back into himself!
OW!
Well, almost. He realized he now bled sap instead of blood!
There is a legend that says a spirit sleeps within each of us and that a childhood trauma will awaken it. Such is the rise of the Zelphire...

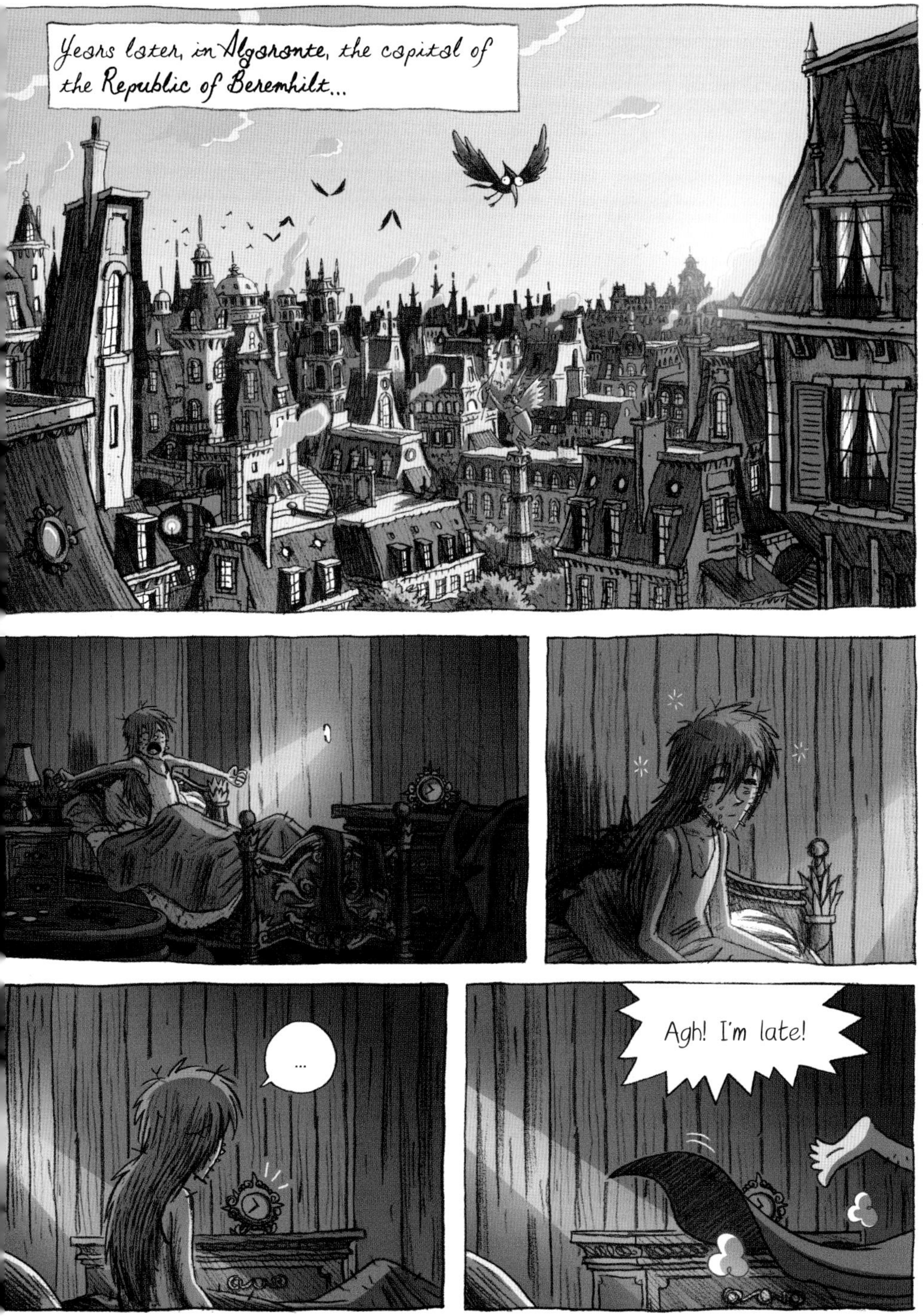
Years later, in Algaronte, the capital of the Republic of Beremhilt...
...
Agh! I'm late!

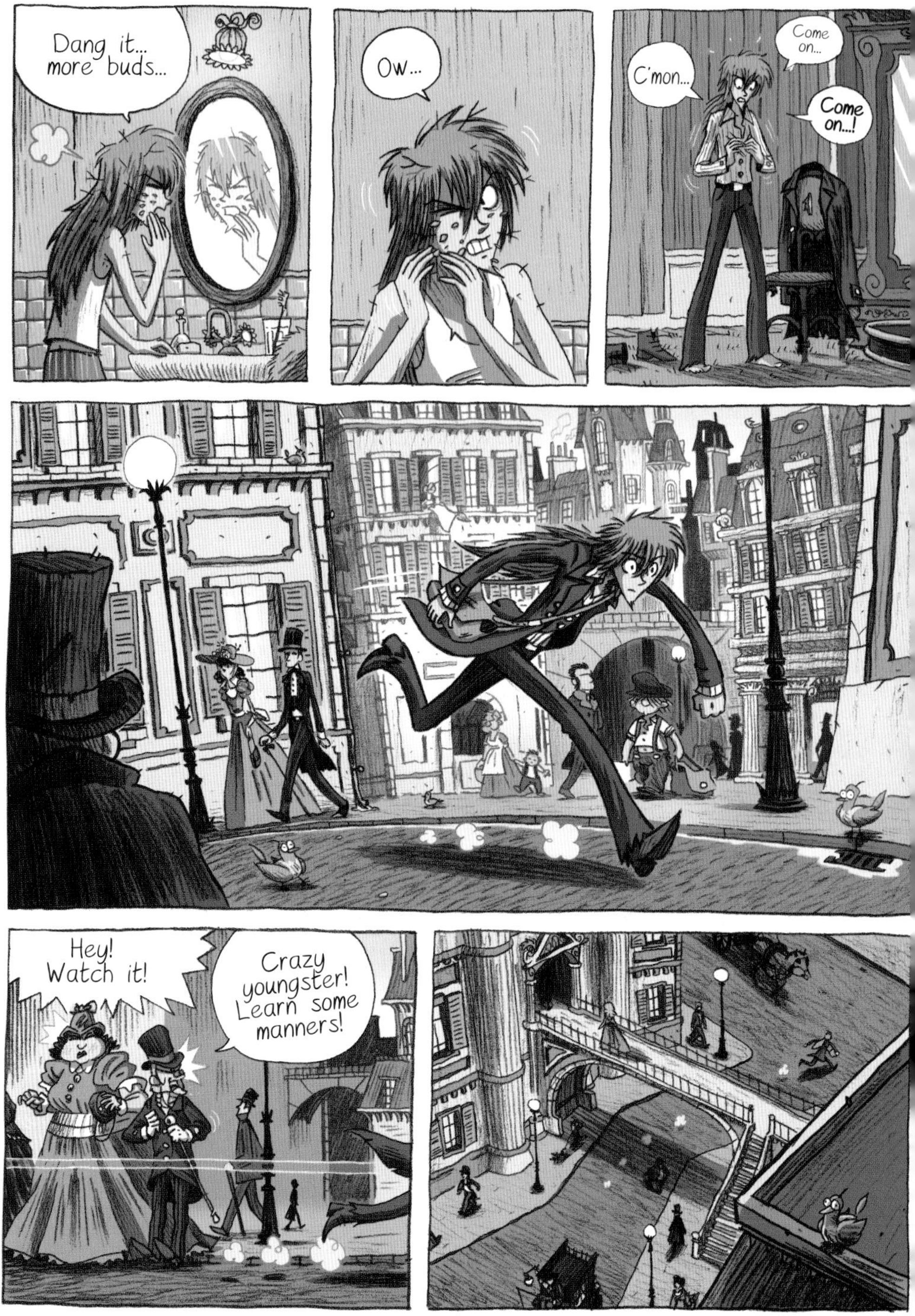
Dang it... more buds...
Ow...
C'mon...
Come on...
Come on...!
Hey! Watch it!
Crazy youngster! Learn some manners!

ycads /ˈsaɪkædz/ are seed plants with a long fossil history that were formerly more abundant and more diverse than they are today. They have a sto...

Cycads are gymnosperms (naked seeded) meaning their unfertilized seeds are open to the air to be directly fertilized by pollination, contrasted with...

...his neurotoxin may enter a sort of human food chain as the cycad toxin seeds may be eaten directly as a source of flour by humans or by feral animals such as b...

Sylvan Khelmann!

This is the third time this week you've been late... and it's only Tuesday!

I'll never understand why Professor Wernes agreed to your request...

...despite my objections...

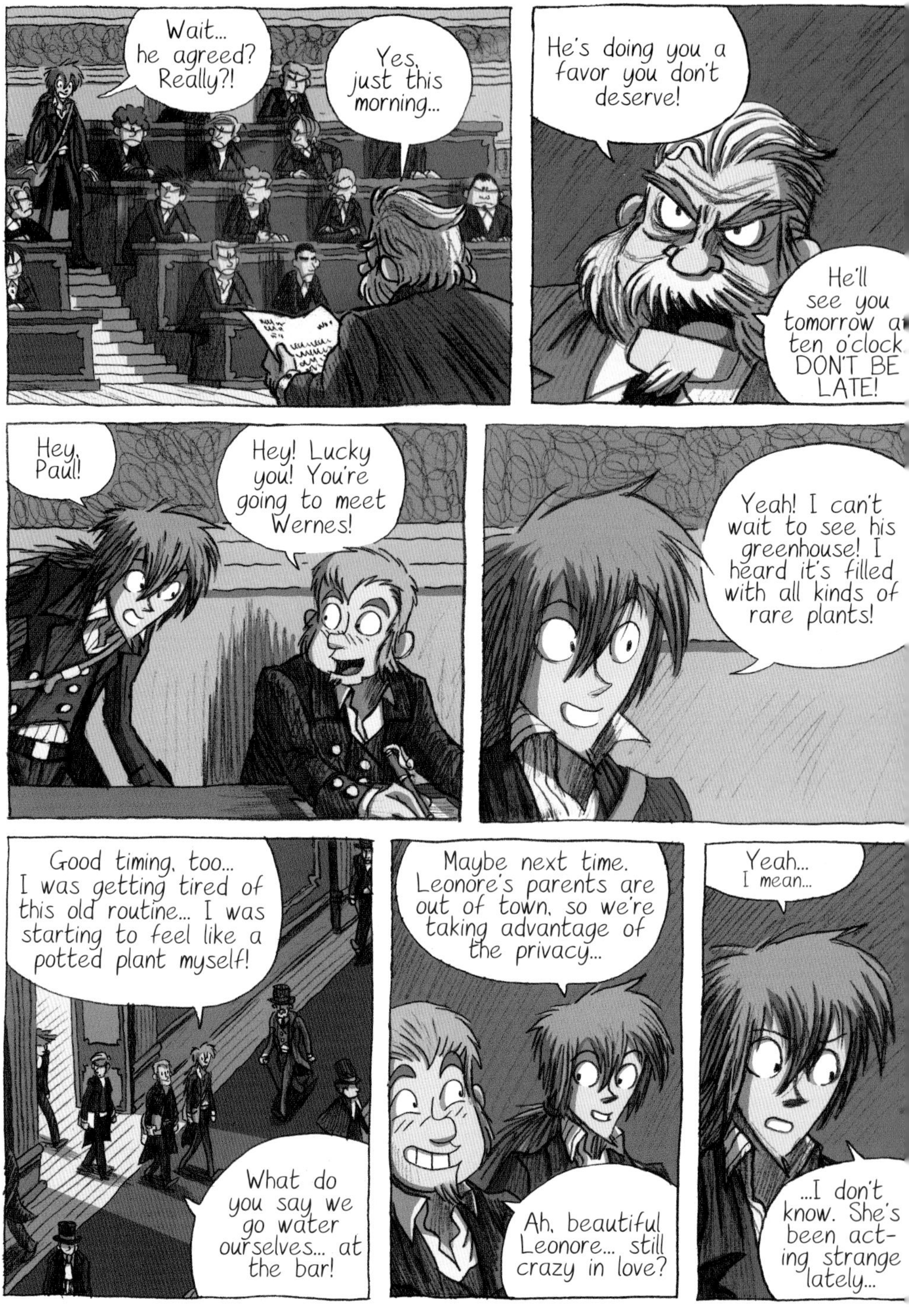
Wait... he agreed? Really?!
Yes, just this morning...
He's doing you a favor you don't deserve!
He'll see you tomorrow at ten o'clock DON'T BE LATE!
Hey, Paul!
Hey! Lucky you! You're going to meet Wernes!
Yeah! I can't wait to see his greenhouse! I heard it's filled with all kinds of rare plants!
Good timing, too... I was getting tired of this old routine... I was starting to feel like a potted plant myself!
What do you say we go water ourselves... at the bar!
Maybe next time. Leonore's parents are out of town, so we're taking advantage of the privacy...
Ah, beautiful Leonore... still crazy in love?
Yeah... I mean...
...I don't know. She's been acting strange lately...

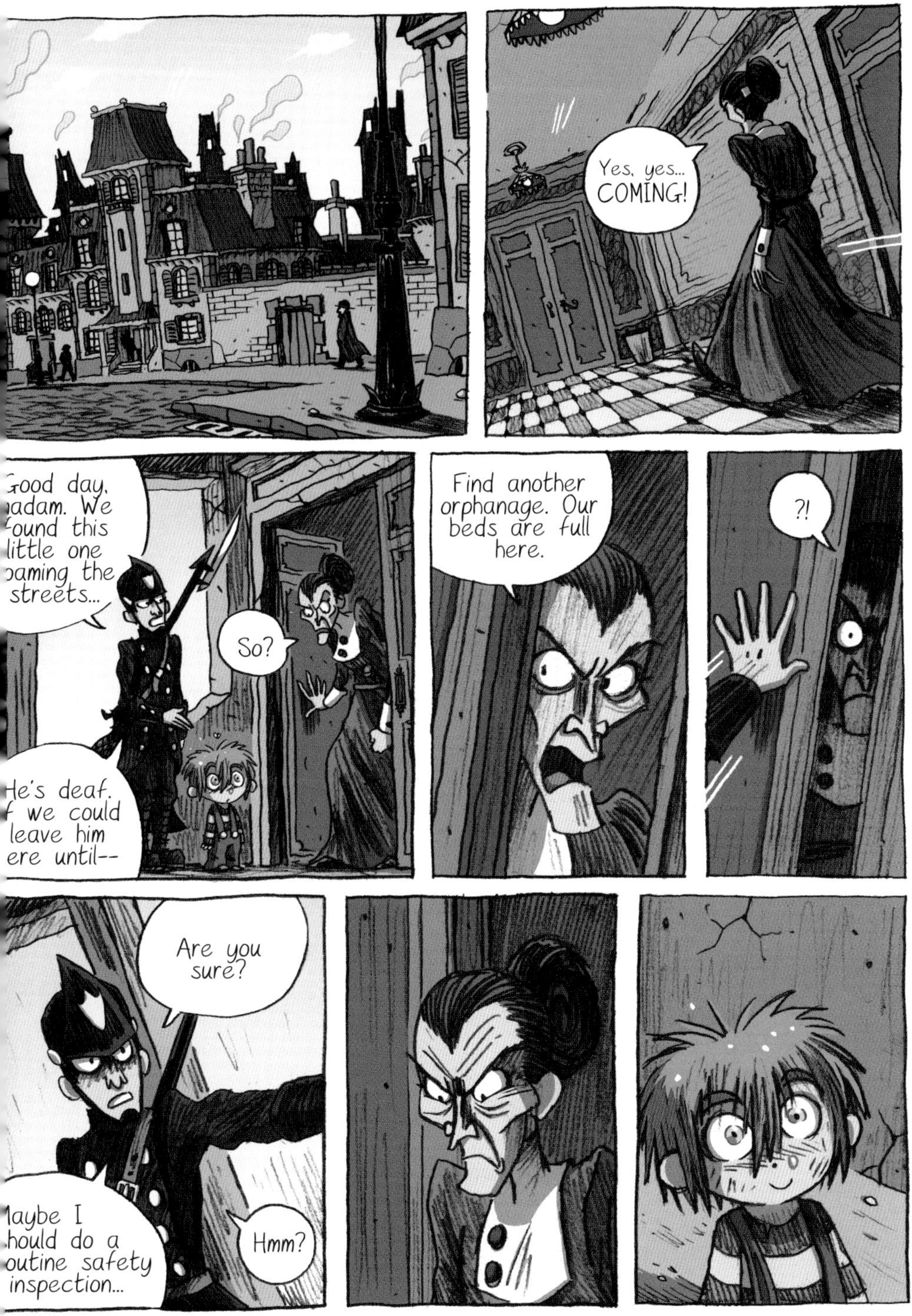
Yes, yes...
COMING!
Good day, adam. We ound this little one oaming the streets...
So?
He's deaf. f we could leave him ere until--
Find another orphanage. Our beds are full here.
?!
Are you sure?
Hmm?
laybe I hould do a outine safety inspection...

Welcome!

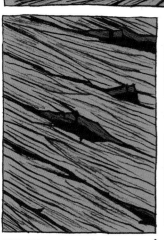

?

OW!
Leave me
alone!

Stop!
AHHH!

OW!

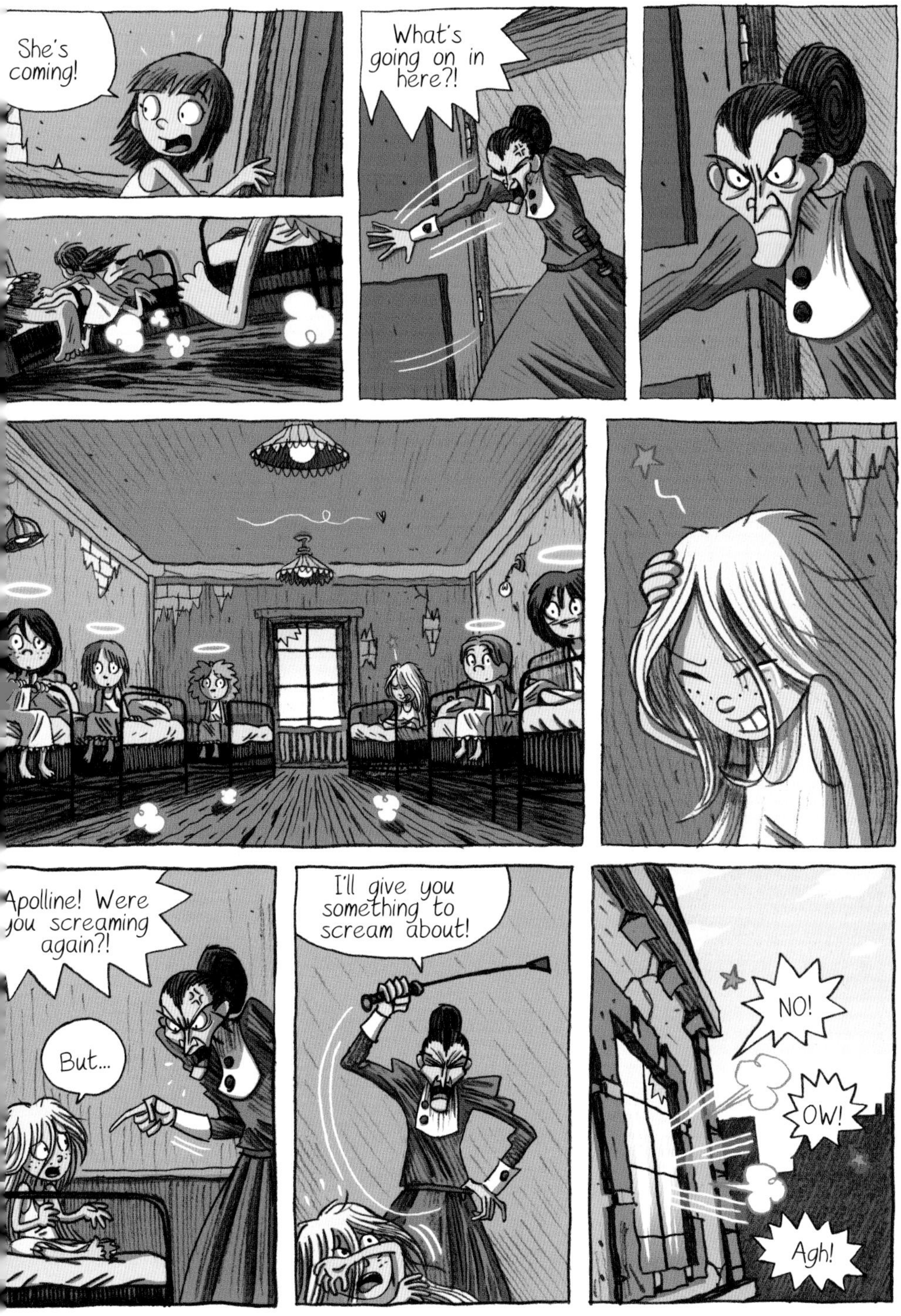
She's coming!
What's going on in here?!
Apolline! Were you screaming again?!
But...
I'll give you something to scream about!
NO!
OW!
Agh!

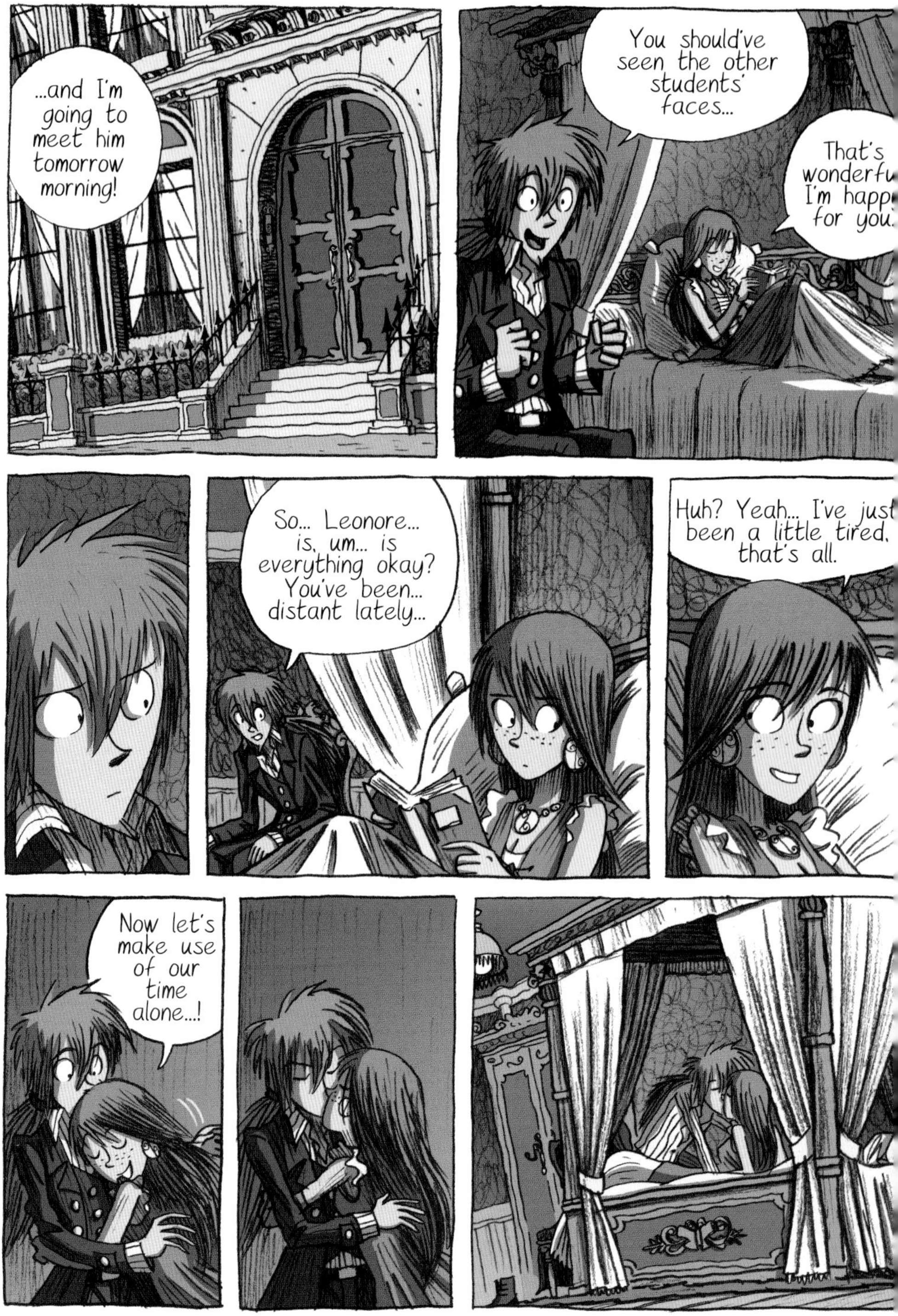
...and I'm going to meet him tomorrow morning!
You should've seen the other students' faces...
That's wonderfu
I'm happ
for you.
So... Leonore... is, um... is everything okay? You've been... distant lately...
Huh? Yeah... I've just been a little tired, that's all.
Now let's make use of our time alone...!

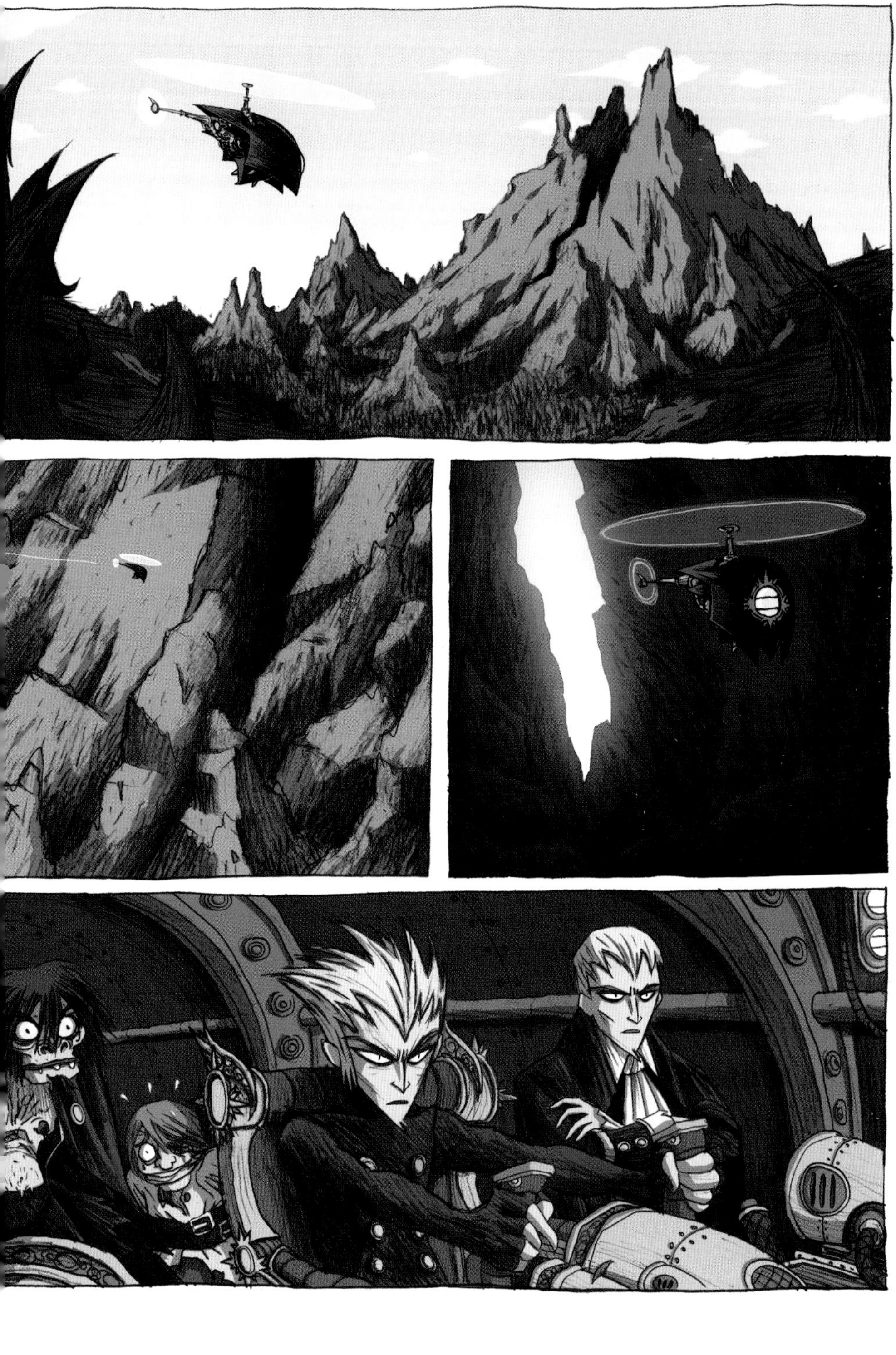

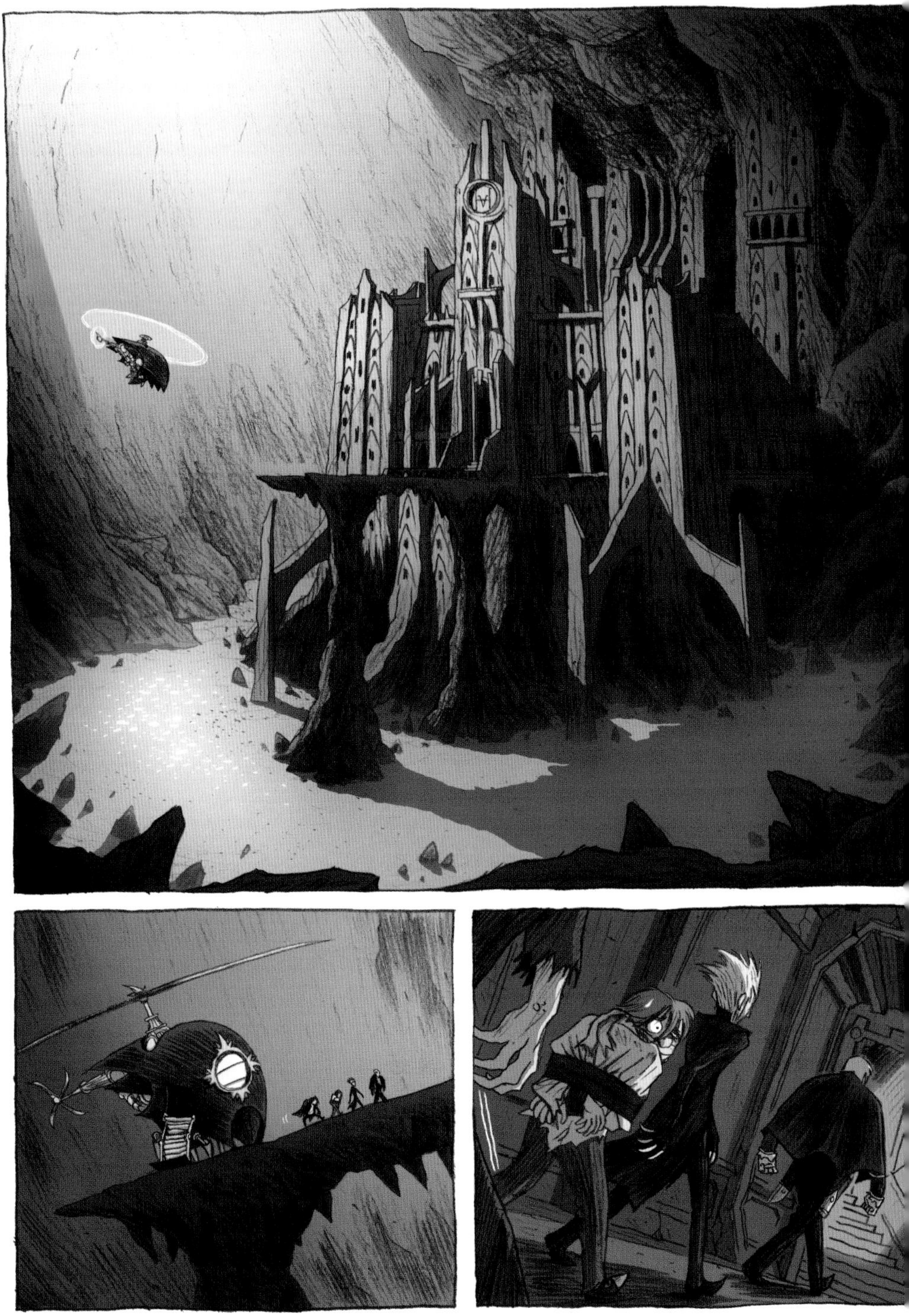

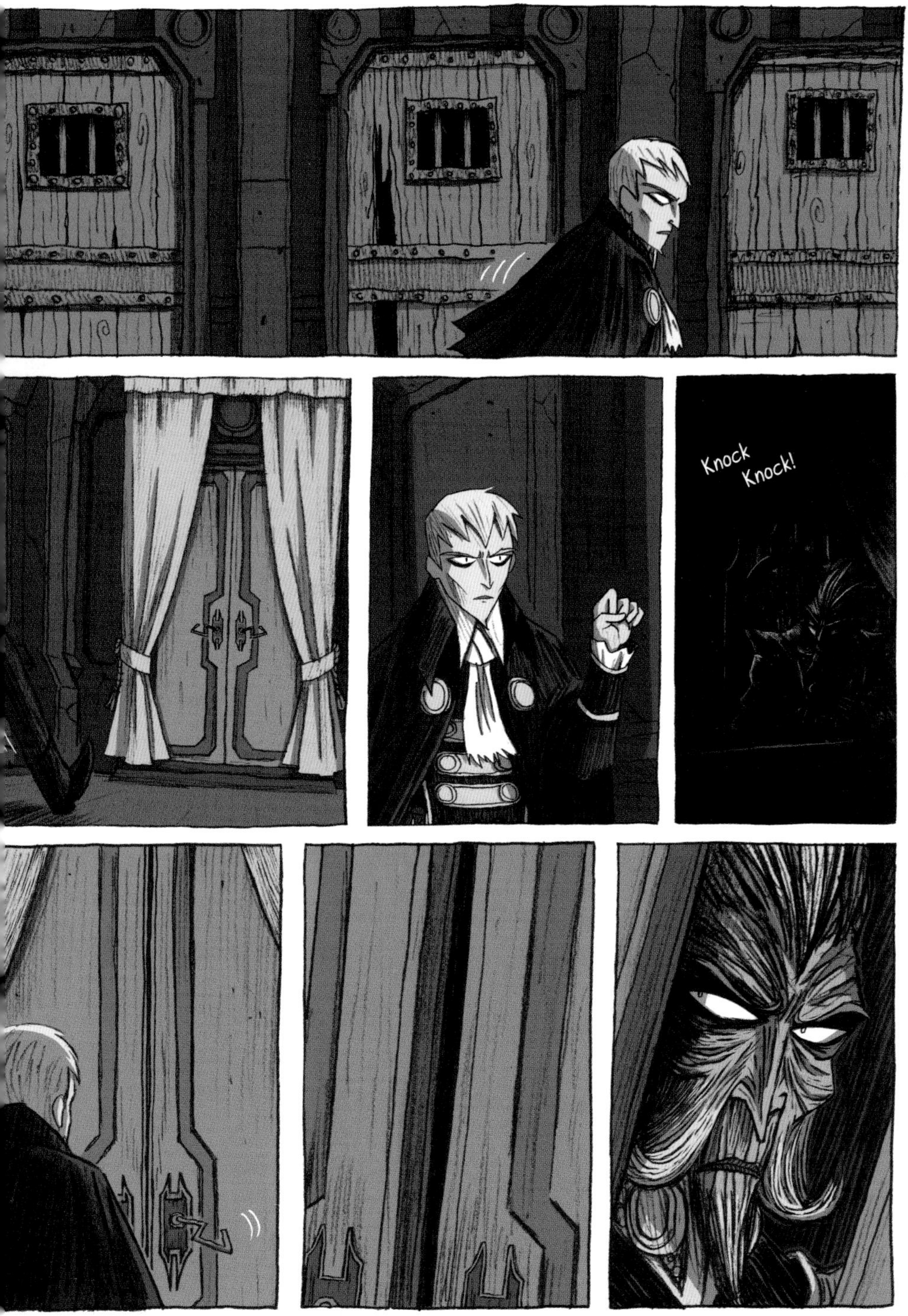
Knock
Knock!

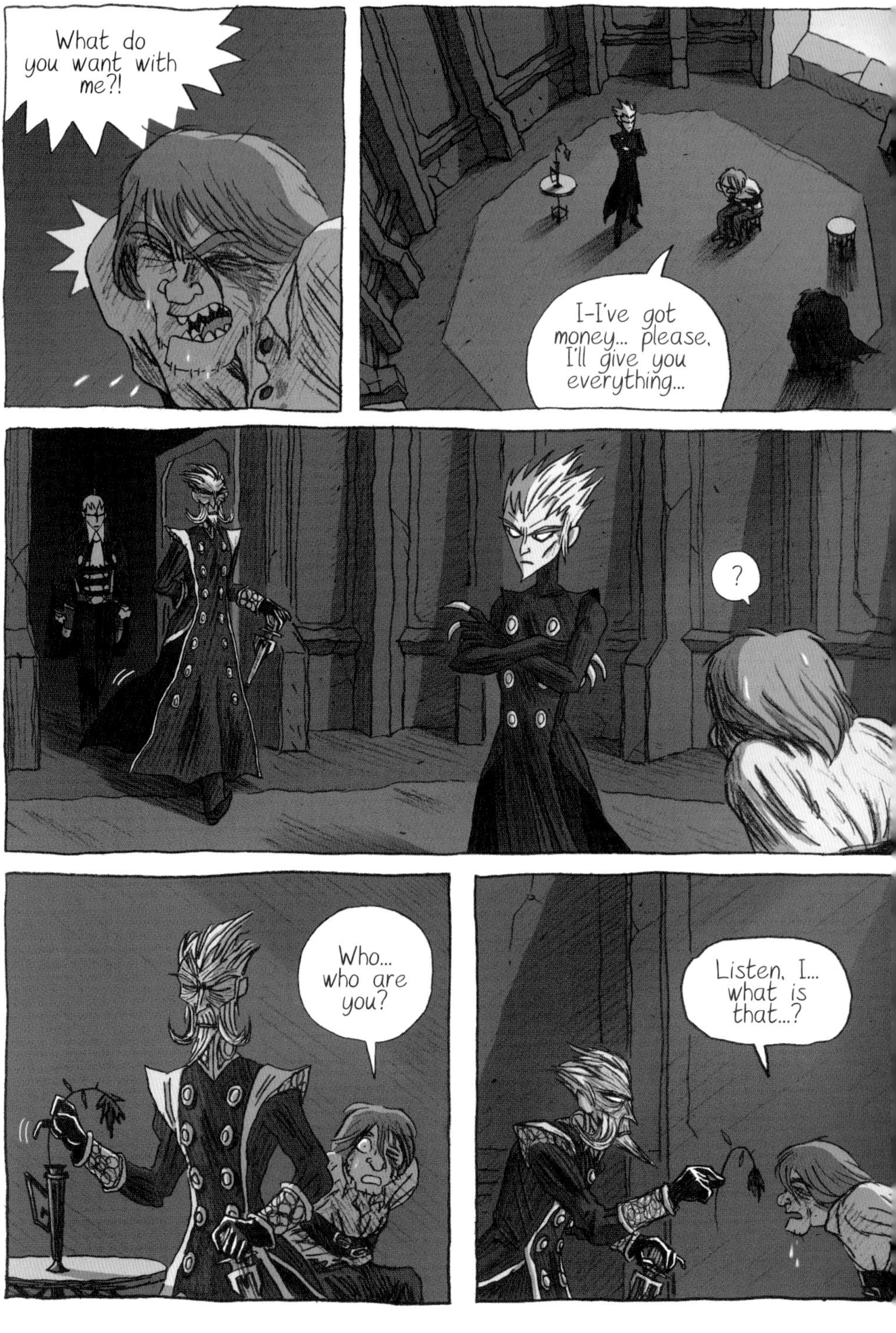
What do you want with me?!
I-I've got money... please. I'll give you everything...
?
Who... who are you?
Listen, I... what is that...?

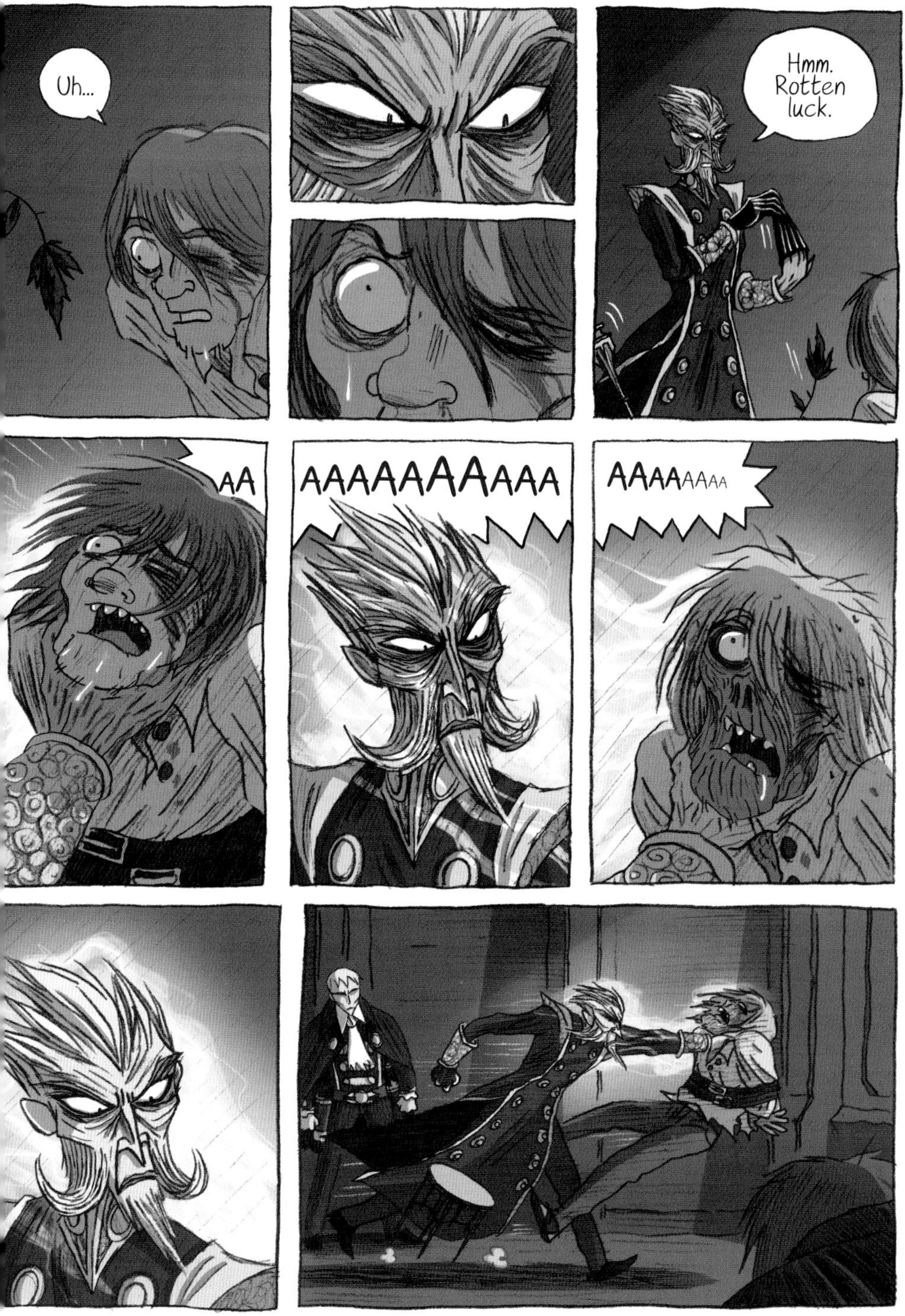
Uh...
Hmm. Rotten luck.
AA
AAAAAAAAAAA
AAAAAAAA

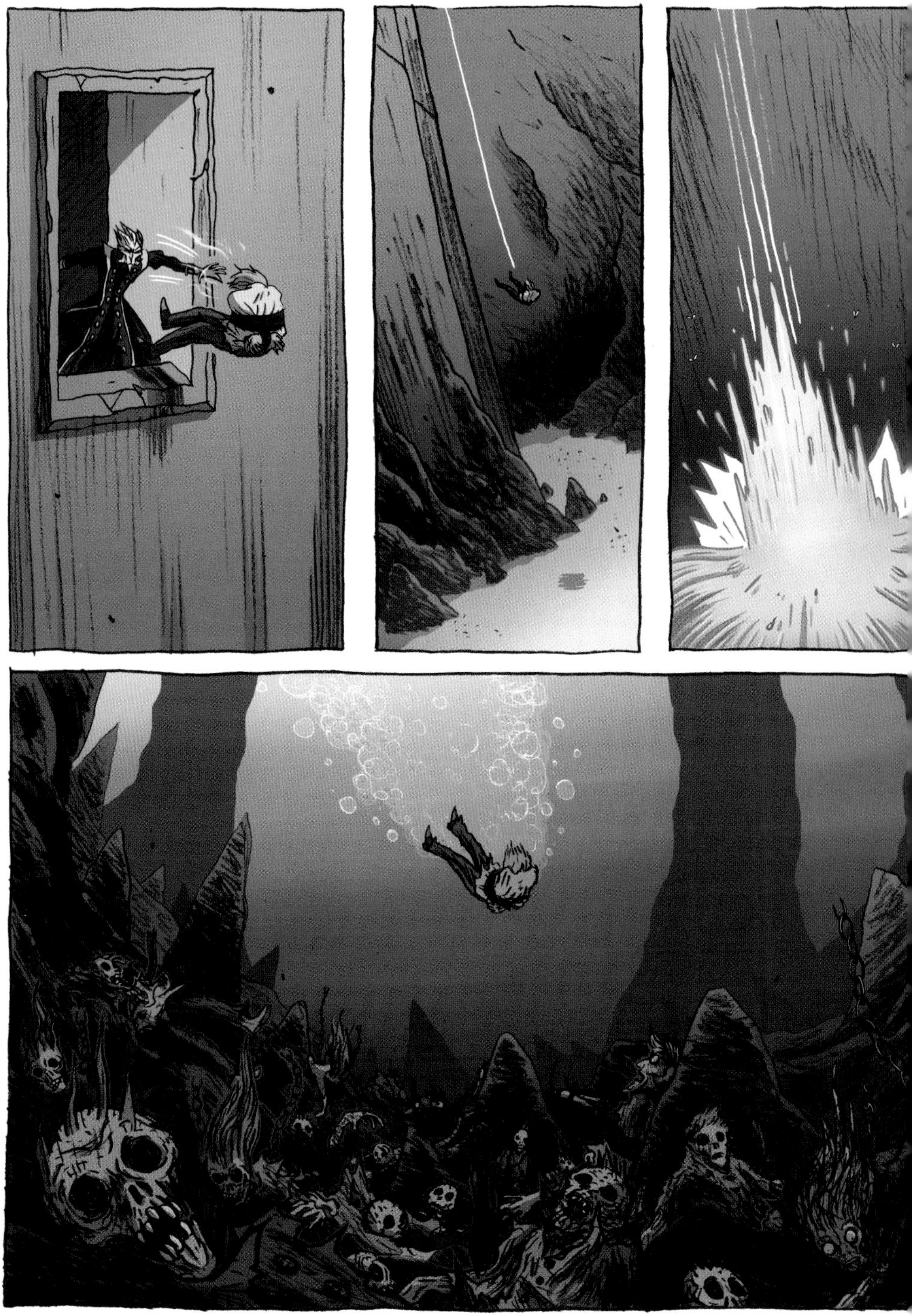

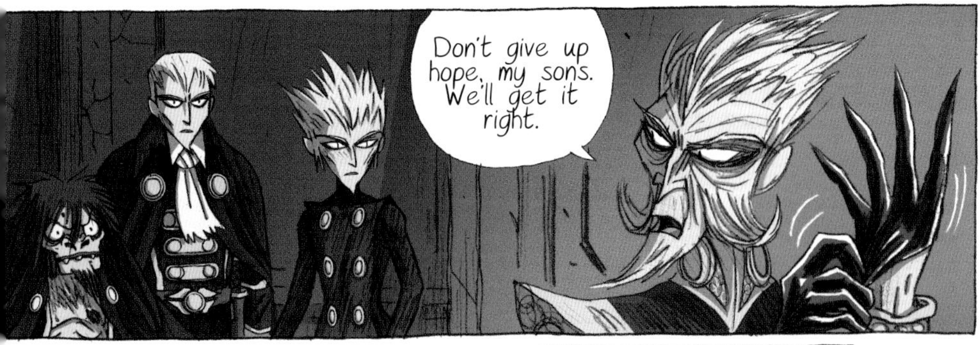
Don't give up hope, my sons. We'll get it right.

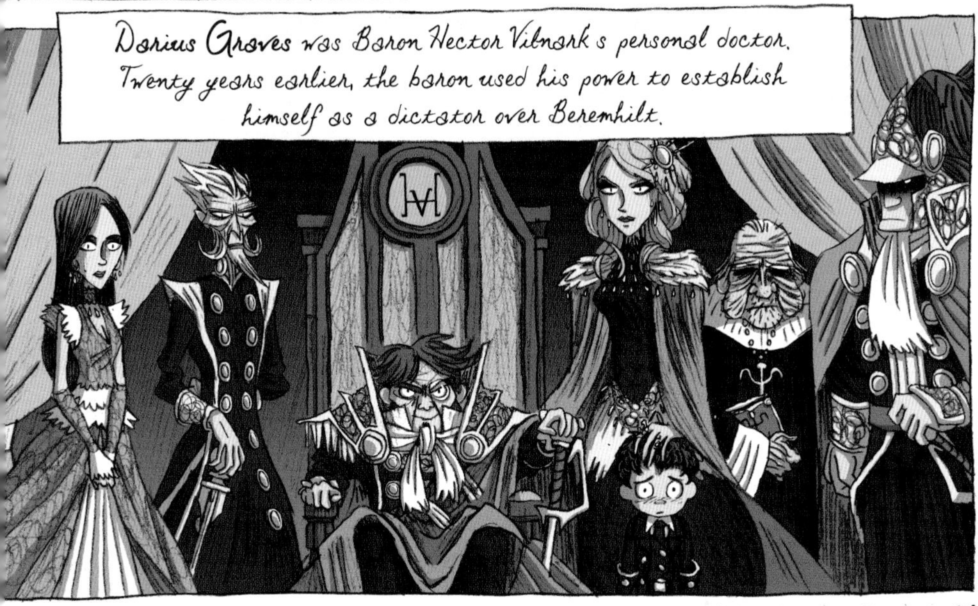
Darius Graves was Baron Hector Vilnark's personal doctor. Twenty years earlier, the baron used his power to establish himself as a dictator over Beremhilt.

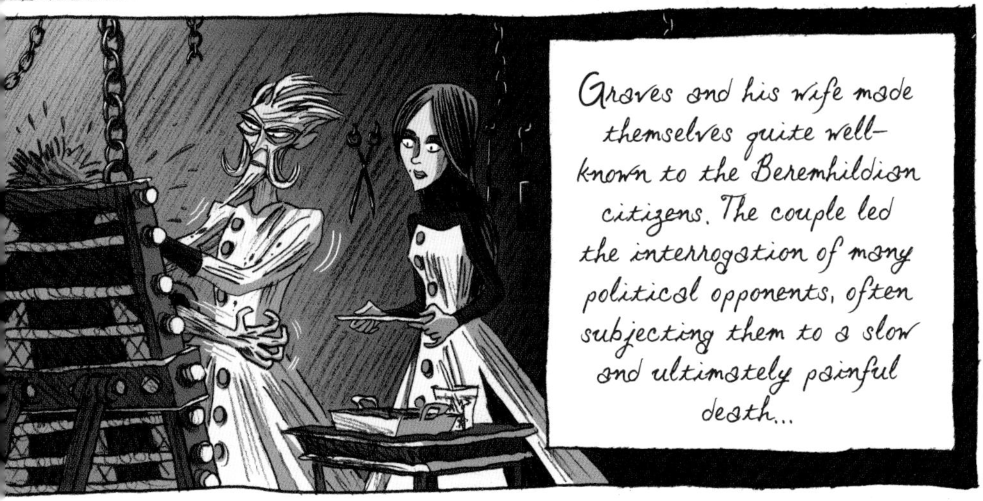
Graves and his wife made themselves quite well-known to the Beremhildian citizens. The couple led the interrogation of many political opponents, often subjecting them to a slow and ultimately painful death...

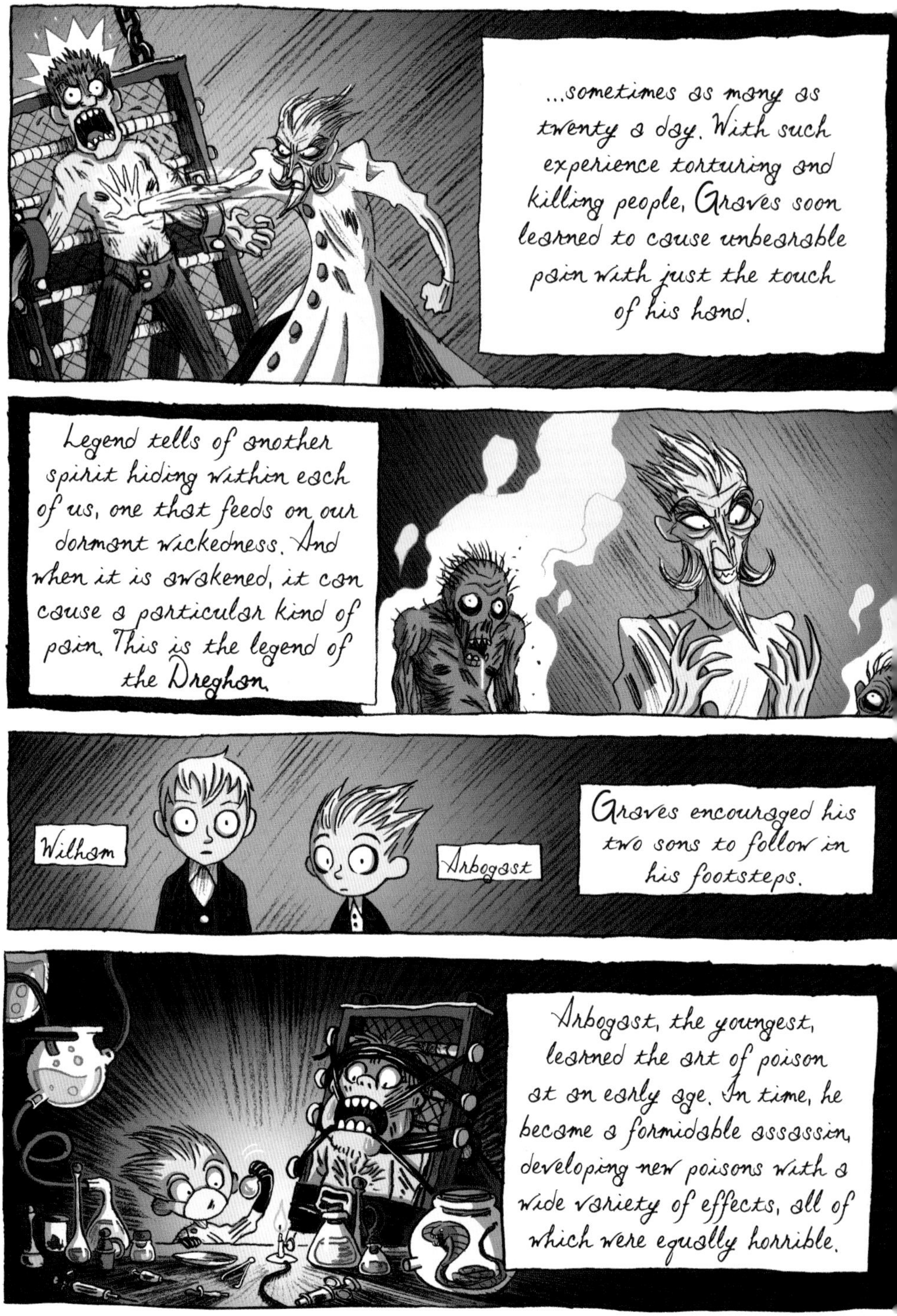
...sometimes as many as twenty a day. With such experience torturing and killing people, Graves soon learned to cause unbearable pain with just the touch of his hand.
Legend tells of another spirit hiding within each of us, one that feeds on our dormant wickedness. And when it is awakened, it can cause a particular kind of pain. This is the legend of the Dreghon.
Wilham
Arbogast
Graves encouraged his two sons to follow in his footsteps.
Arbogast, the youngest, learned the art of poison at an early age. In time, he became a formidable assassin, developing new poisons with a wide variety of effects, all of which were equally horrible.

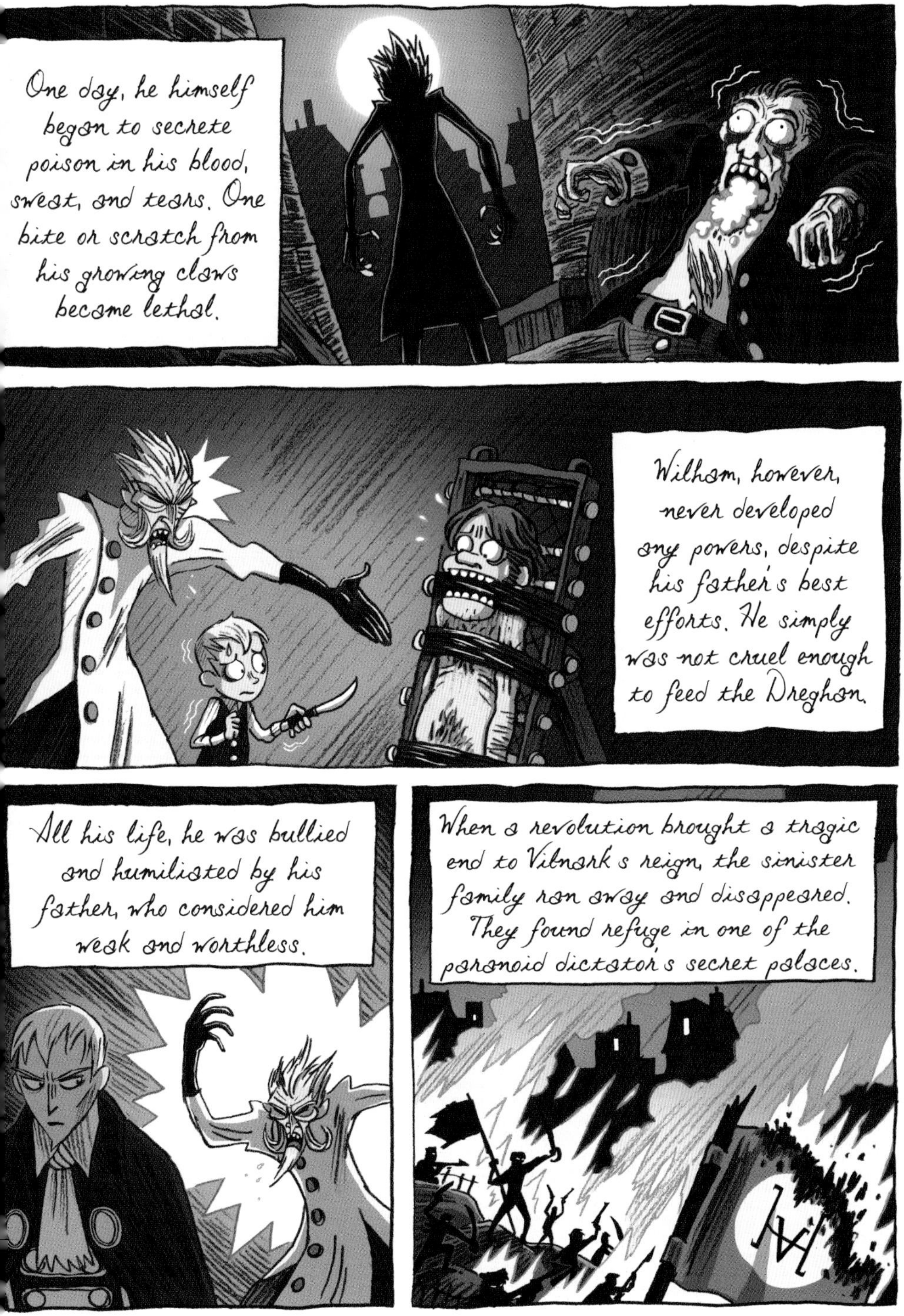
One day, he himself began to secrete poison in his blood, sweat, and tears. One bite or scratch from his growing claws became lethal.
Wilham, however, never developed any powers, despite his father's best efforts. He simply was not cruel enough to feed the Dreghan.
All his life, he was bullied and humiliated by his father, who considered him weak and worthless.
When a revolution brought a tragic end to Vibnark's reign, the sinister family ran away and disappeared. They found refuge in one of the paranoid dictator's secret palaces.

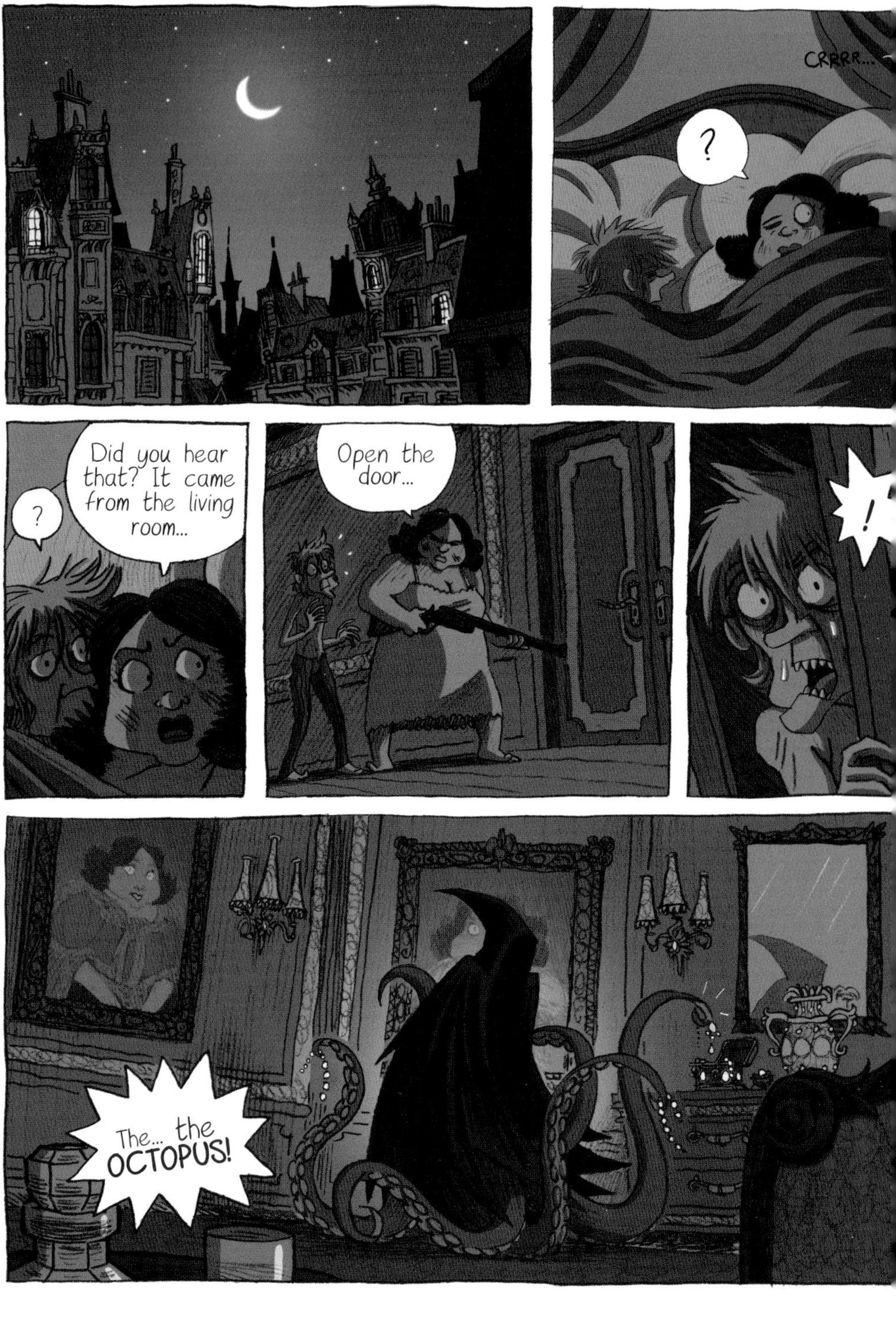
CRRRR...
?
?
Did you hear that? It came from the living room...
Open the door...
!
The... the OCTOPUS!

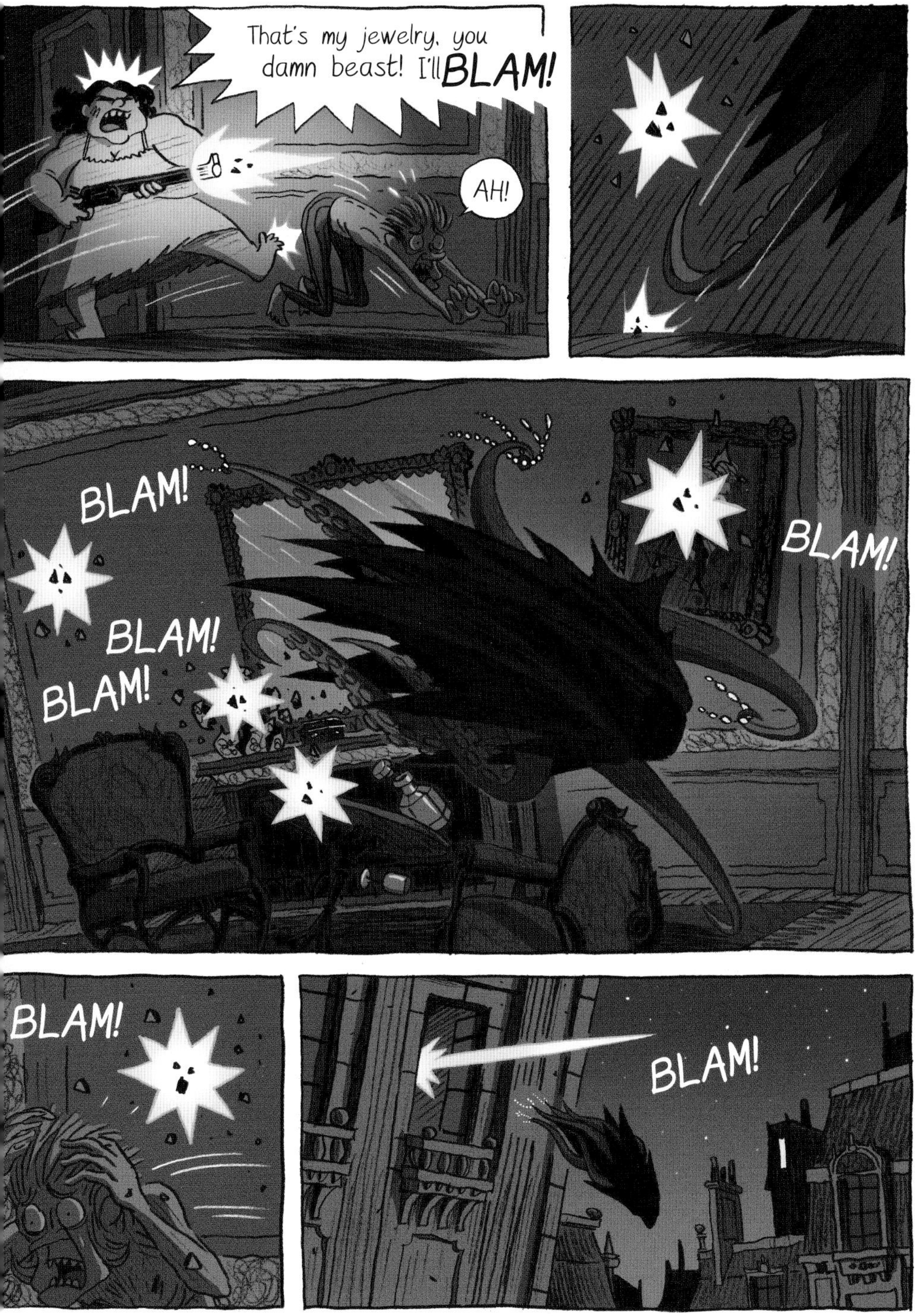
That's my jewelry, you damn beast! I'll
BLAM!
AH!
BLAM!
BLAM!
BLAM!
BLAM!
BLAM!
BLAM!

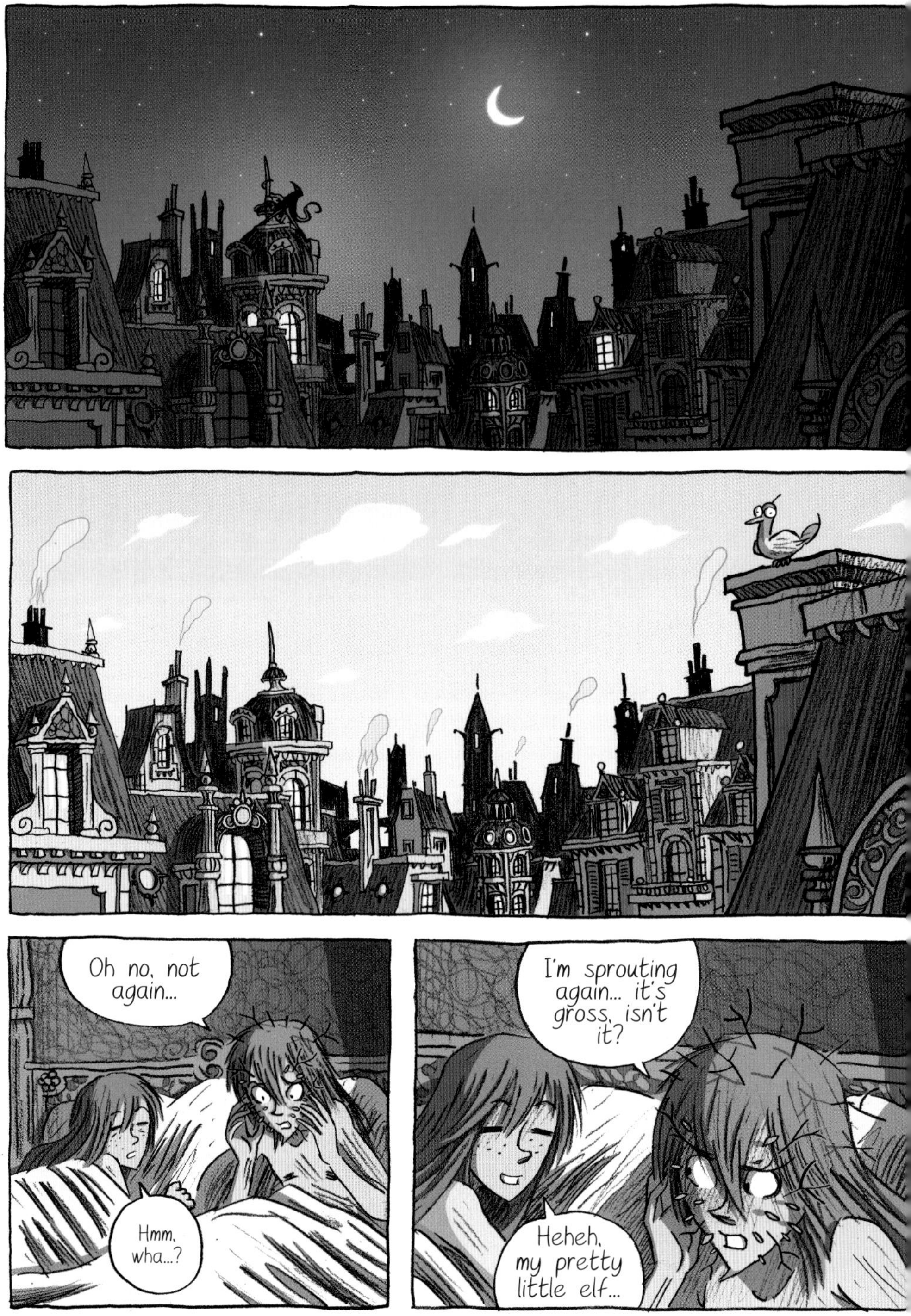
Oh no, not again...
Hmm, wha...?
I'm sprouting again... it's gross, isn't it?
Heheh, my pretty little elf...

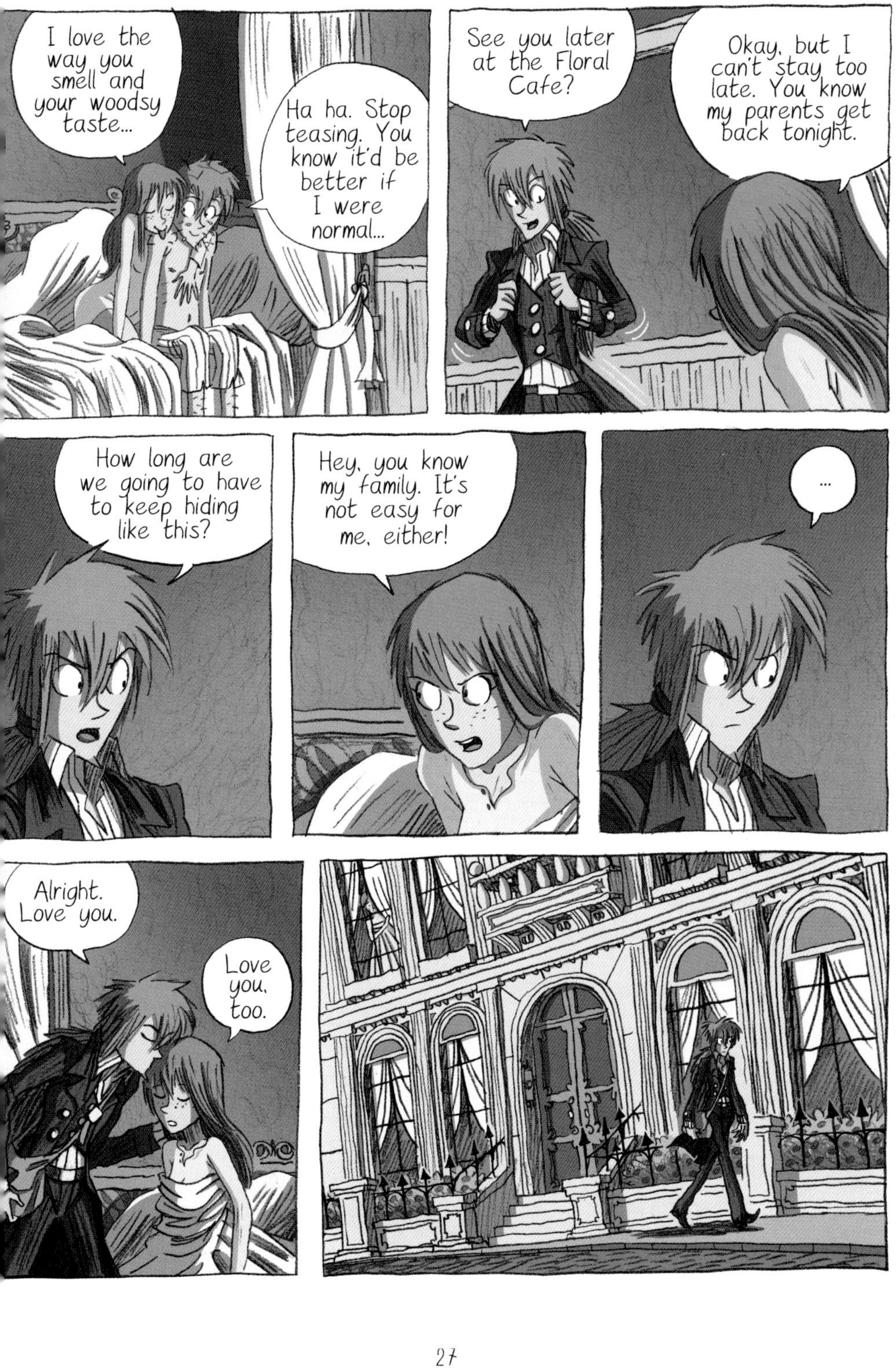

I love the way you smell and your woodsy taste...
Ha ha. Stop teasing. You know it'd be better if I were normal...
See you later at the Floral Cafe?
Okay, but I can't stay too late. You know my parents get back tonight.
How long are we going to have to keep hiding like this?
Hey, you know my family. It's not easy for me, either!
...
Alright. Love you.
Love you, too.

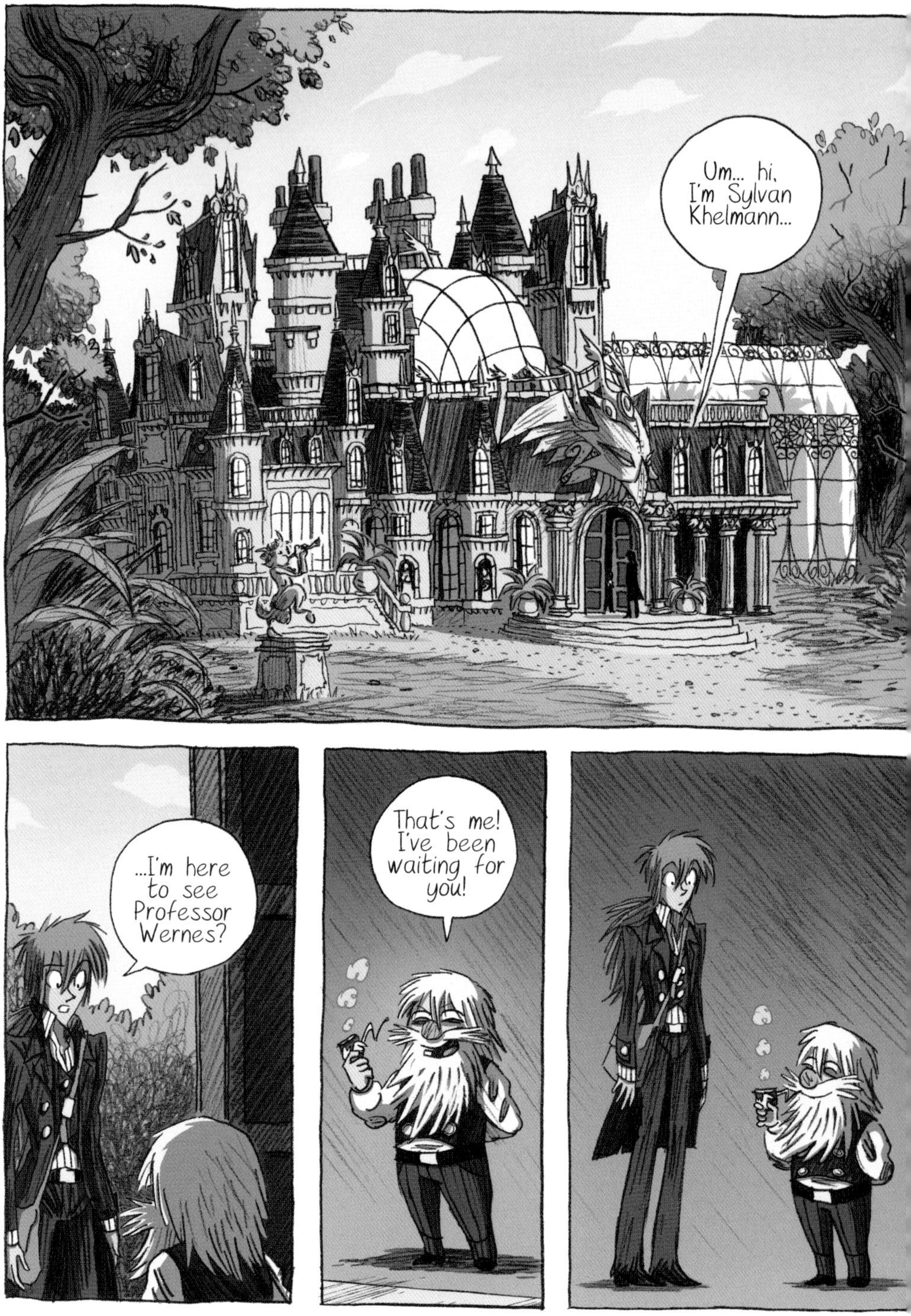
Um... hi, I'm Sylvan Khelmann...
...I'm here to see Professor Wernes?
That's me! I've been waiting for you!

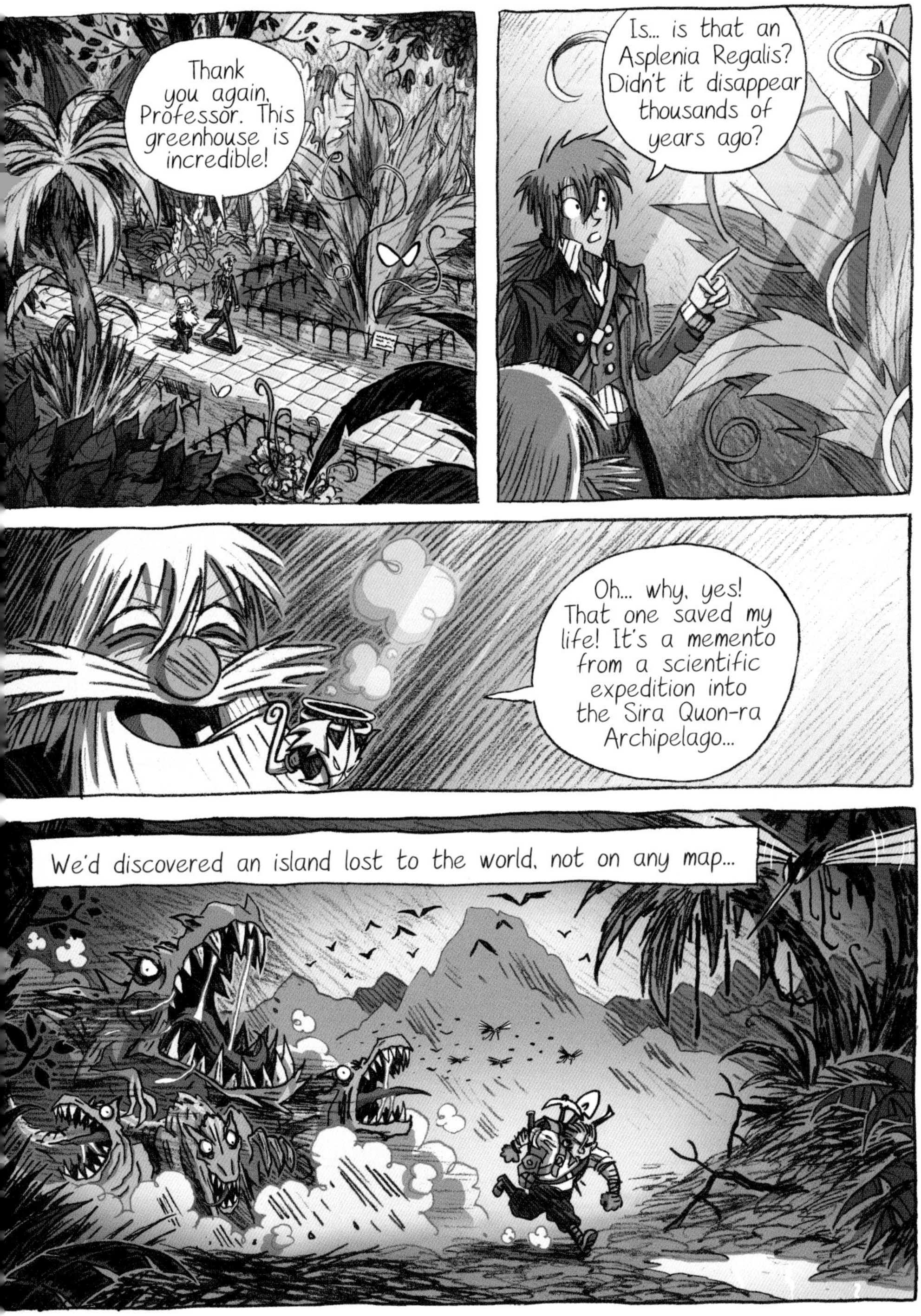
Thank you again, Professor. This greenhouse is incredible!
Is... is that an Asplenia Regalis? Didn't it disappear thousands of years ago?
Oh... why, yes! That one saved my life! It's a memento from a scientific expedition into the Sira Quon-ra Archipelago...
We'd discovered an island lost to the world, not on any map...

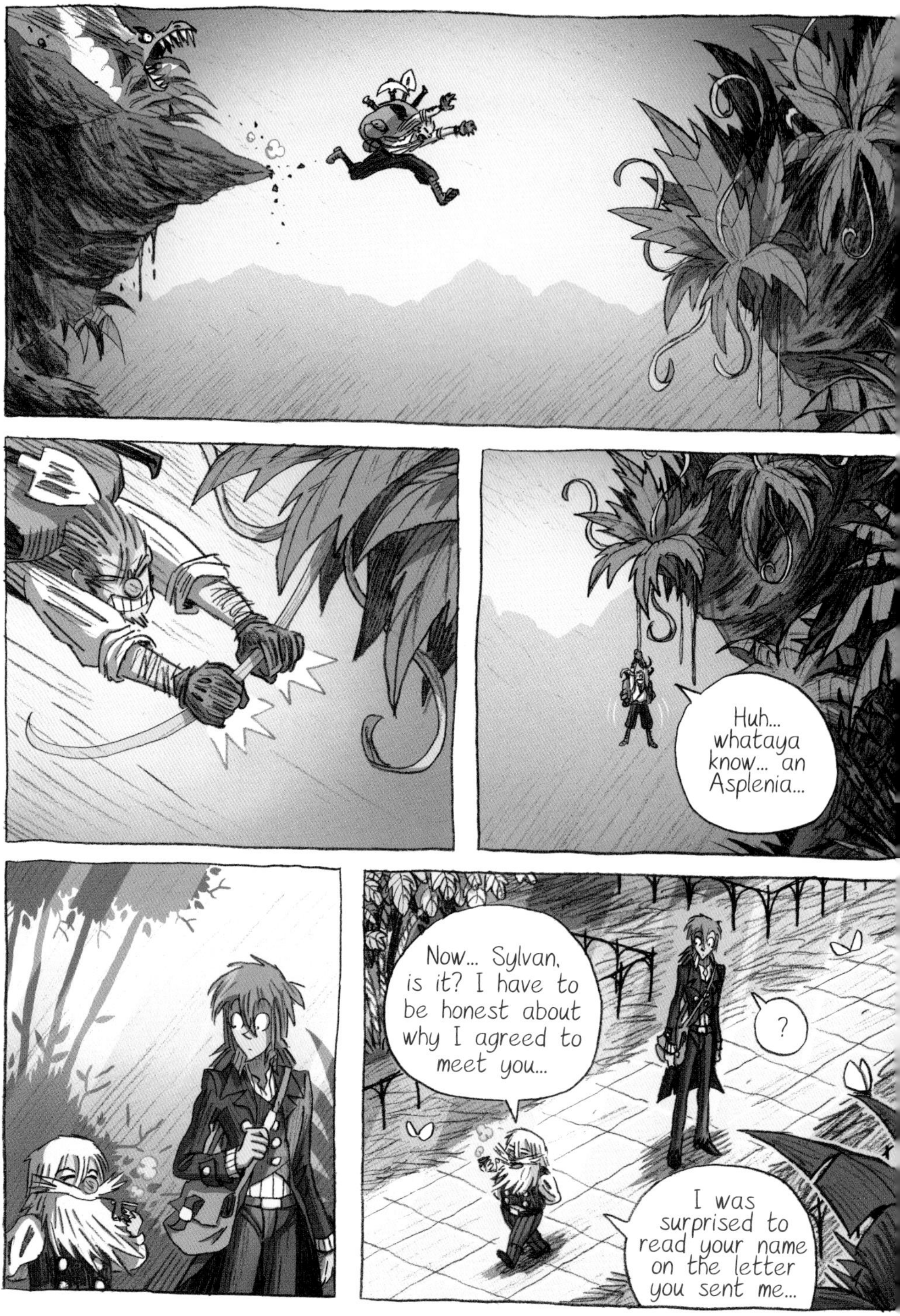
Huh... whataya know... an Asplenia...
Now... Sylvan, is it? I have to be honest about why I agreed to meet you...
?
I was surprised to read your name on the letter you sent me...

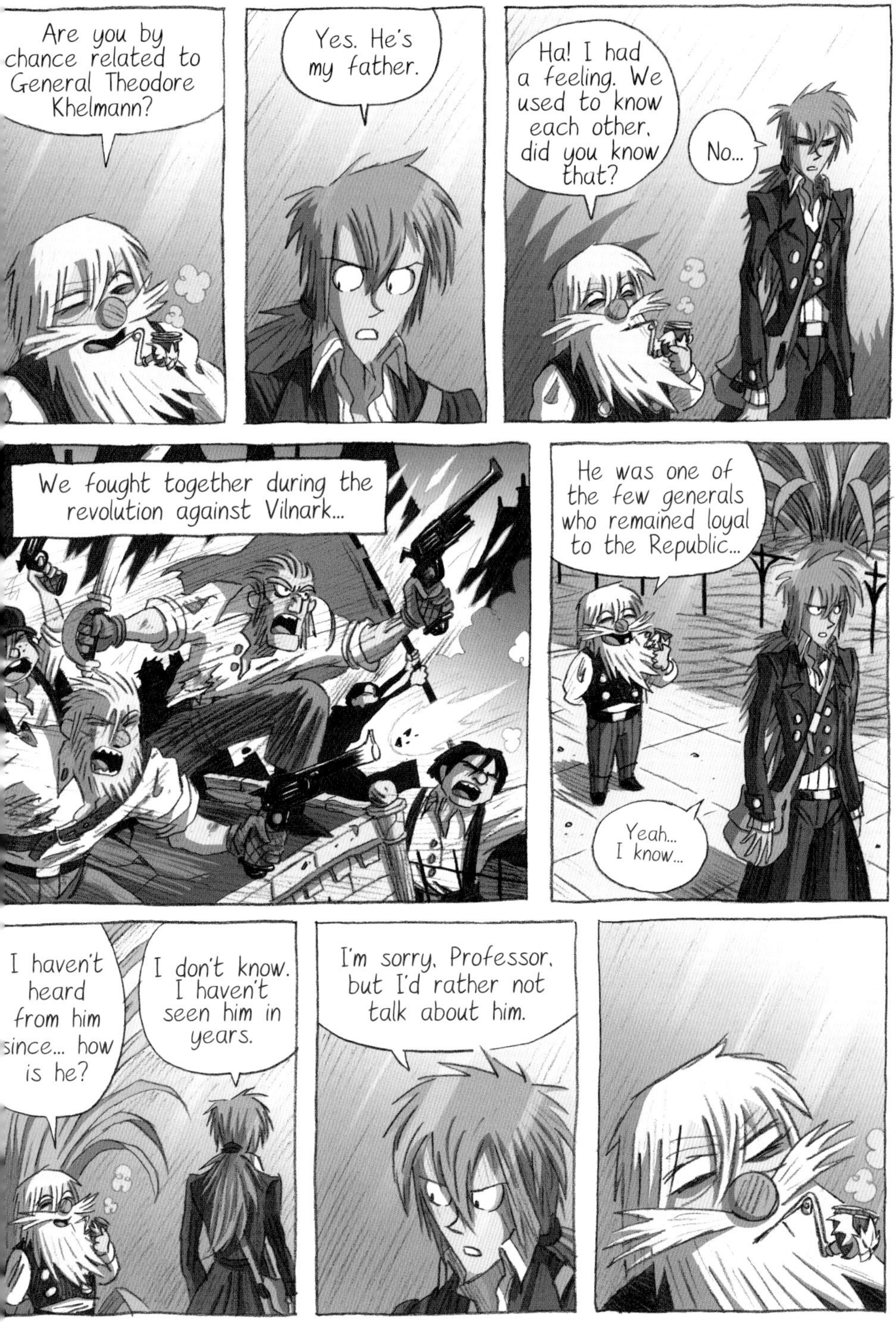

Are you by chance related to General Theodore Khelmann?
Yes. He's my father.
Ha! I had a feeling. We used to know each other, did you know that?
No...
We fought together during the revolution against Vilnark...
He was one of the few generals who remained loyal to the Republic...
Yeah... I know...
I haven't heard from him since... how is he?
I don't know. I haven't seen him in years.
I'm sorry, Professor, but I'd rather not talk about him.

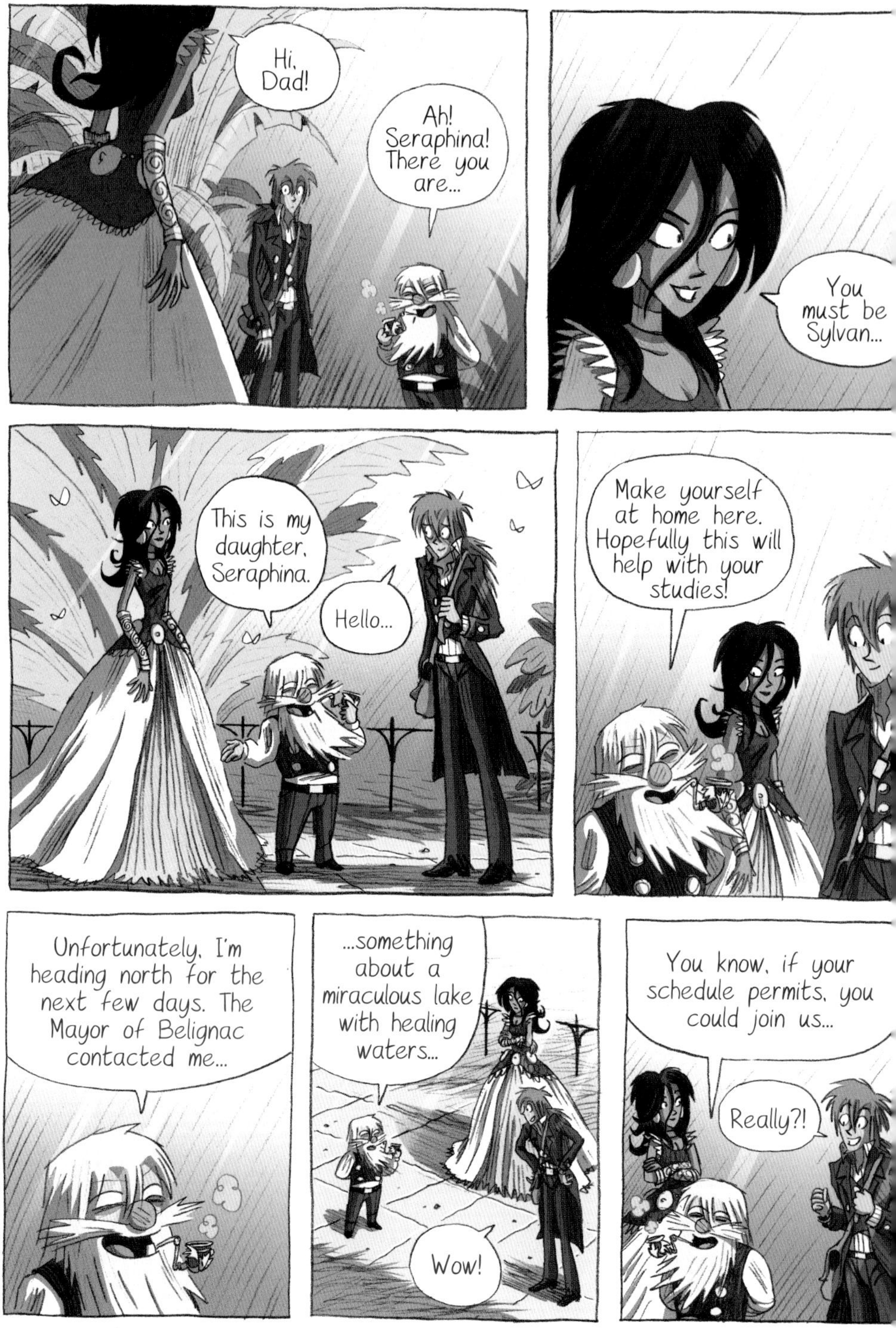
Hi, Dad!
Ah! Seraphina! There you are...
You must be Sylvan...
This is my daughter, Seraphina.
Hello...
Make yourself at home here. Hopefully this will help with your studies!
Unfortunately, I'm heading north for the next few days. The Mayor of Belignac contacted me...
...something about a miraculous lake with healing waters...
Wow!
You know, if your schedule permits, you could join us...
Really?!

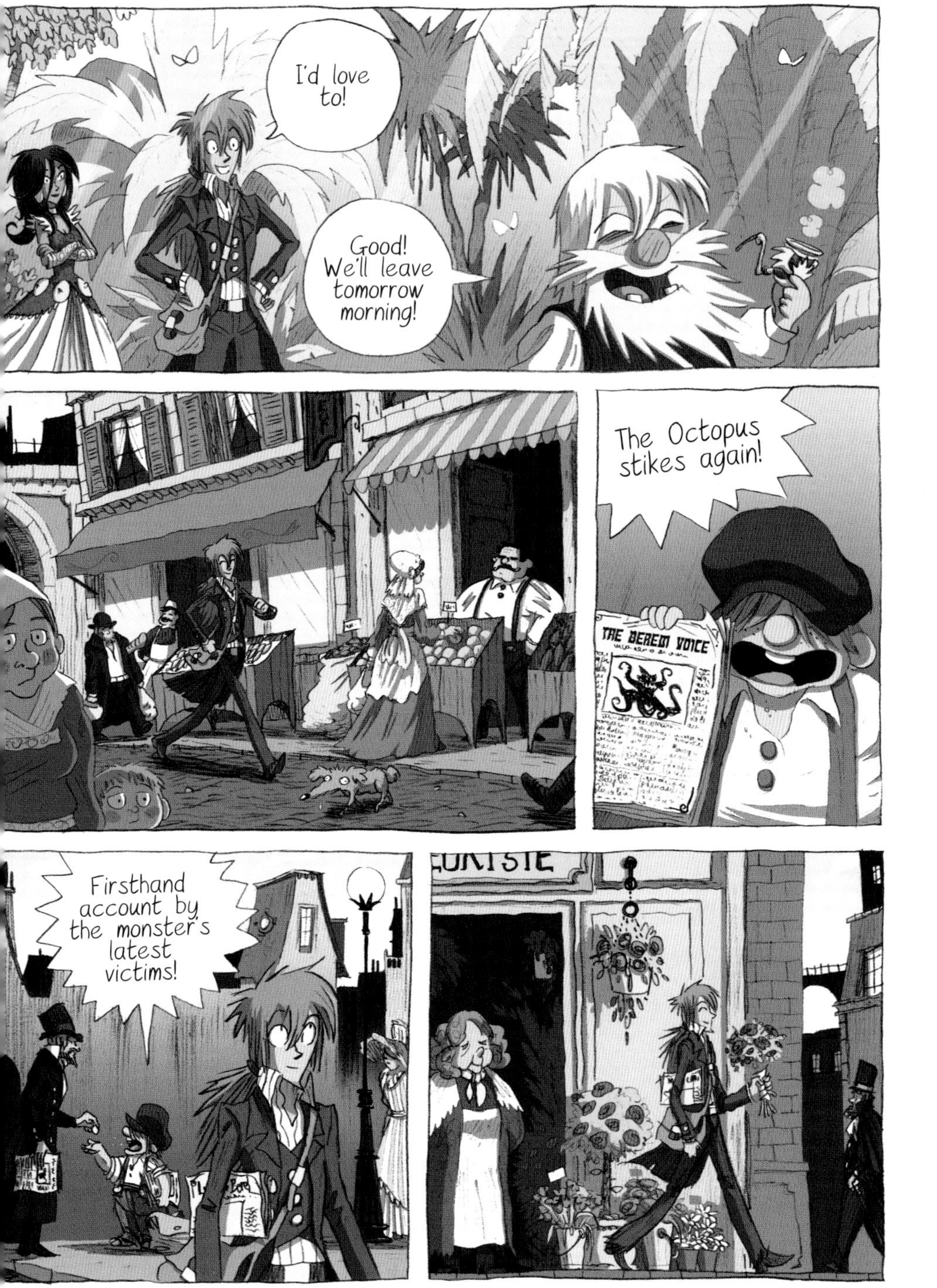
I'd love to!
Good! We'll leave tomorrow morning!
The Octopus stikes again!
THE BEREM VOICE
Firsthand account by the monster's latest victims!

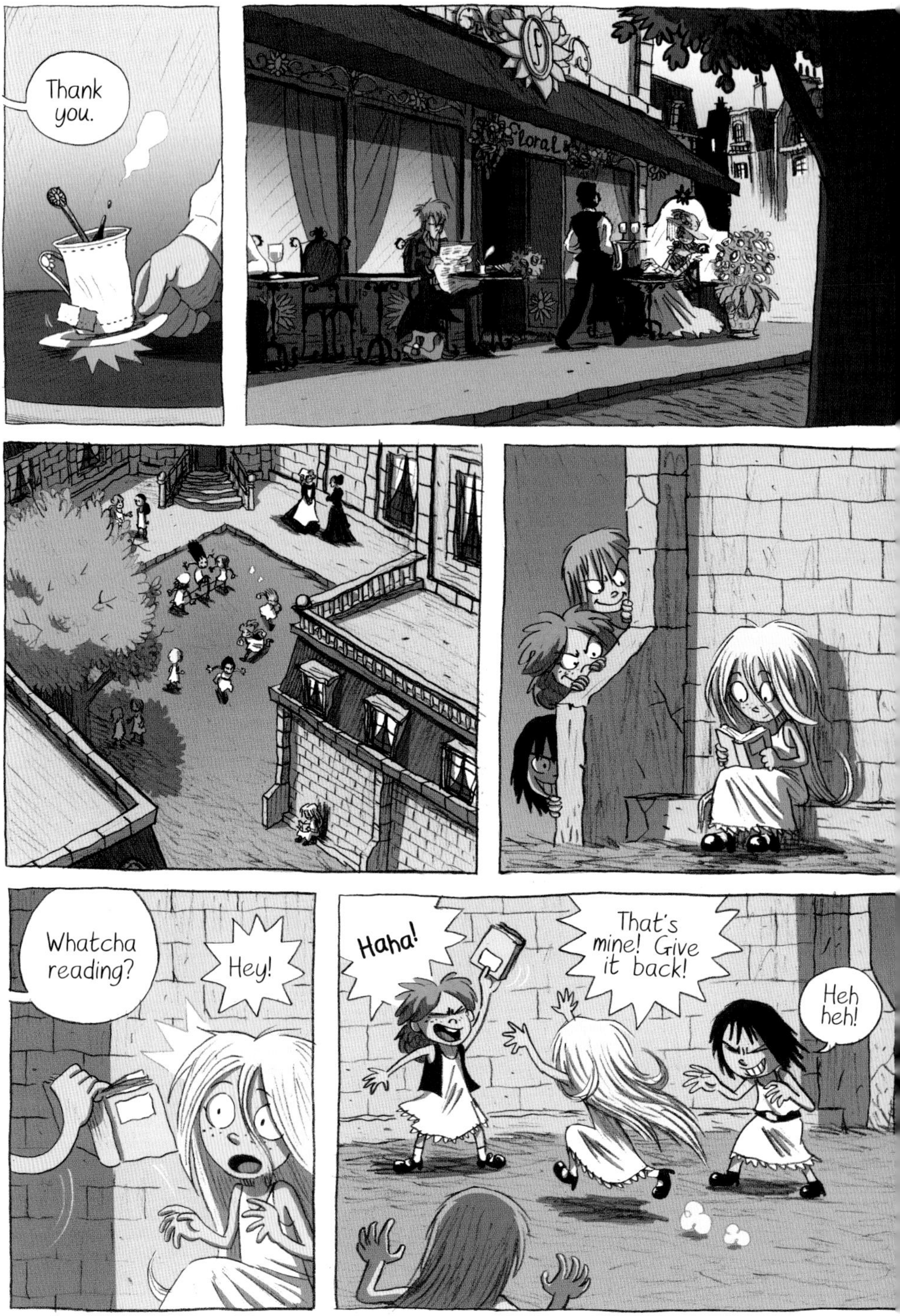
Thank you.
Whatcha reading?
Hey!
Haha!
That's mine! Give it back!
Heh heh!

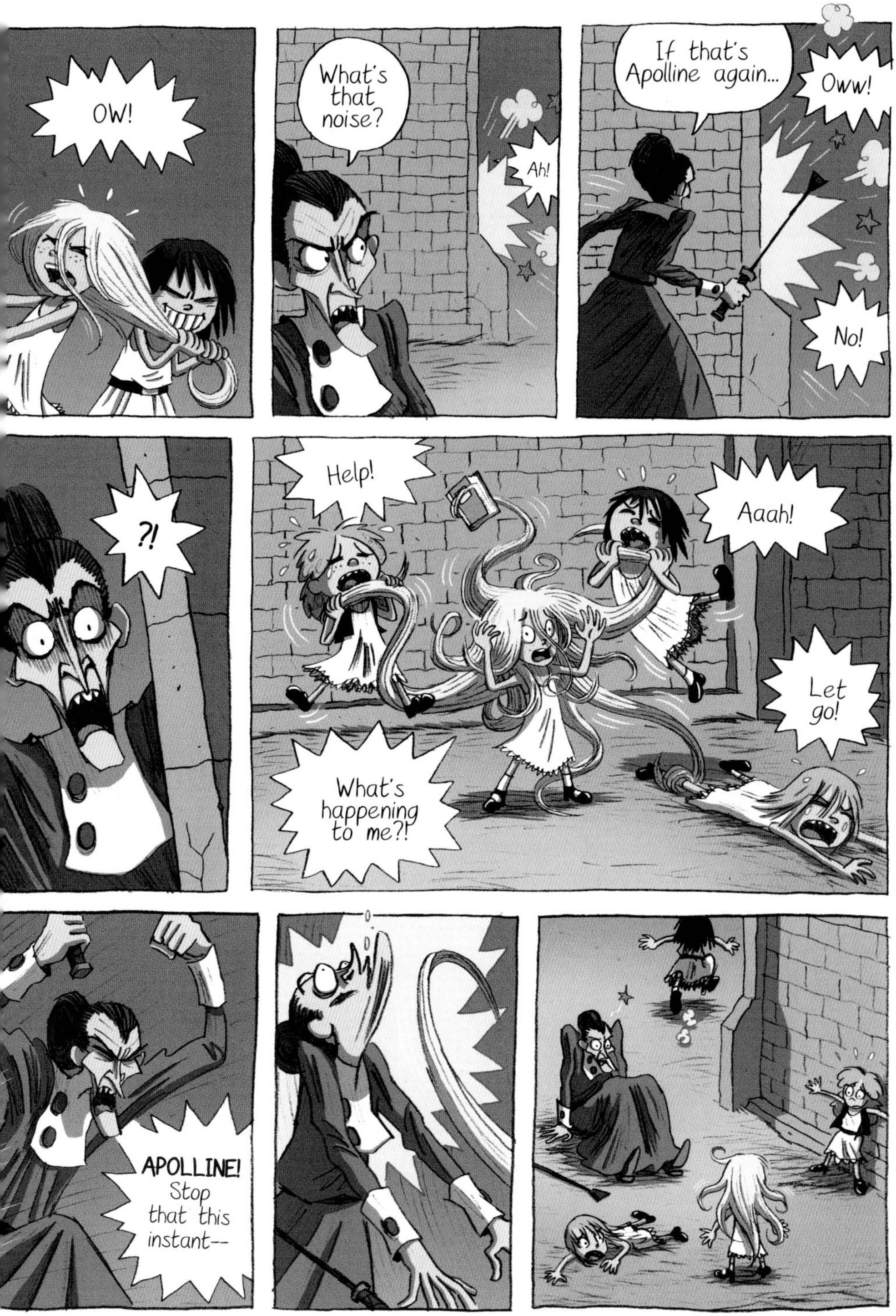
OW!
What's that noise?
Ah!
If that's Apolline again...
Oww!
No!
?!
Help!
Aaah!
Let go!
What's happening to me?!
APOLLINE! Stop that this instant--

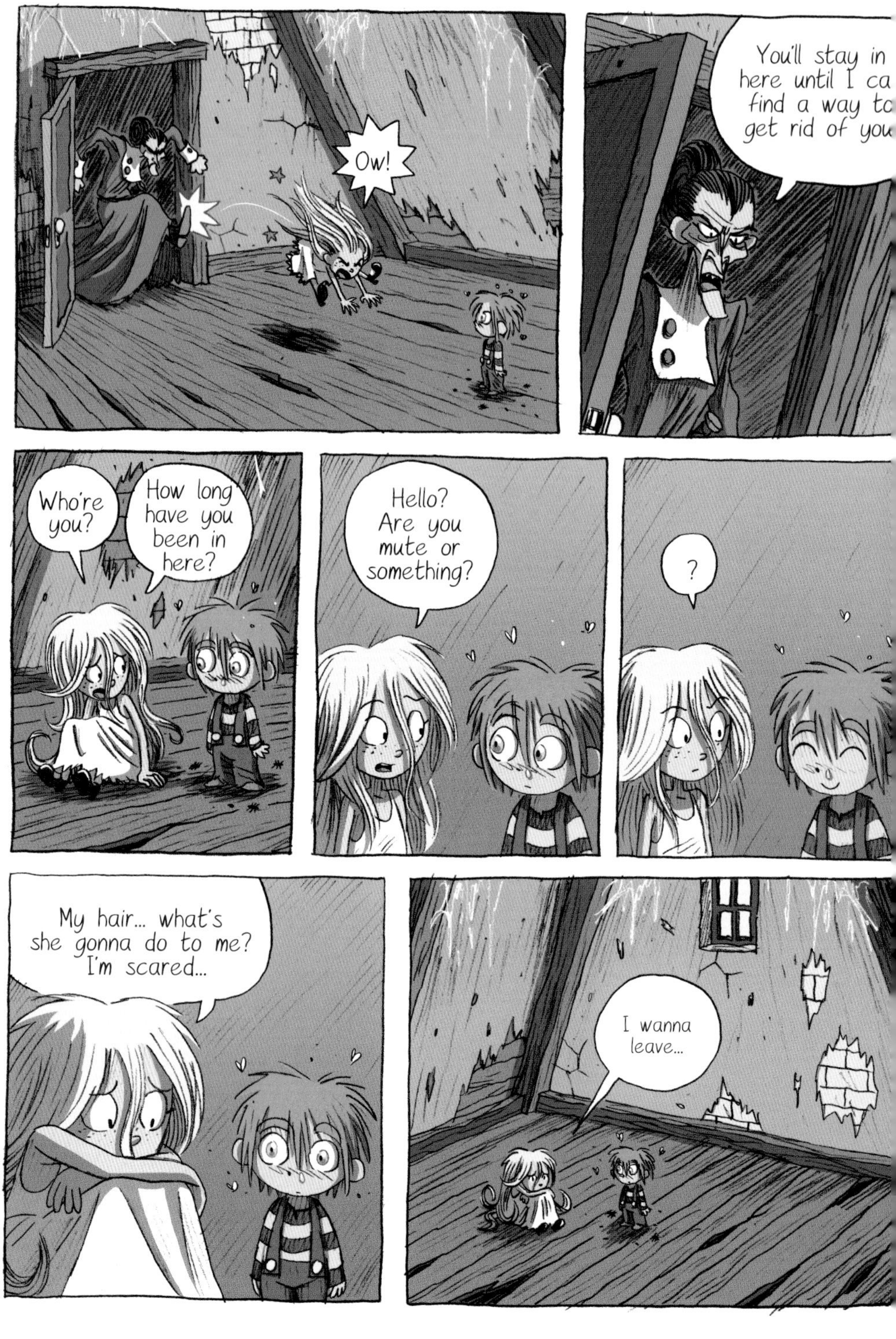
Ow!
You'll stay in here until I ca find a way to get rid of you
Who're you?
How long have you been in here?
Hello? Are you mute or something?
?
My hair... what's she gonna do to me? I'm scared...
I wanna leave...

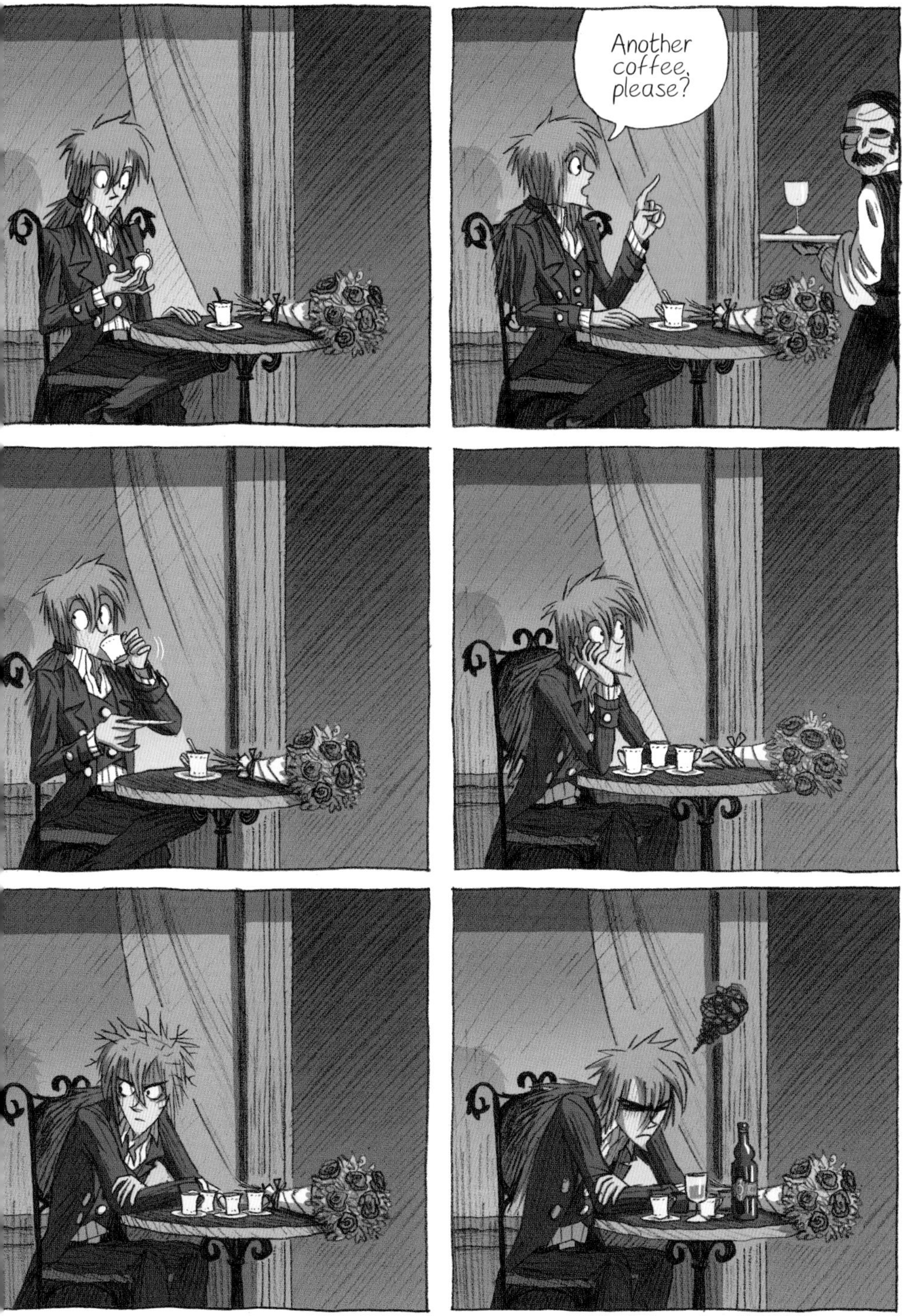
Another coffee, please?

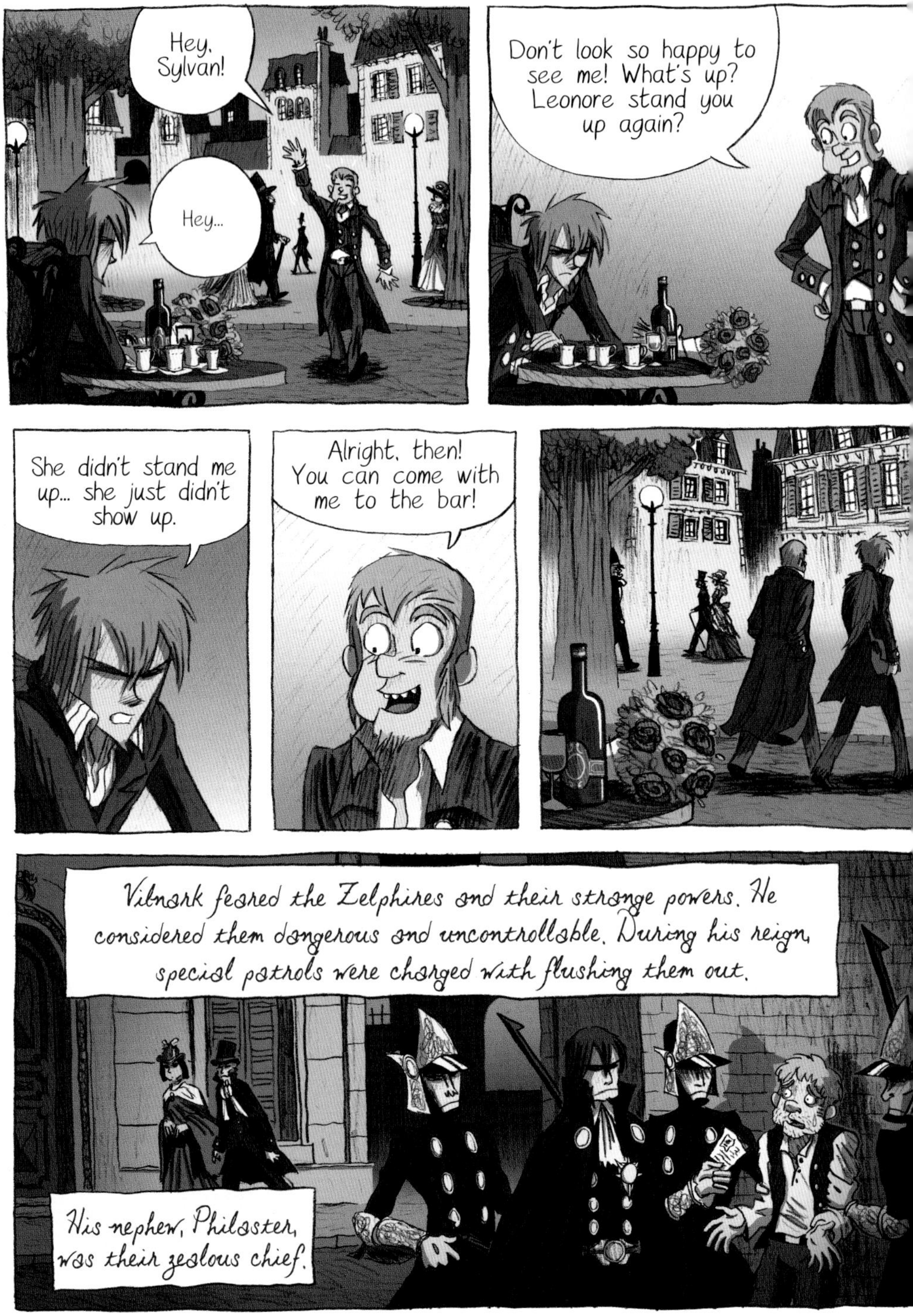
Hey, Sylvan!
Hey...
Don't look so happy to see me! What's up? Leonore stand you up again?
She didn't stand me up... she just didn't show up.
Alright, then! You can come with me to the bar!
Vilnark feared the Zelphires and their strange powers. He considered them dangerous and uncontrollable. During his reign, special patrols were charged with flushing them out.
His nephew, Philaster, was their zealous chief.

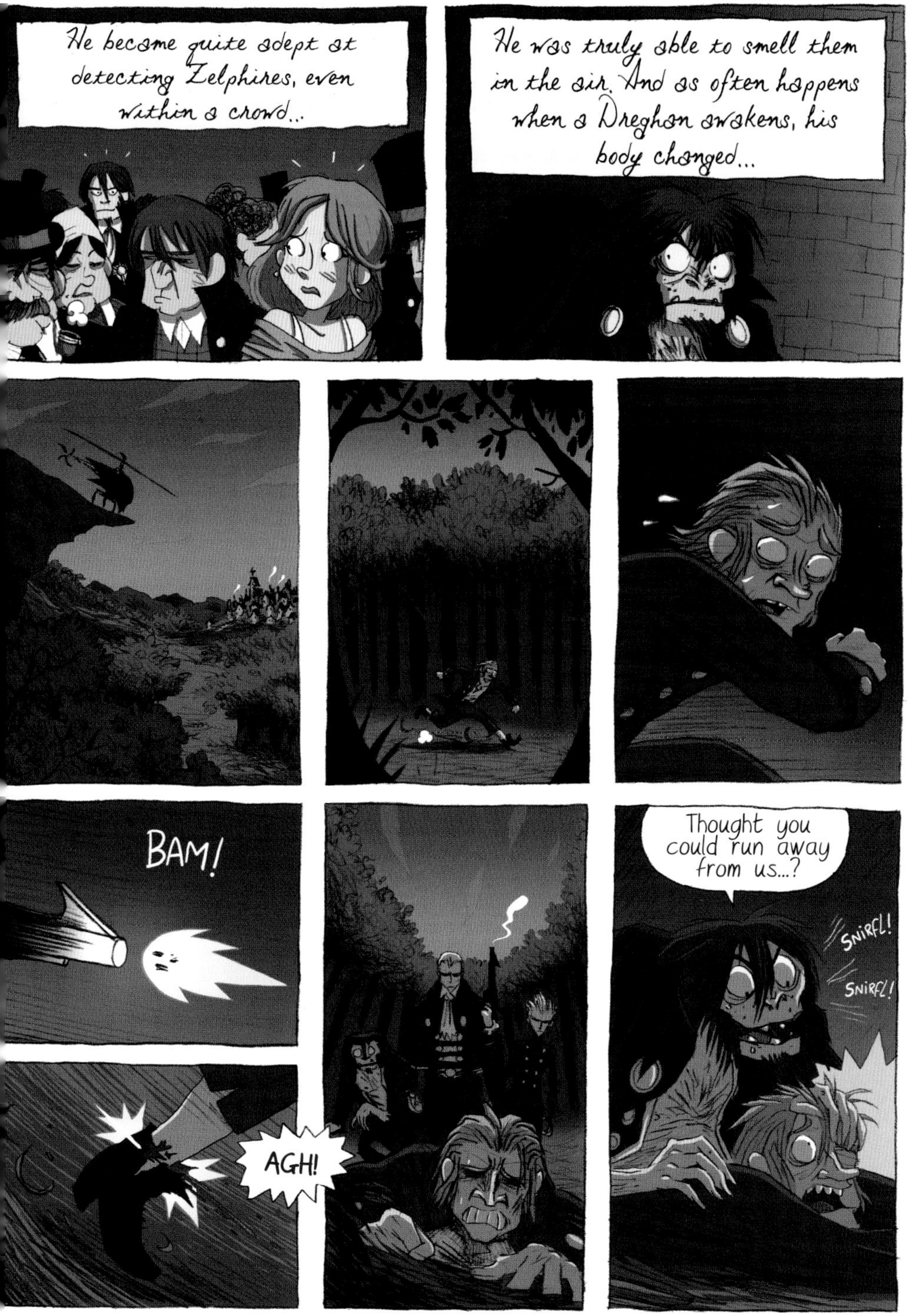
He became quite adept at detecting Zelphires, even within a crowd...
He was truly able to smell them in the air. And as often happens when a Dreghon awakens, his body changed...
BAM!
AGH!
Thought you could run away from us...?
SNIRFL!
SNIRFL!

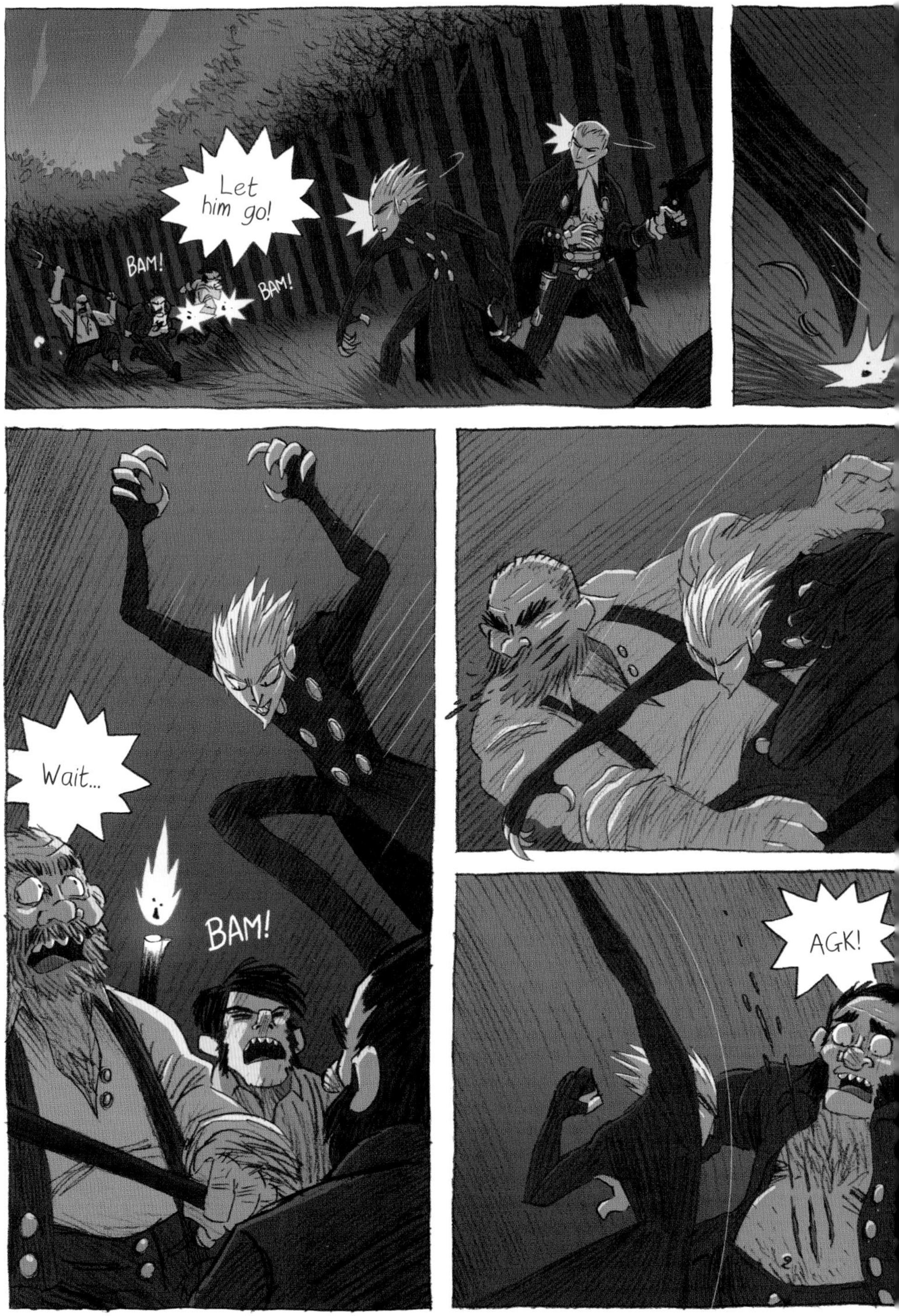
Let him go!
BAM!
BAM!
Wait...
BAM!
AGK!

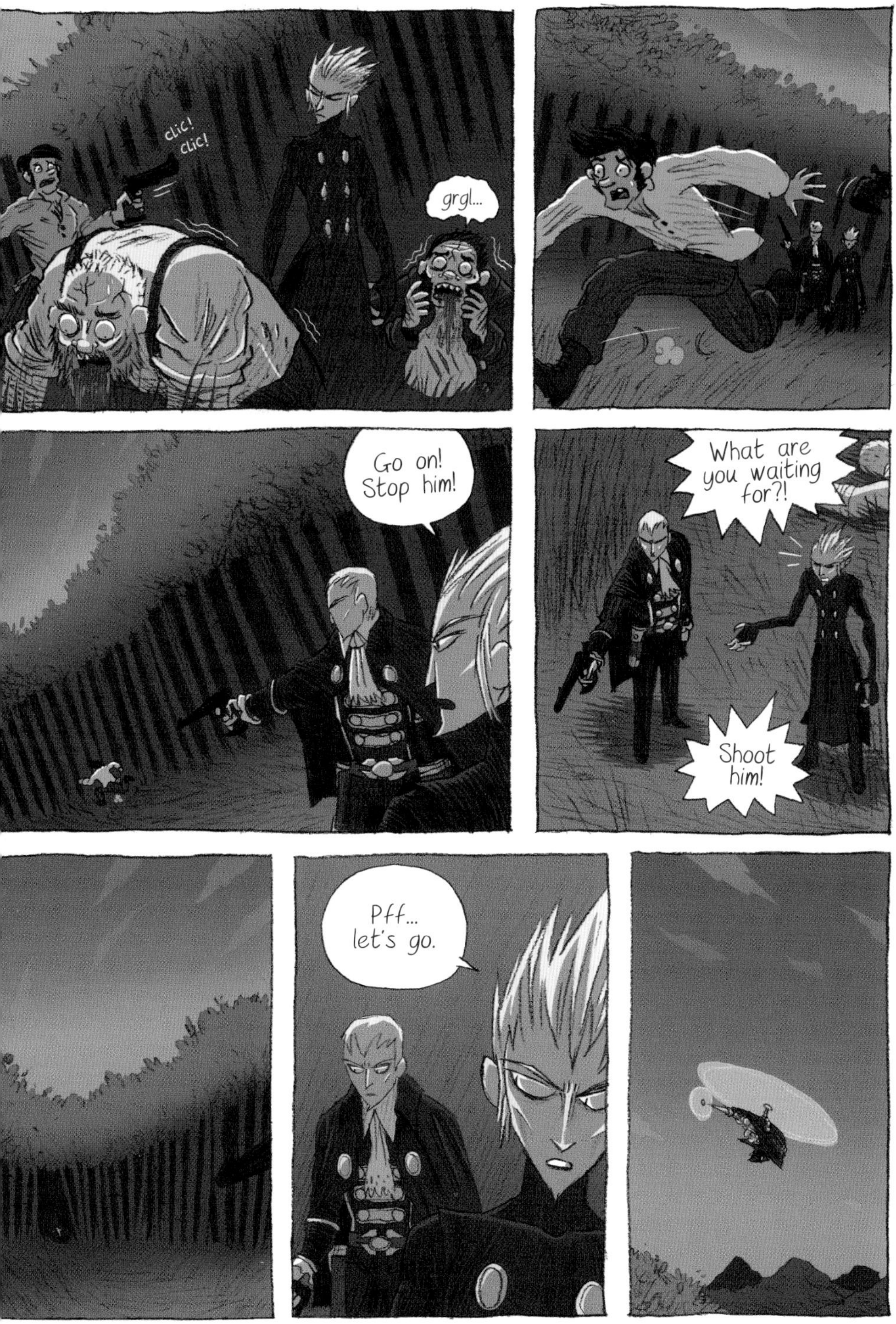
clic! clic!
grgl...
Go on! Stop him!
What are you waiting for?!
Shoot him!
Pff... let's go.

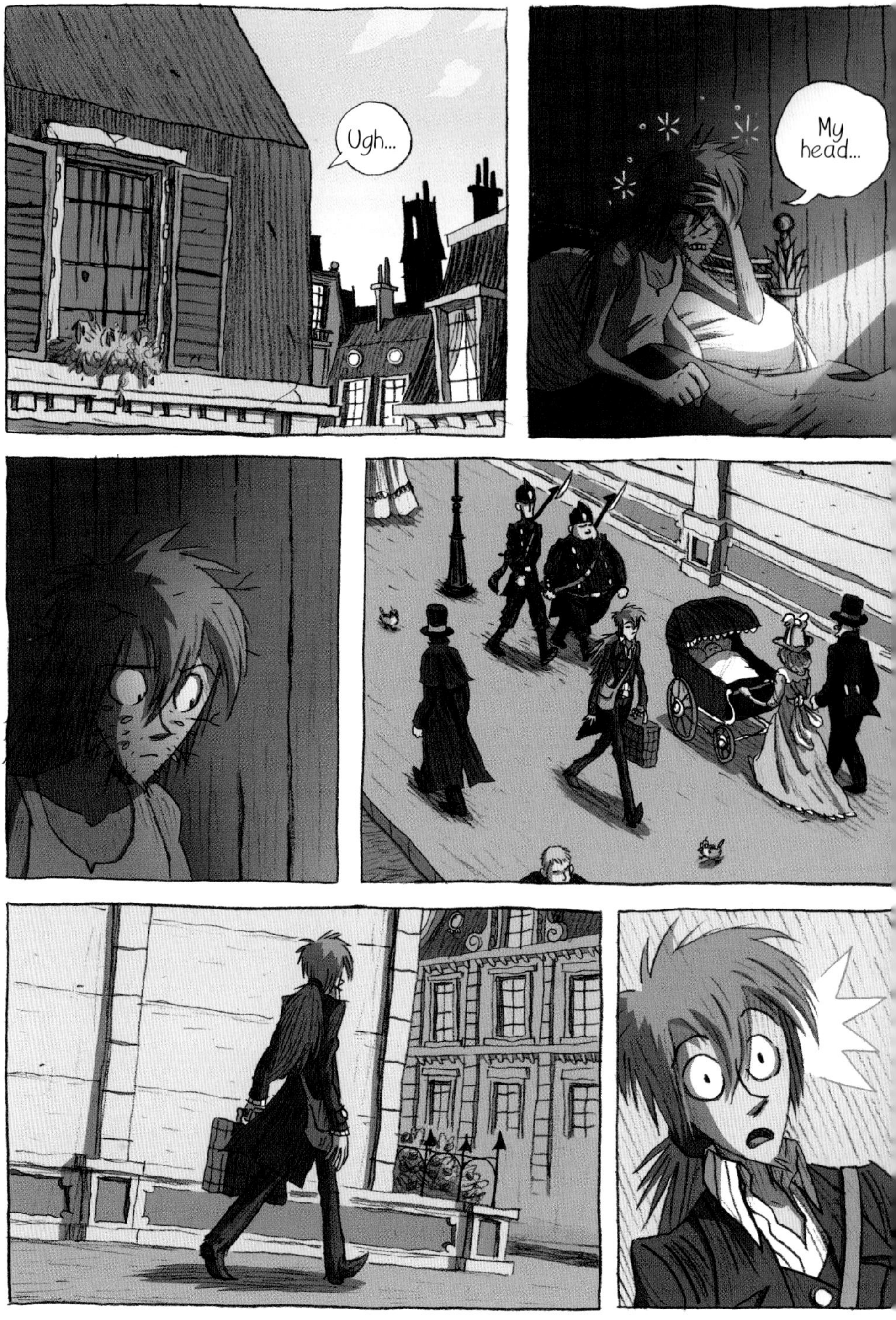
Ugh...
My head...

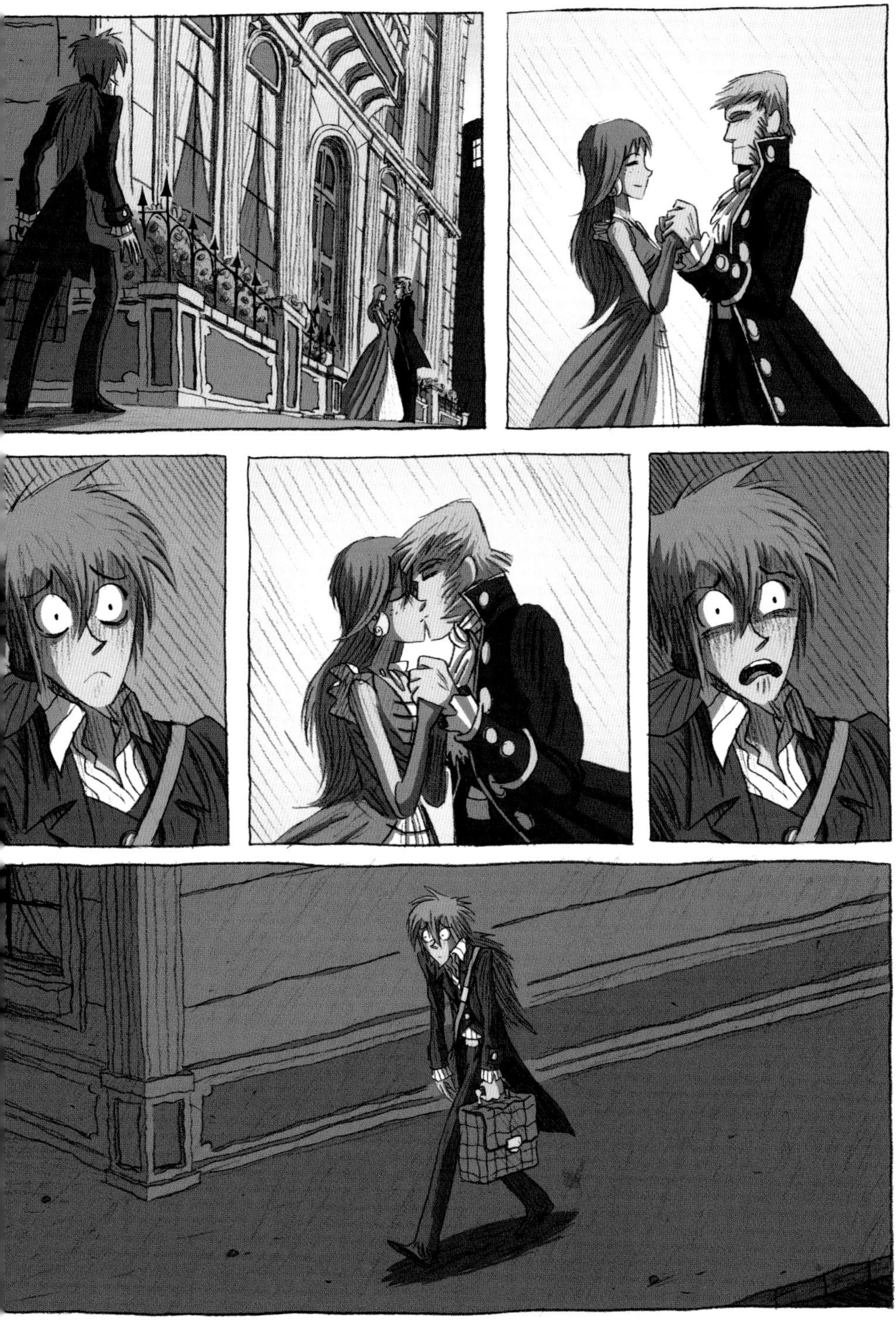

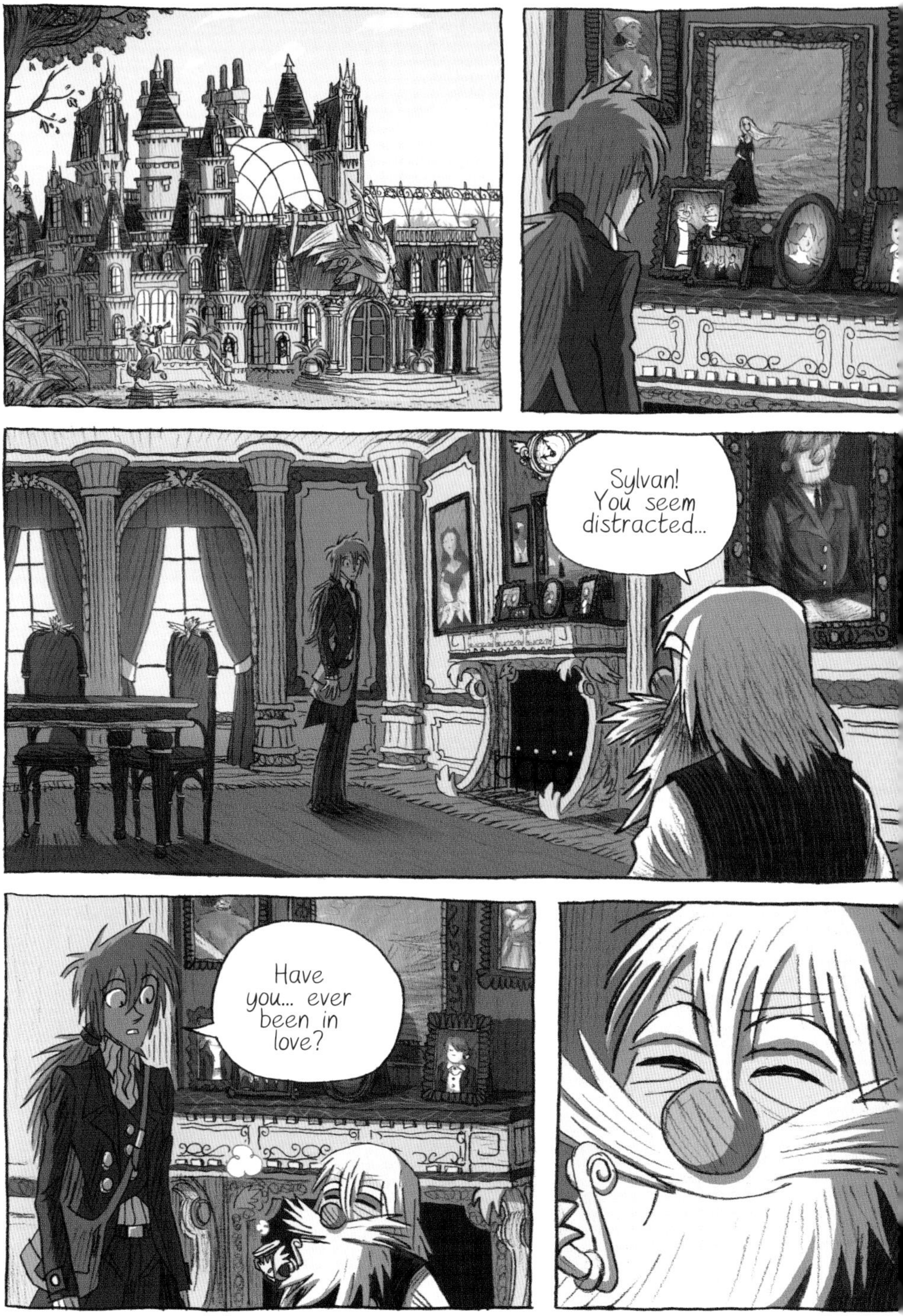
Sylvan! You seem distracted...
Have you... ever been in love?

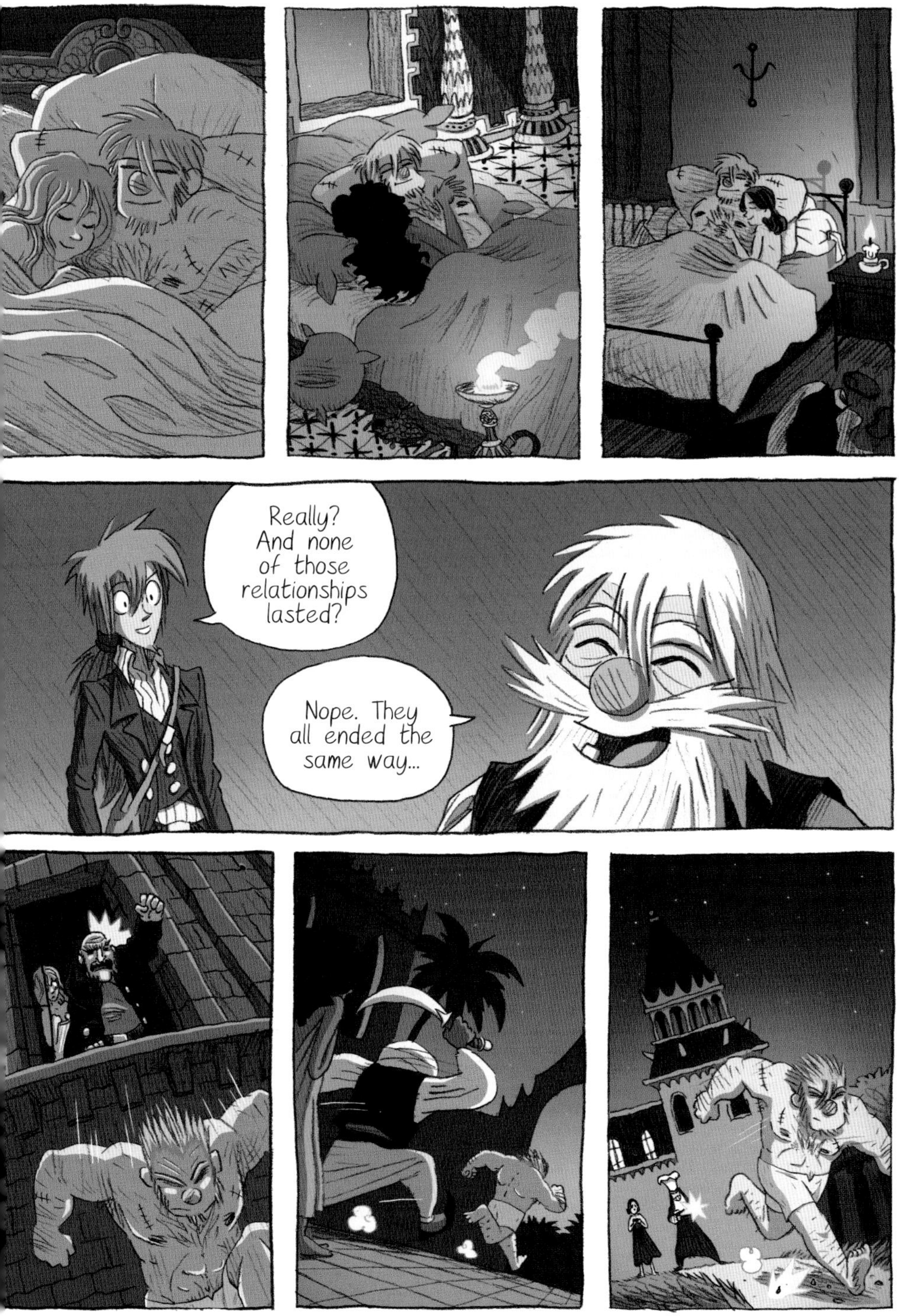
Really? And none of those relationships lasted?
Nope. They all ended the same way...

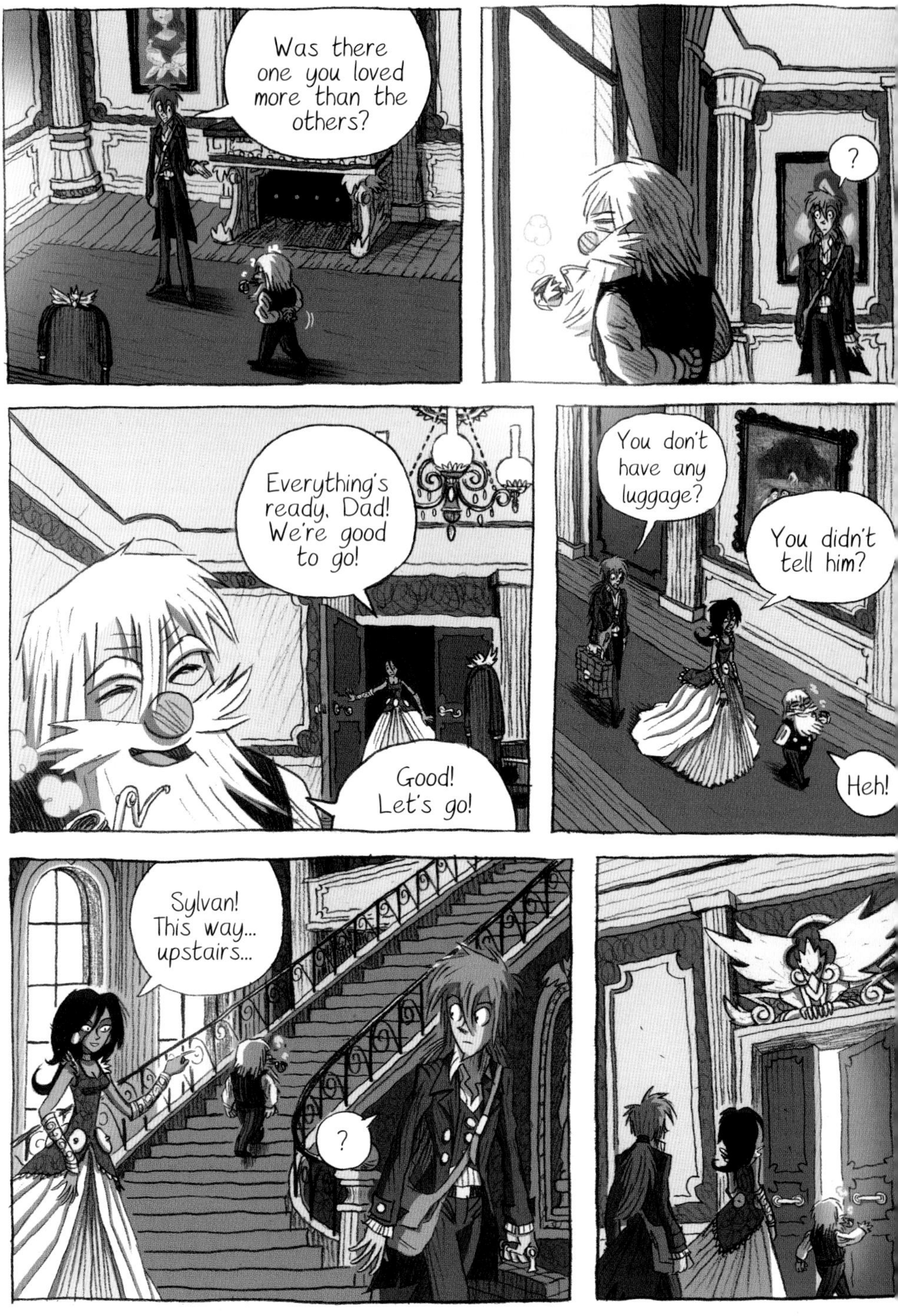

Was there one you loved more than the others?
?
Everything's ready, Dad! We're good to go!
Good! Let's go!
You don't have any luggage?
You didn't tell him?
Heh!
Sylvan! This way... upstairs...
?

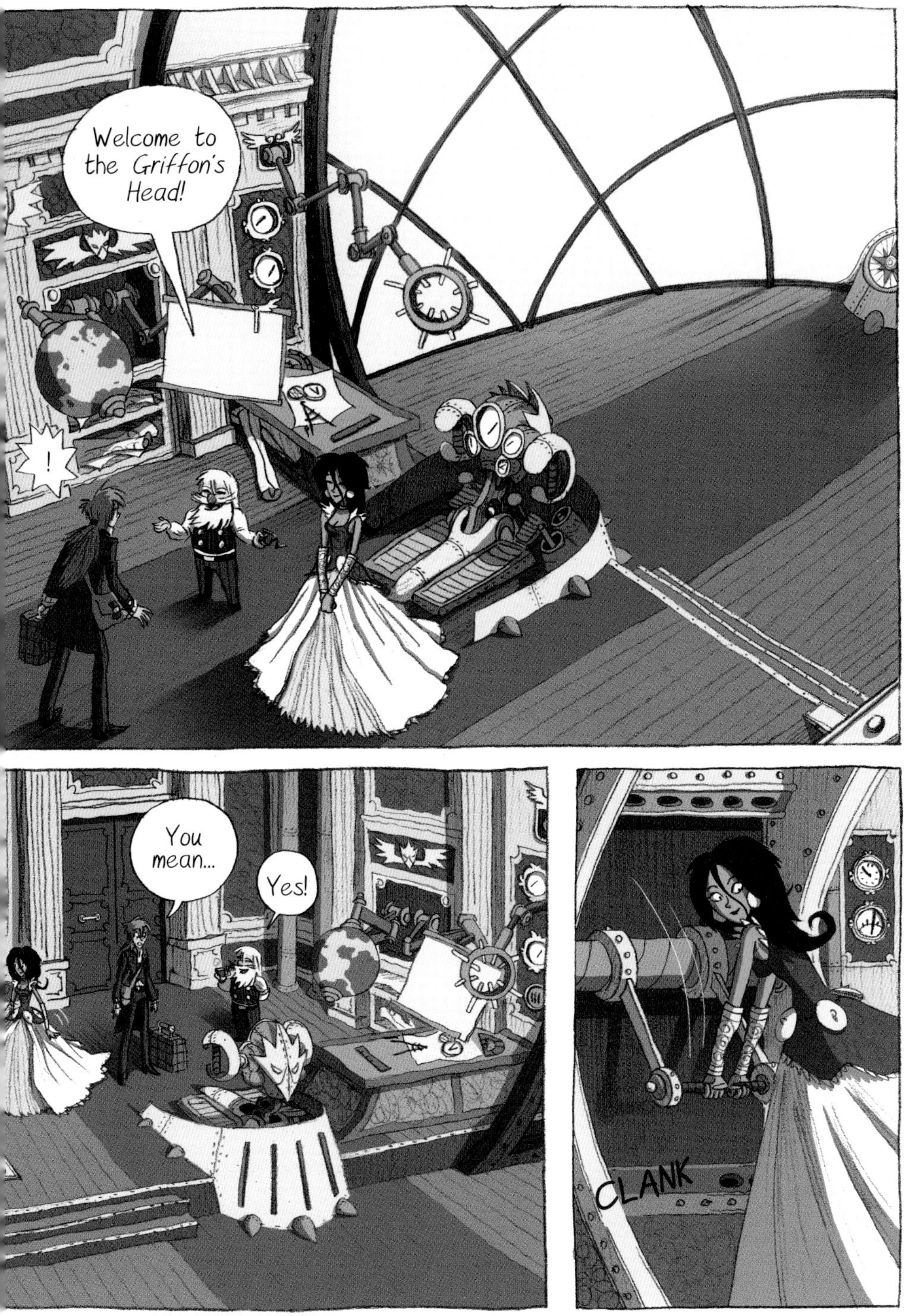
Welcome to the Griffon's Head!
!
You mean...
Yes!
CLANK

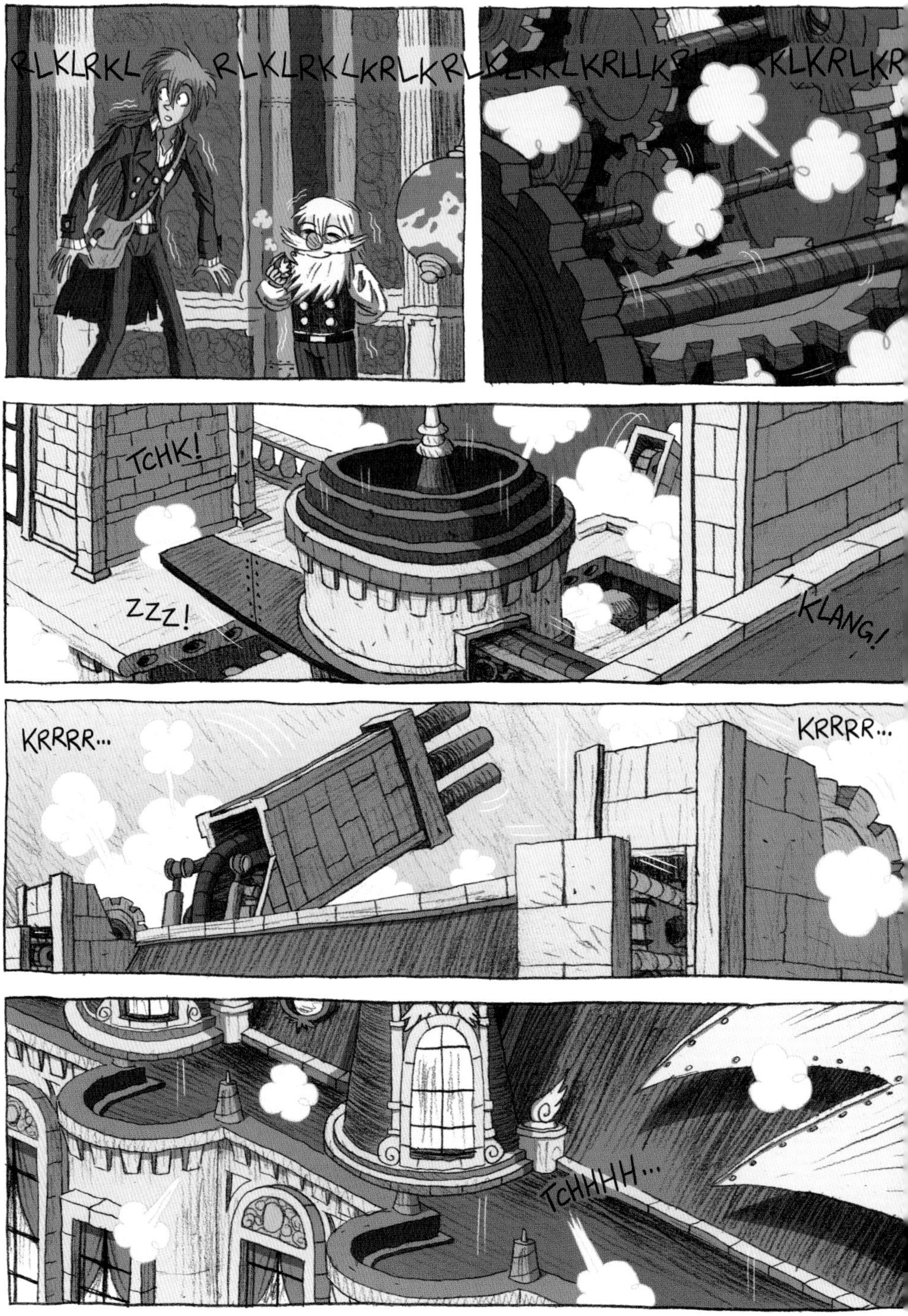
RLKLRKL RLKLRKLKRLKRLKLRKLKRLLKR KRKLKRLKR
TCHK!
ZZZ!
KLANG!
KRRRR...
KRRRR...
TCHHHH...

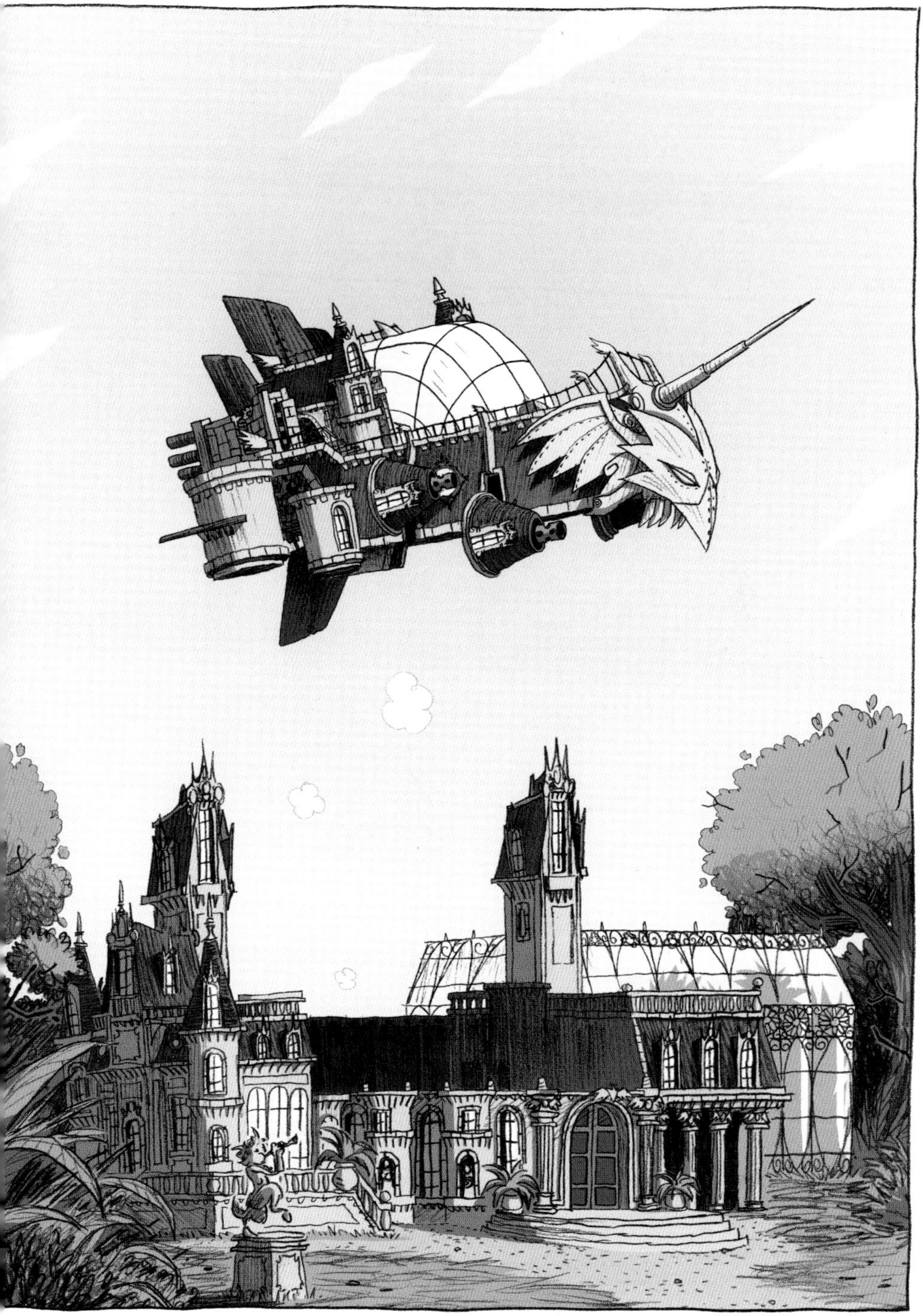

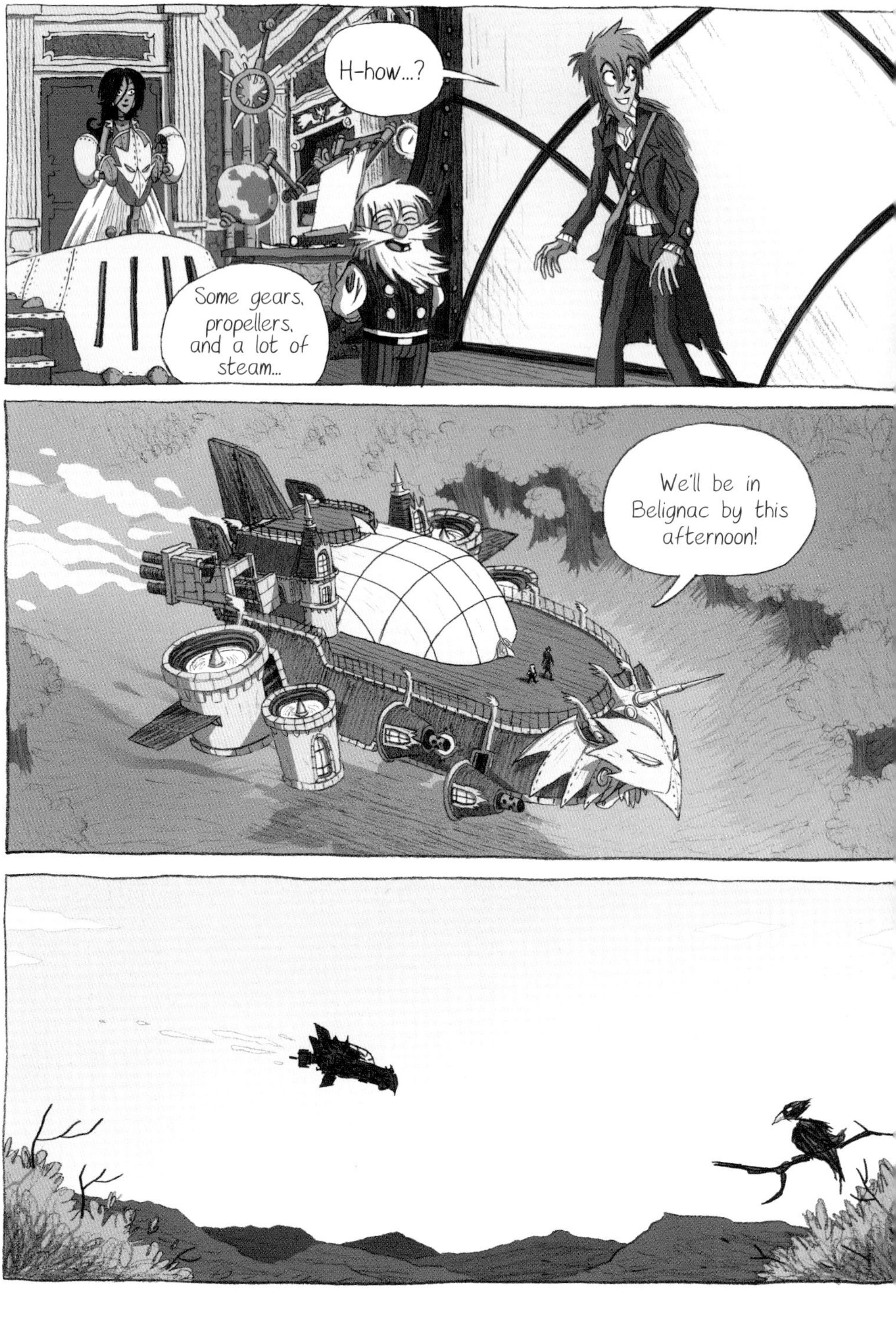
H-how...?
Some gears, propellers, and a lot of steam...
We'll be in Belignac by this afternoon!

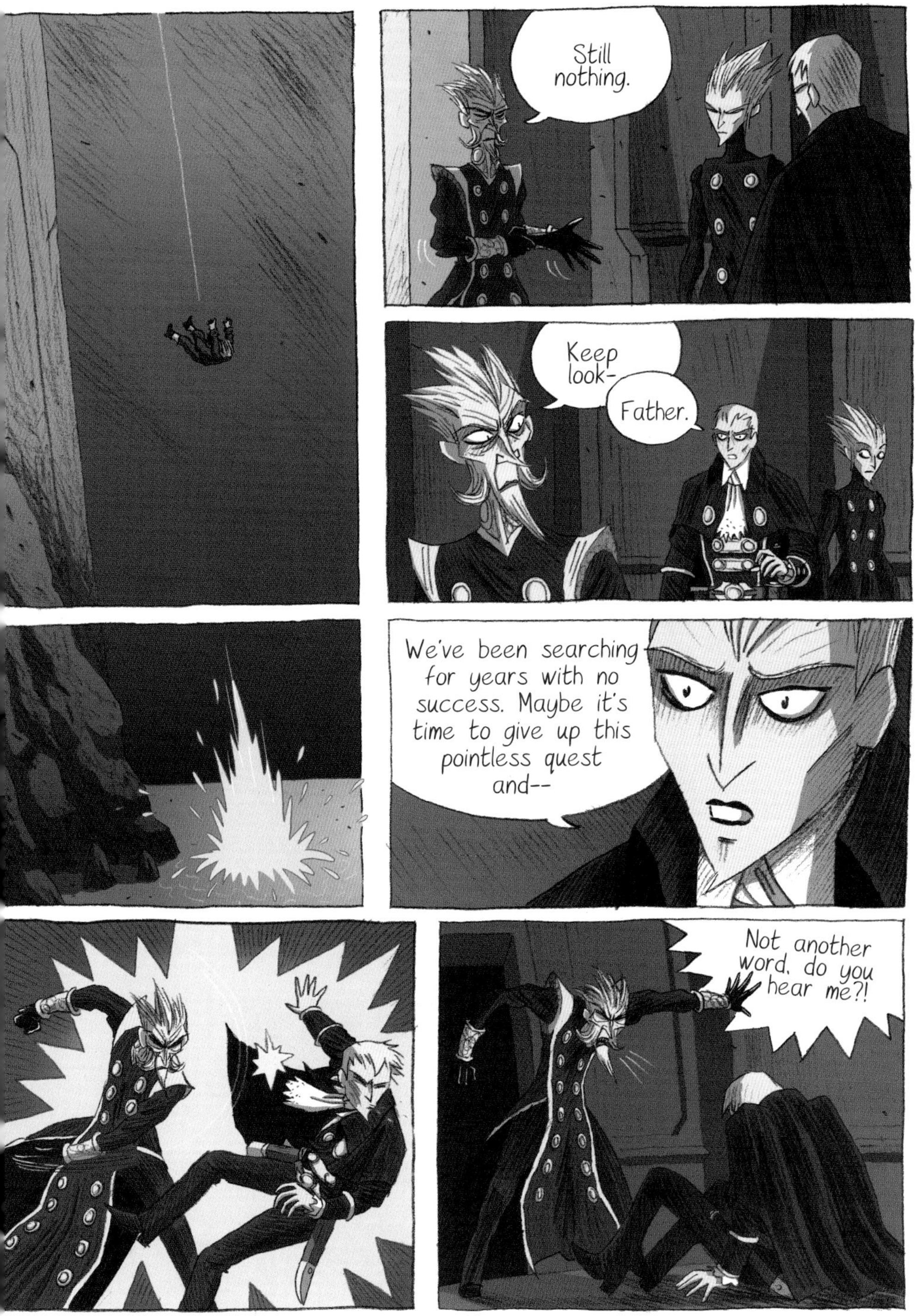
Still nothing.
Keep look-
Father.
We've been searching for years with no success. Maybe it's time to give up this pointless quest and--
Not another word, do you hear me?!

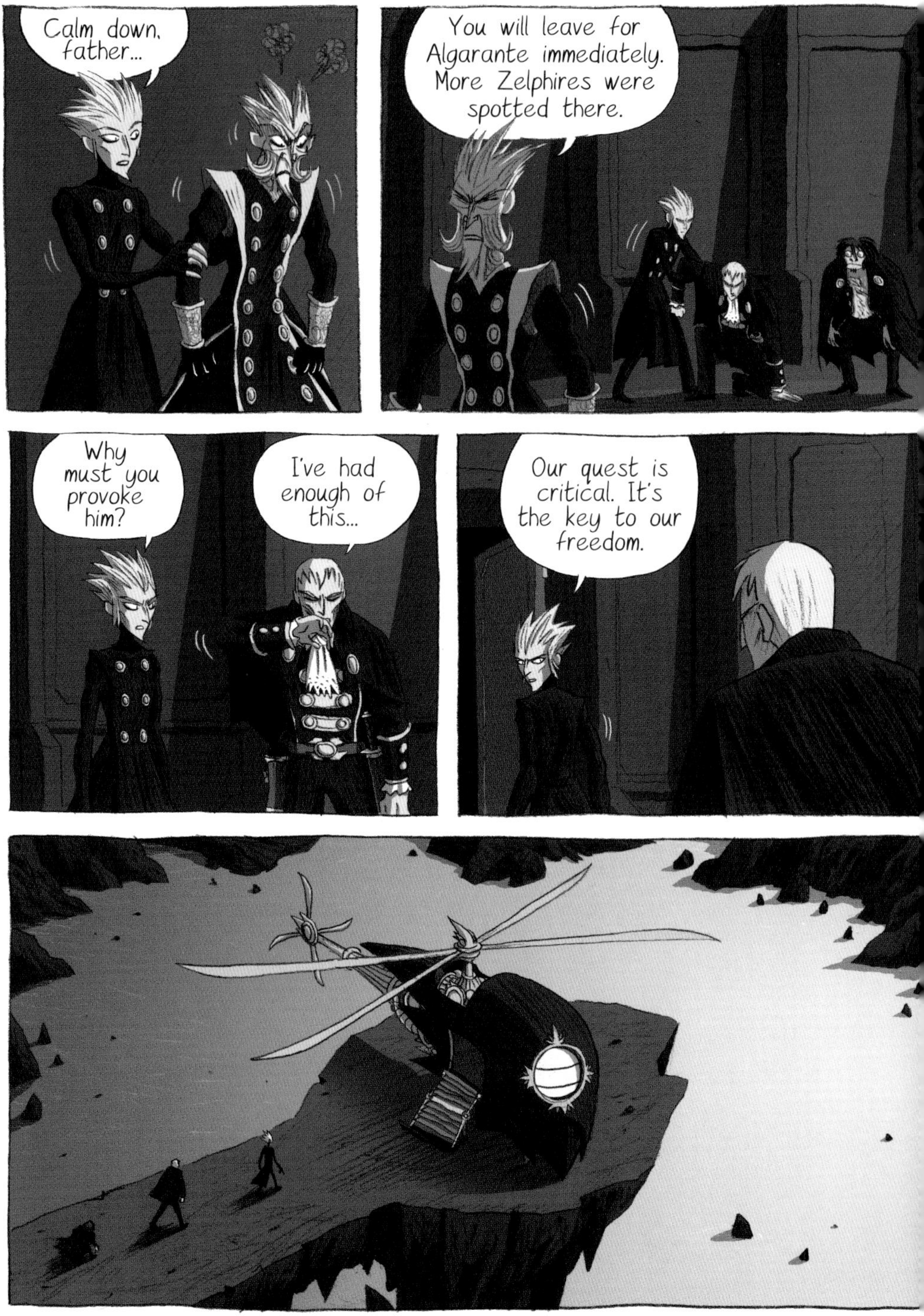
Calm down, father...
You will leave for Algarante immediately. More Zelphires were spotted there.
Why must you provoke him?
I've had enough of this...
Our quest is critical. It's the key to our freedom.

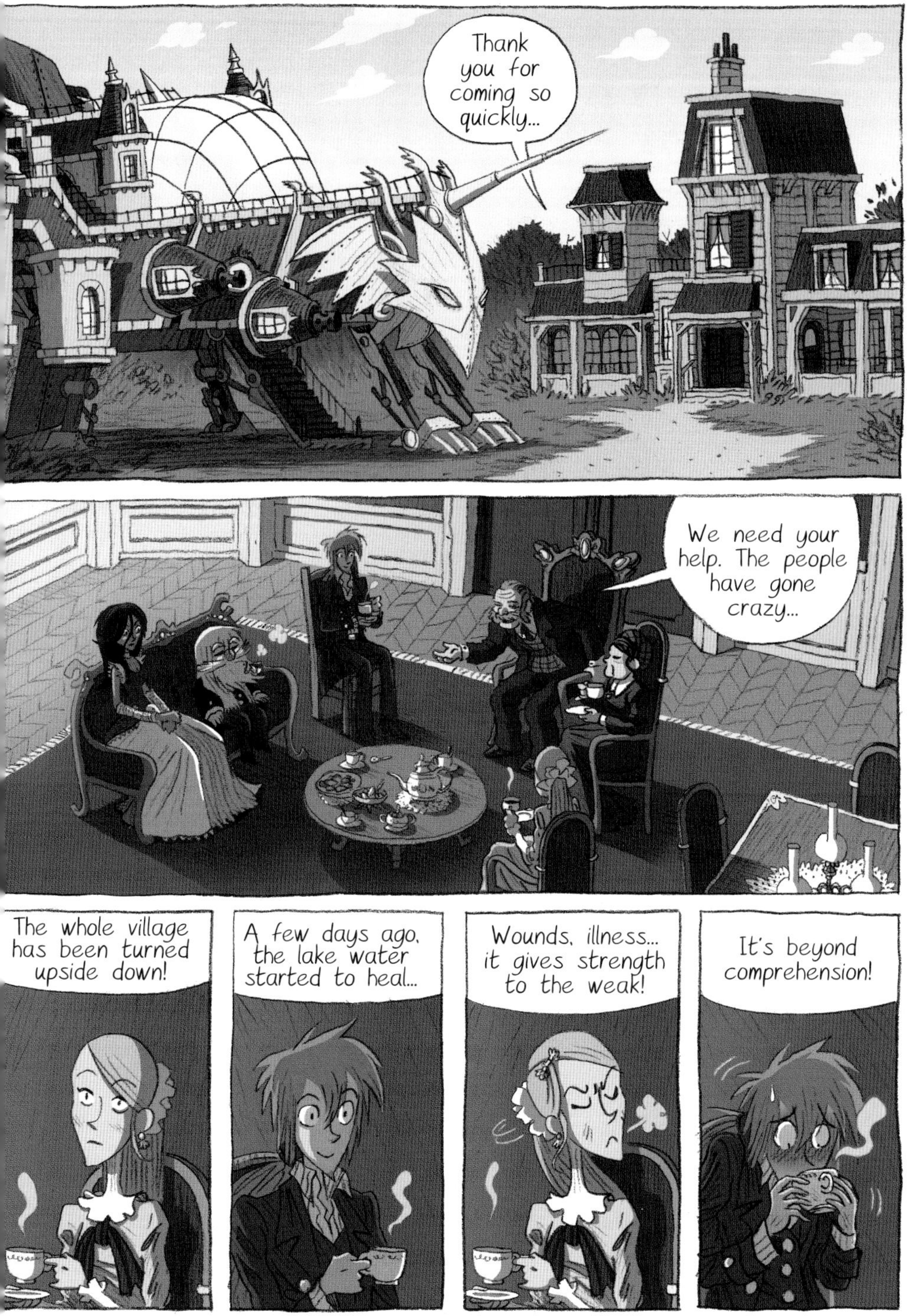
Thank you for coming so quickly...
We need your help. The people have gone crazy...
The whole village has been turned upside down!
A few days ago, the lake water started to heal...
Wounds, illness... it gives strength to the weak!
It's beyond comprehension!

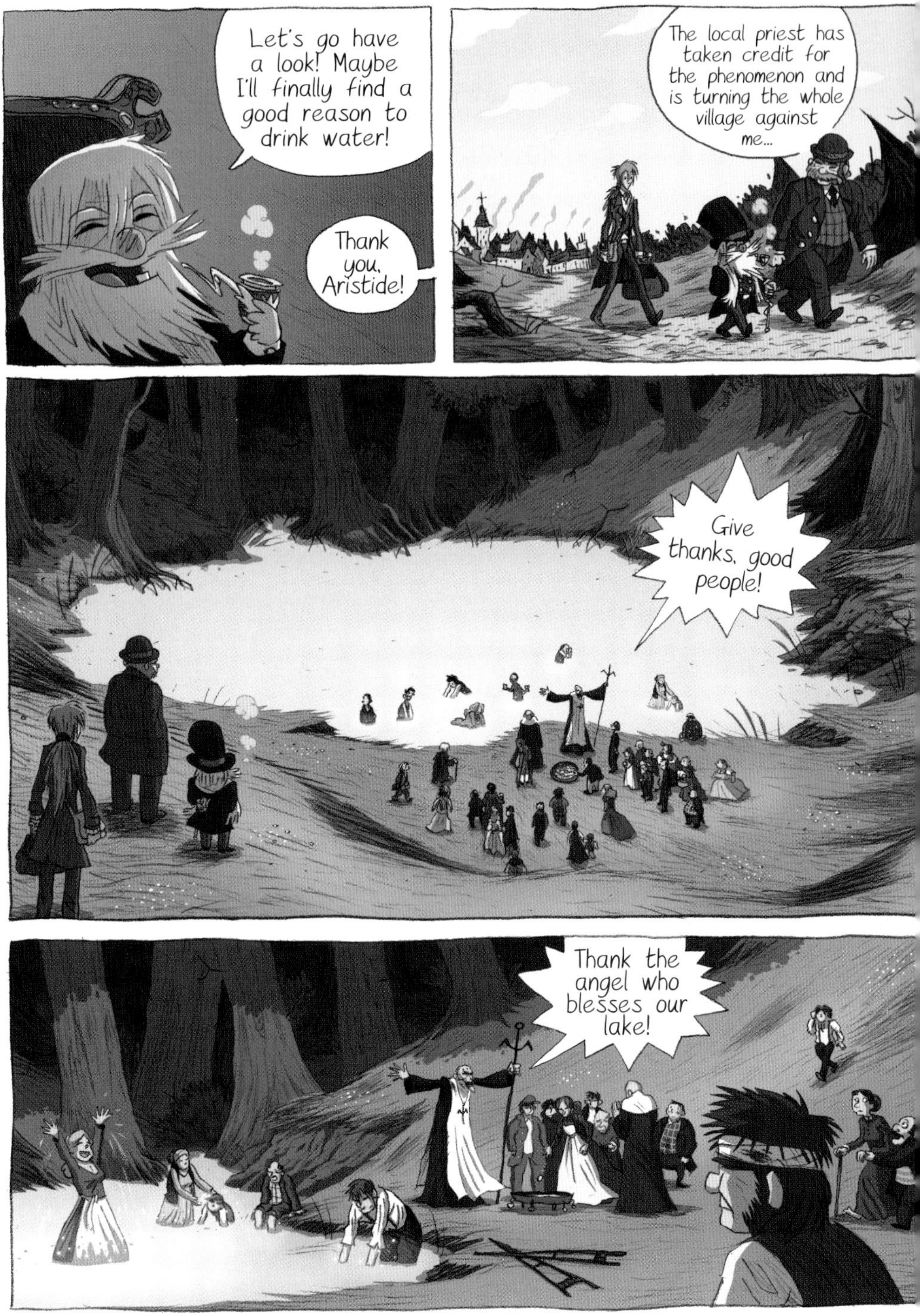
Let's go have a look! Maybe I'll finally find a good reason to drink water!
Thank you, Aristide!
The local priest has taken credit for the phenomenon and is turning the whole village against me...
Give thanks, good people!
Thank the angel who blesses our lake!

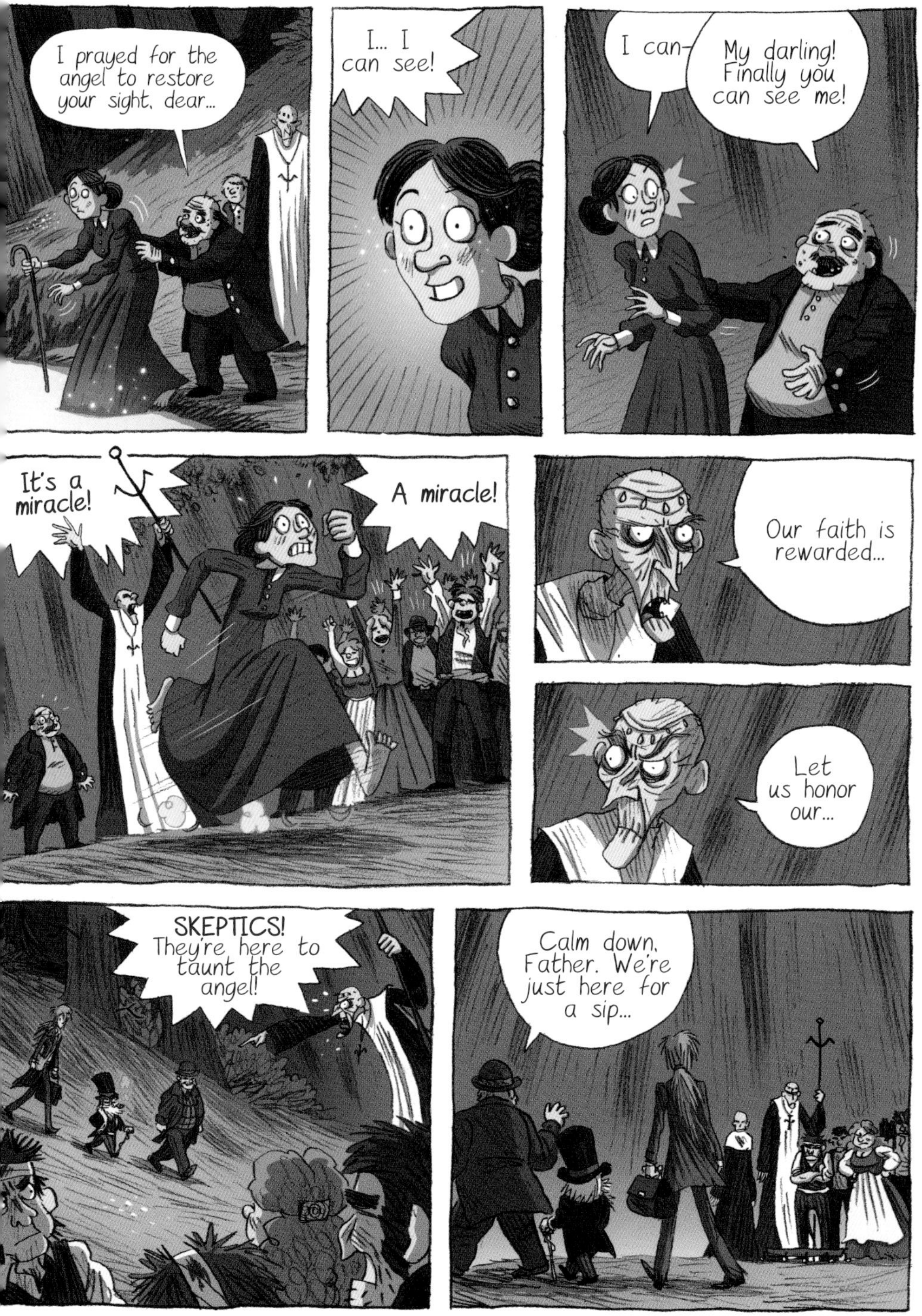
I prayed for the angel to restore your sight, dear...
I... I can see!
I can-
My darling! Finally you can see me!
It's a miracle!
A miracle!
Our faith is rewarded...
Let us honor our...
SKEPTICS! They're here to taunt the angel!
Calm down, Father. We're just here for a sip...

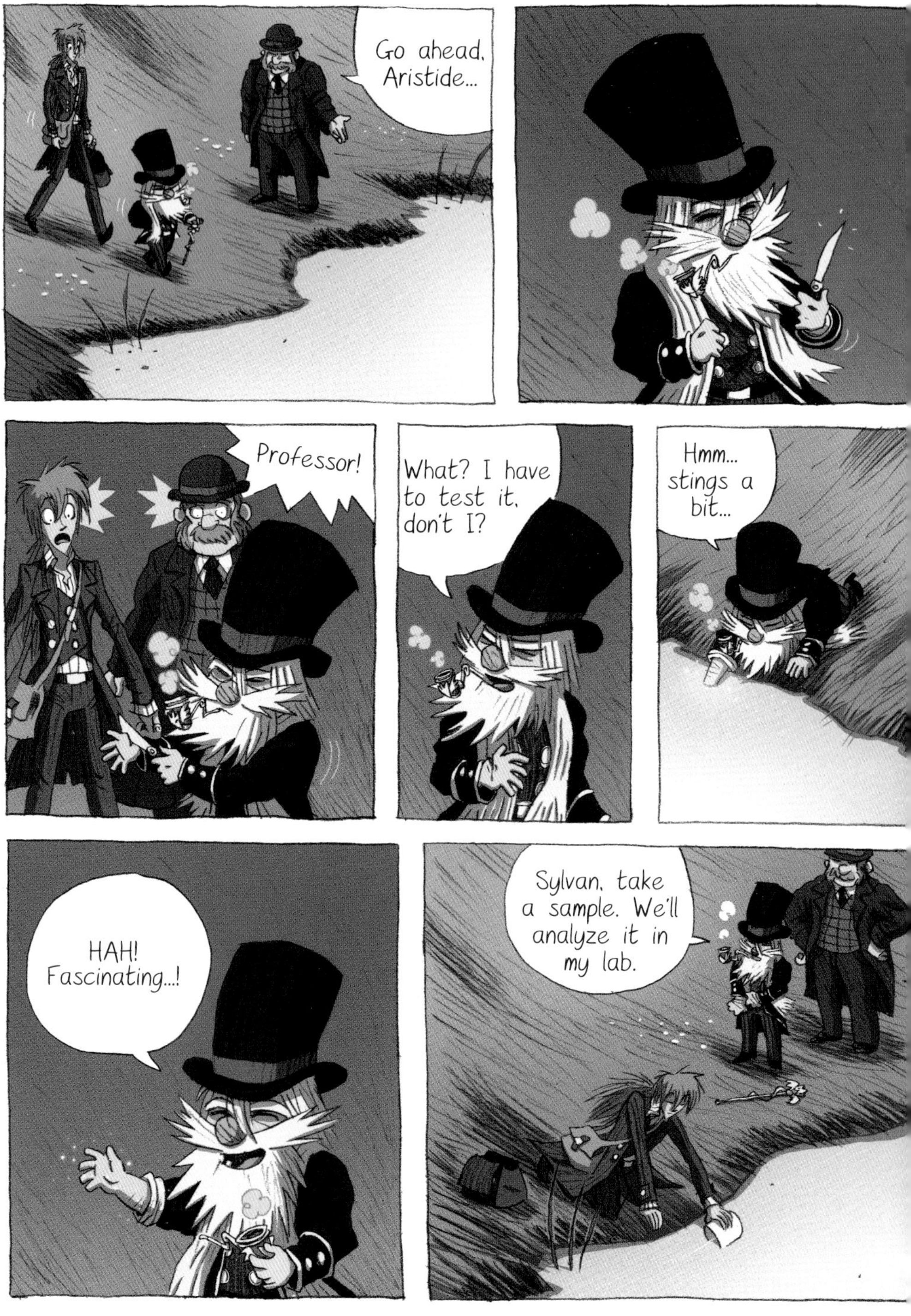

Go ahead, Aristide...
Professor!
What? I have to test it, don't I?
Hmm... stings a bit...
HAH! Fascinating...!
Sylvan, take a sample. We'll analyze it in my lab.

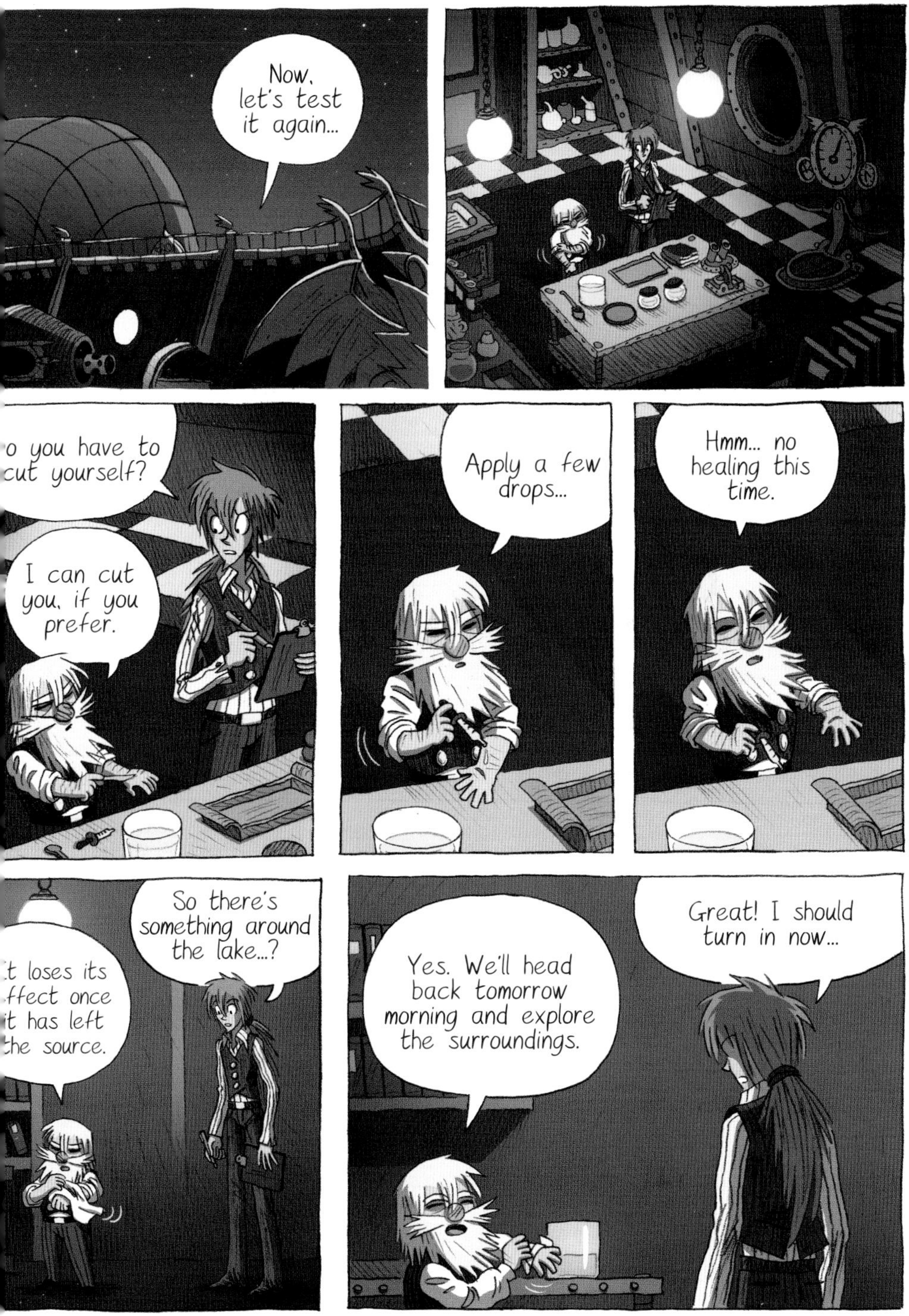
Now, let's test it again...
o you have to cut yourself?
I can cut you, if you prefer.
Apply a few drops...
Hmm... no healing this time.
t loses its ffect once it has left the source.
So there's something around the lake...?
Yes. We'll head back tomorrow morning and explore the surroundings.
Great! I should turn in now...

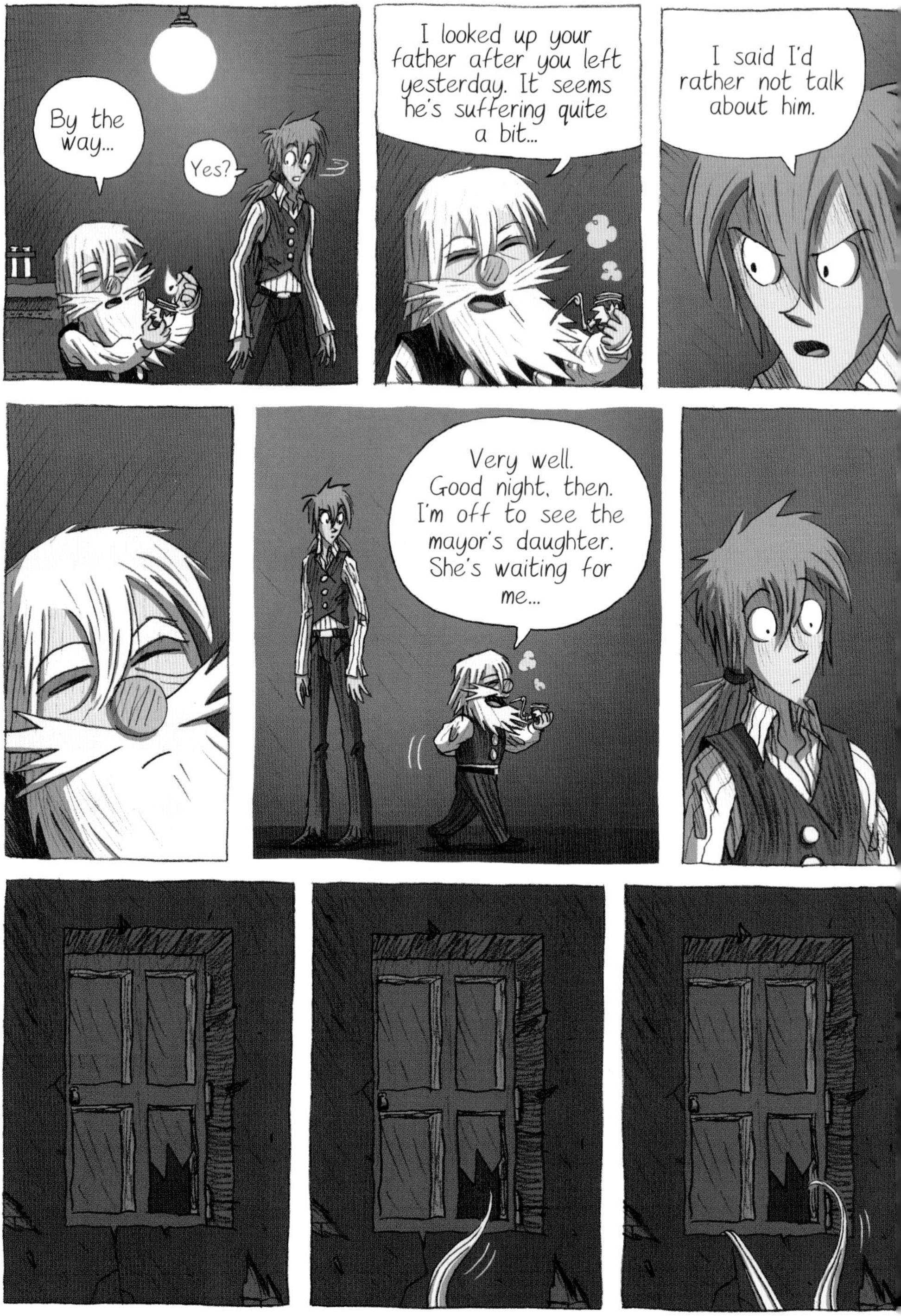
By the way...
Yes?
I looked up your father after you left yesterday. It seems he's suffering quite a bit...
I said I'd rather not talk about him.
Very well. Good night, then. I'm off to see the mayor's daughter. She's waiting for me...

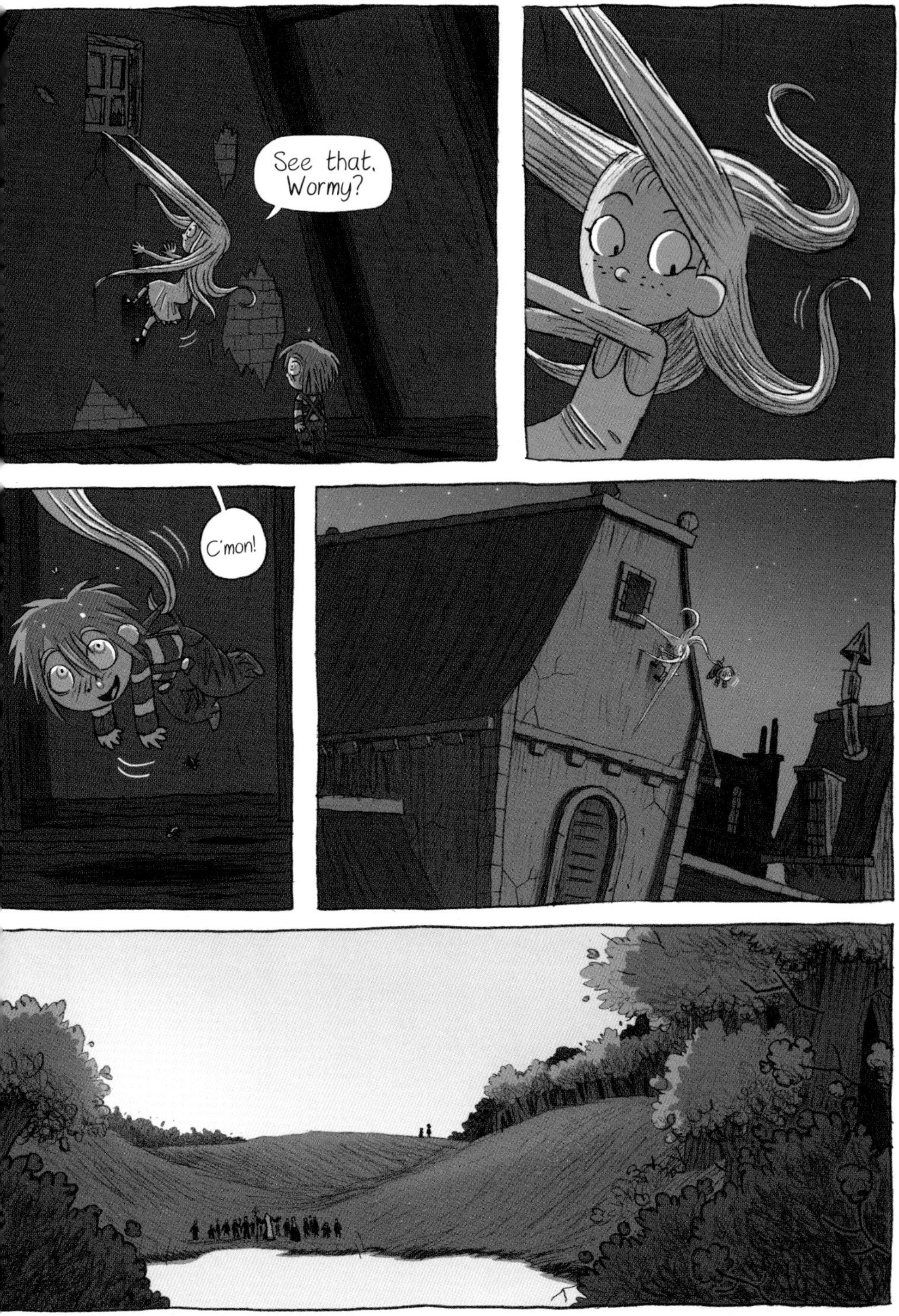
See that, Wormy?
C'mon!

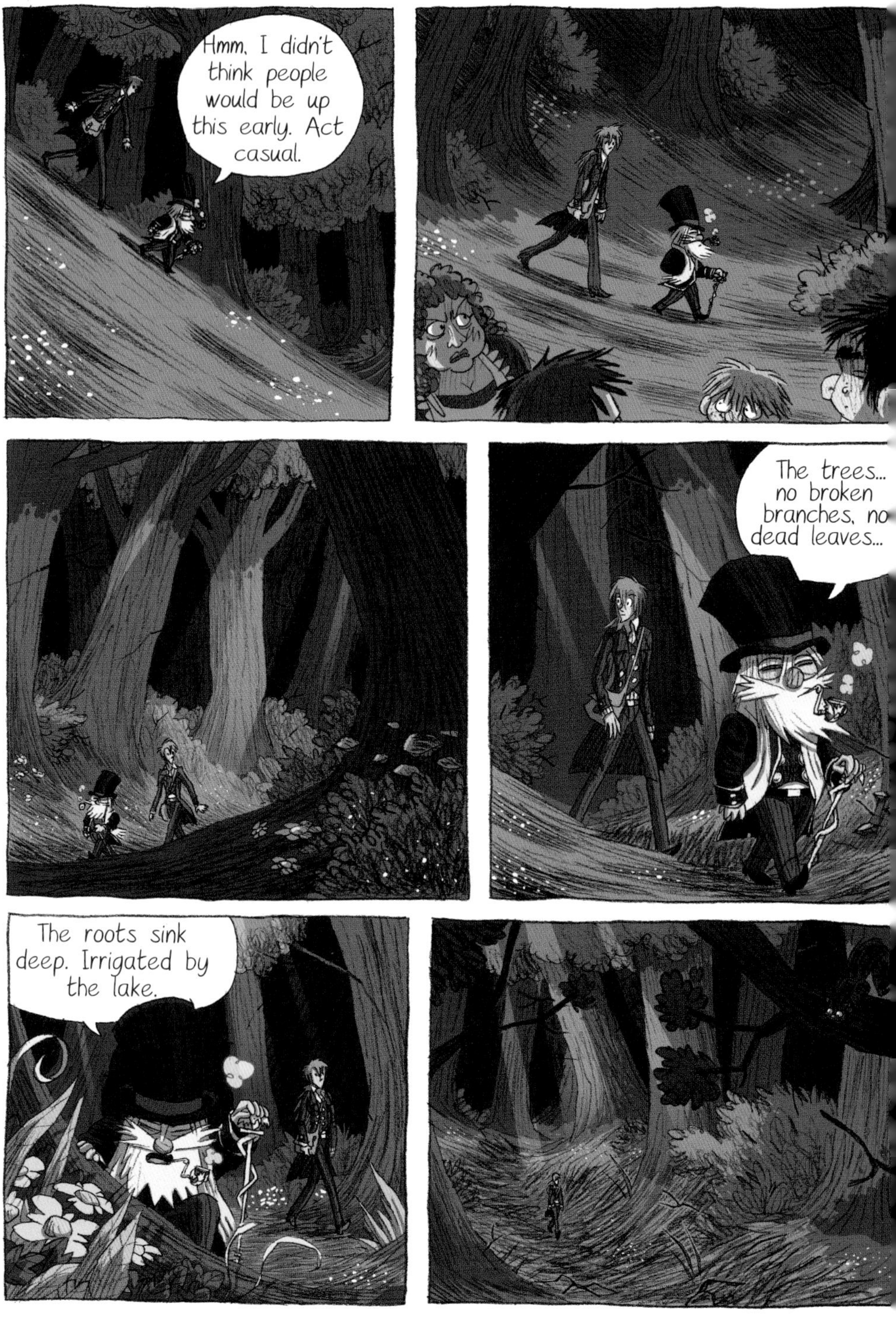
Hmm, I didn't think people would be up this early. Act casual.
The trees... no broken branches, no dead leaves...
The roots sink deep. Irrigated by the lake.

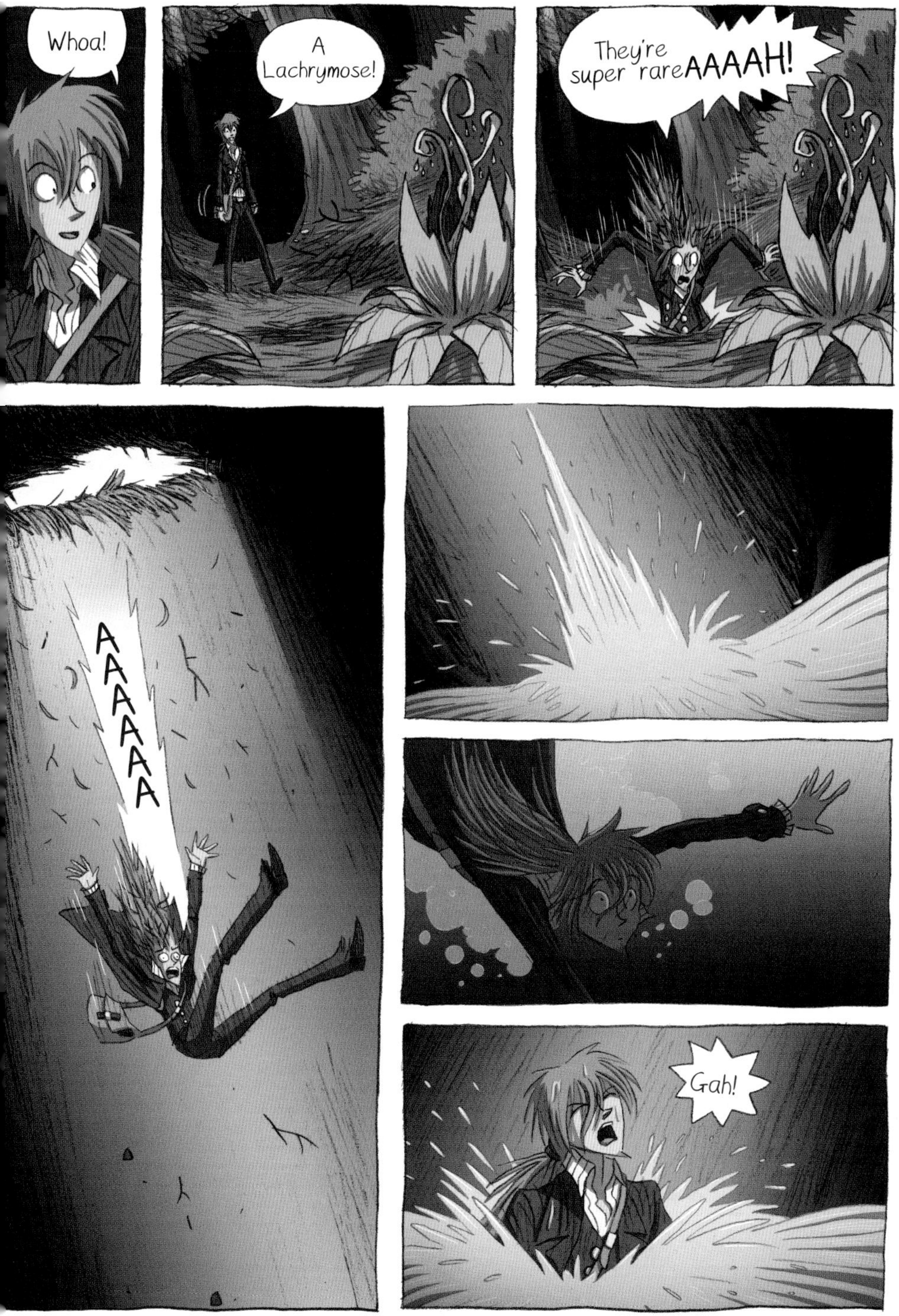
Whoa!
A Lachrymose!
They're super rareAAAAH!
AAAAAA
Gah!

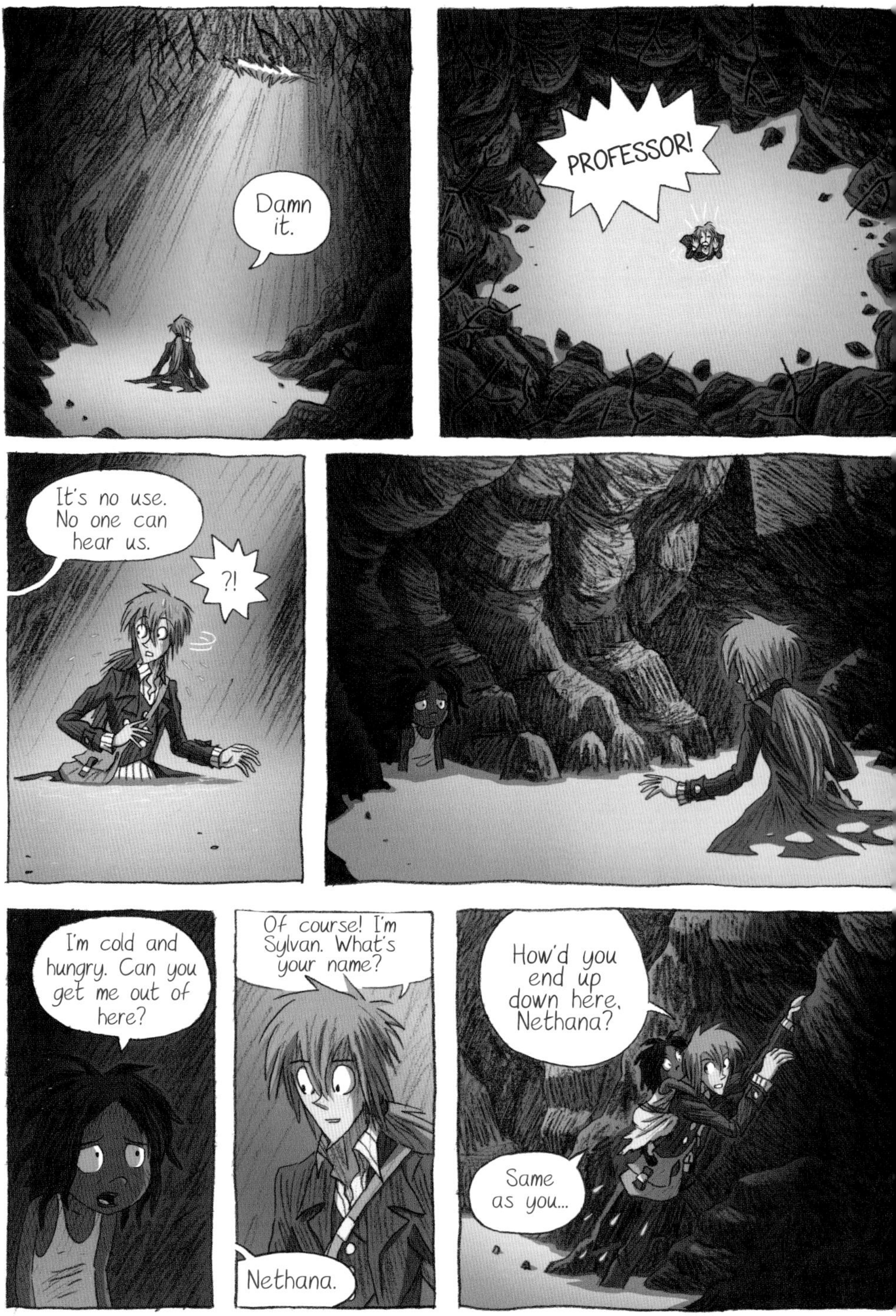
Damn it.
PROFESSOR!
It's no use. No one can hear us.
?!
I'm cold and hungry. Can you get me out of here?
Of course! I'm Sylvan. What's your name?
Nethana.
How'd you end up down here, Nethana?
Same as you...

?

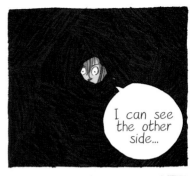

I can see the other side...

Ngn... it's too tough...

I might have to...

...Nethana, don't be scared, okay?

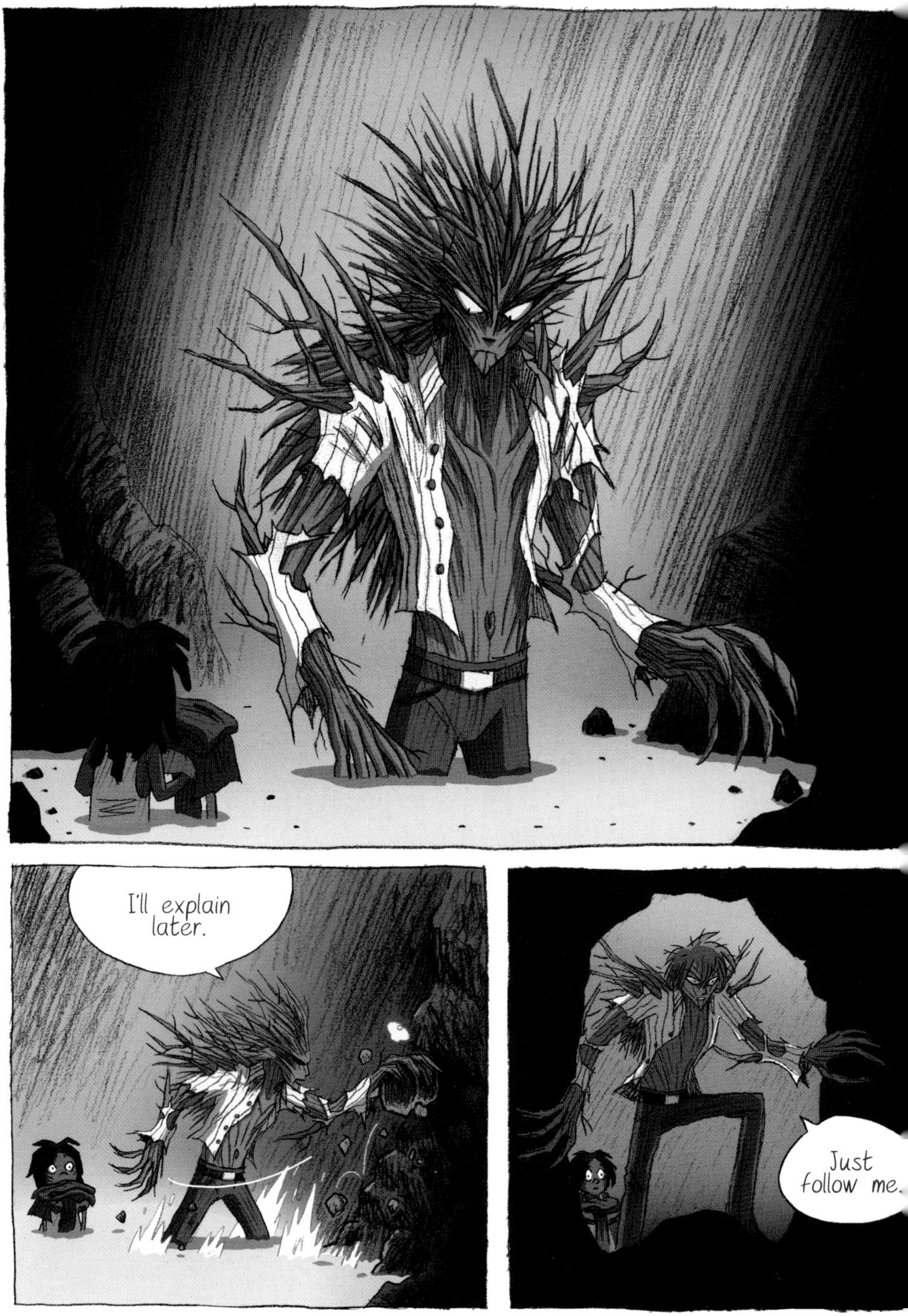
I'll explain later.
Just follow me.

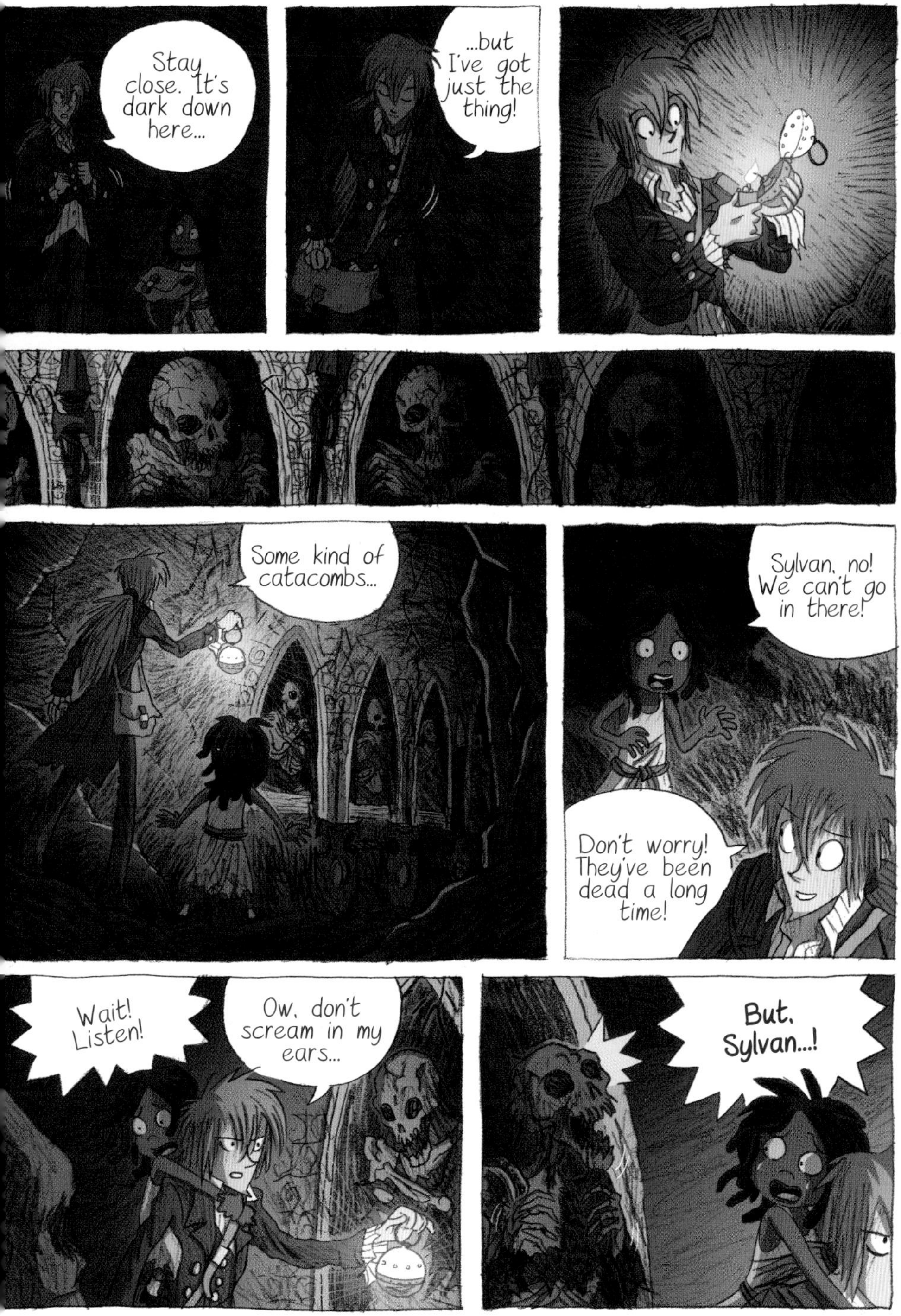
Stay close. It's dark down here...
...but I've got just the thing!
Some kind of catacombs...
Sylvan, no! We can't go in there!
Don't worry! They've been dead a long time!
Wait! Listen!
Ow, don't scream in my ears...
But, Sylvan...!

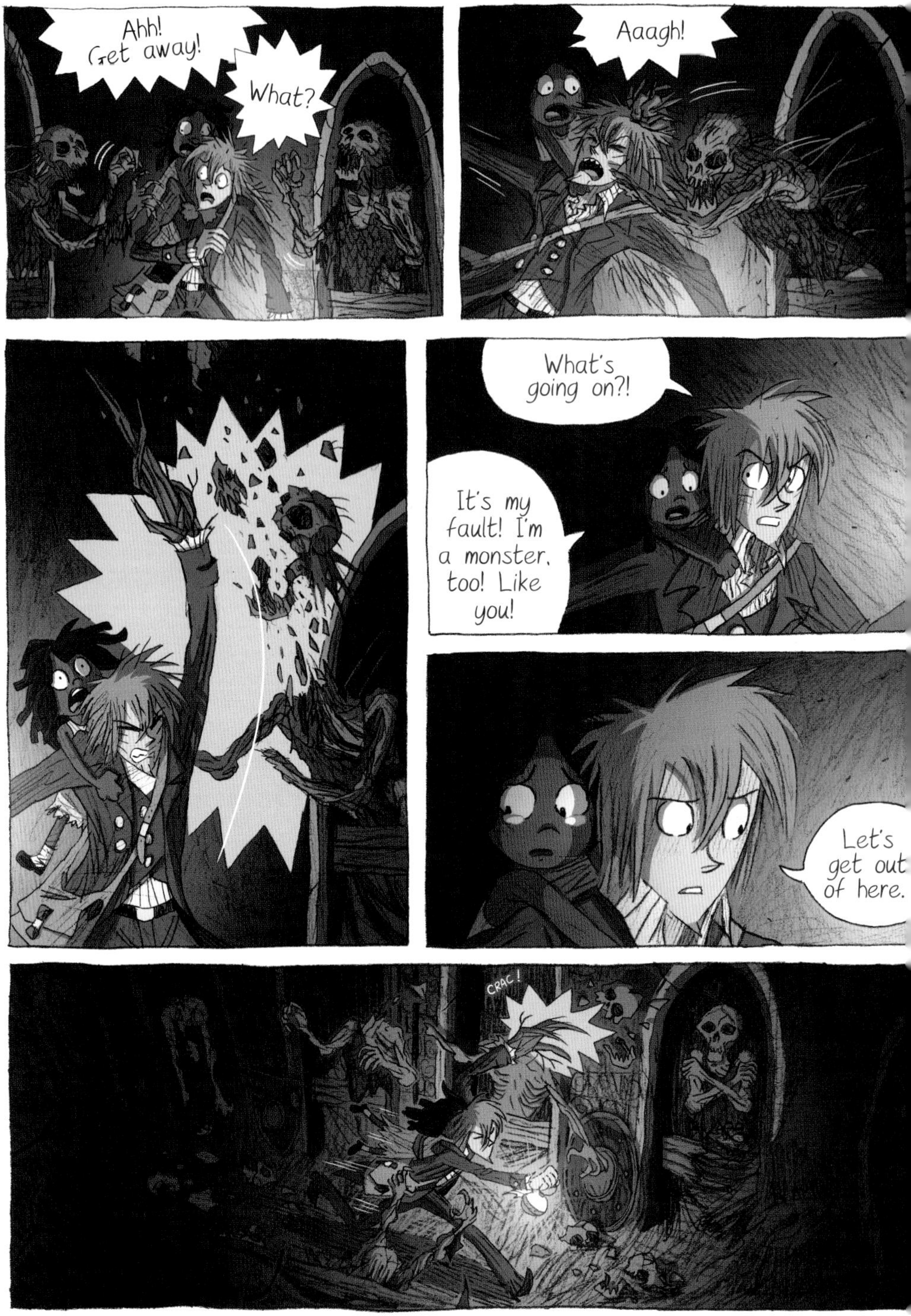
Ahh! Get away!
What?
Aaagh!
What's going on?!
It's my fault! I'm a monster, too! Like you!
Let's get out of here.
CRAC!

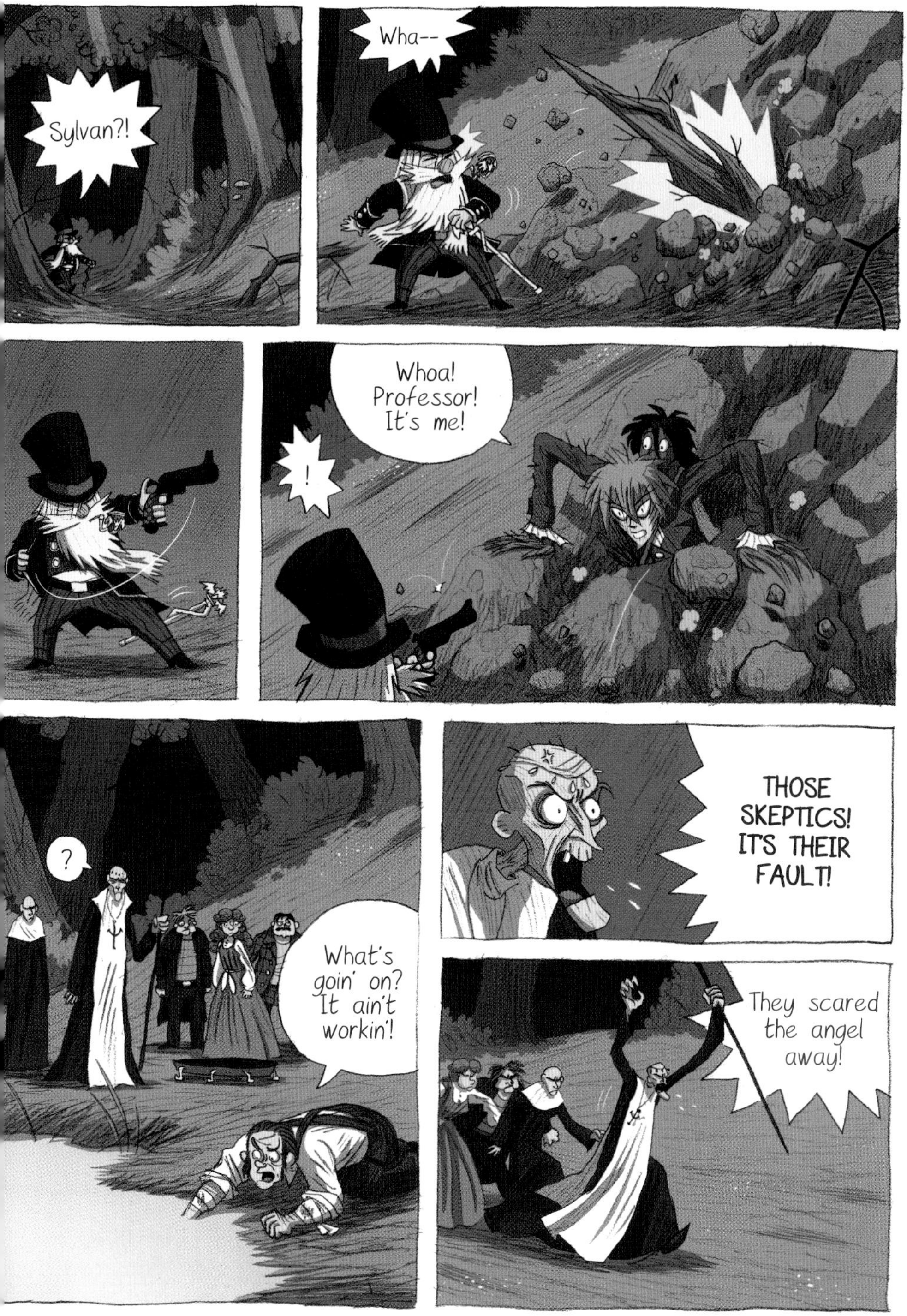
Sylvan?!
Wha--
Whoa! Professor! It's me!
!
?
What's goin' on? It ain't workin'!
THOSE SKEPTICS! IT'S THEIR FAULT!
They scared the angel away!

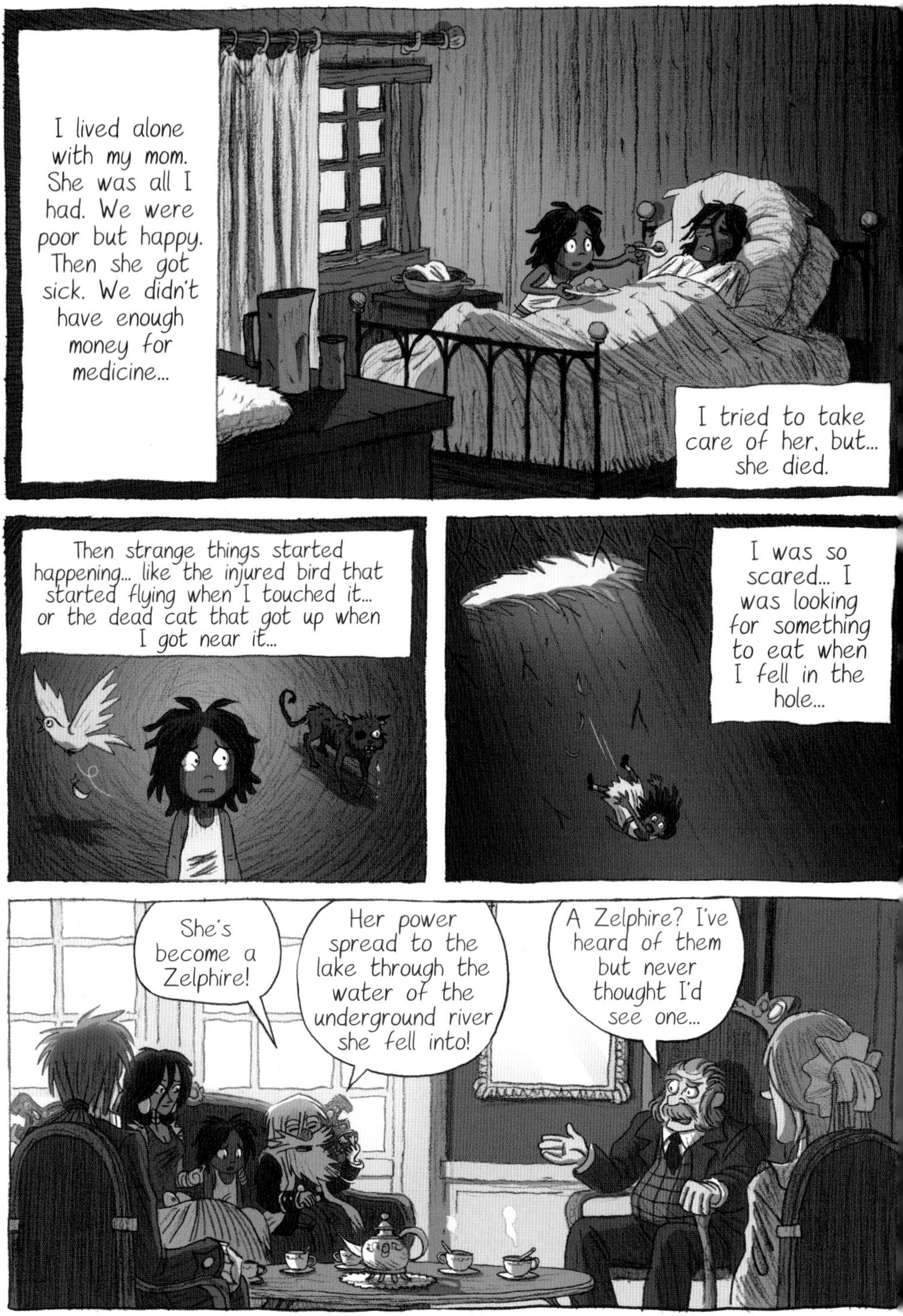
I lived alone with my mom. She was all I had. We were poor but happy. Then she got sick. We didn't have enough money for medicine...
I tried to take care of her, but... she died.
Then strange things started happening... like the injured bird that started flying when I touched it... or the dead cat that got up when I got near it...
I was so scared... I was looking for something to eat when I fell in the hole...
She's become a Zelphire!
Her power spread to the lake through the water of the underground river she fell into!
A Zelphire? I've heard of them but never thought I'd see one...

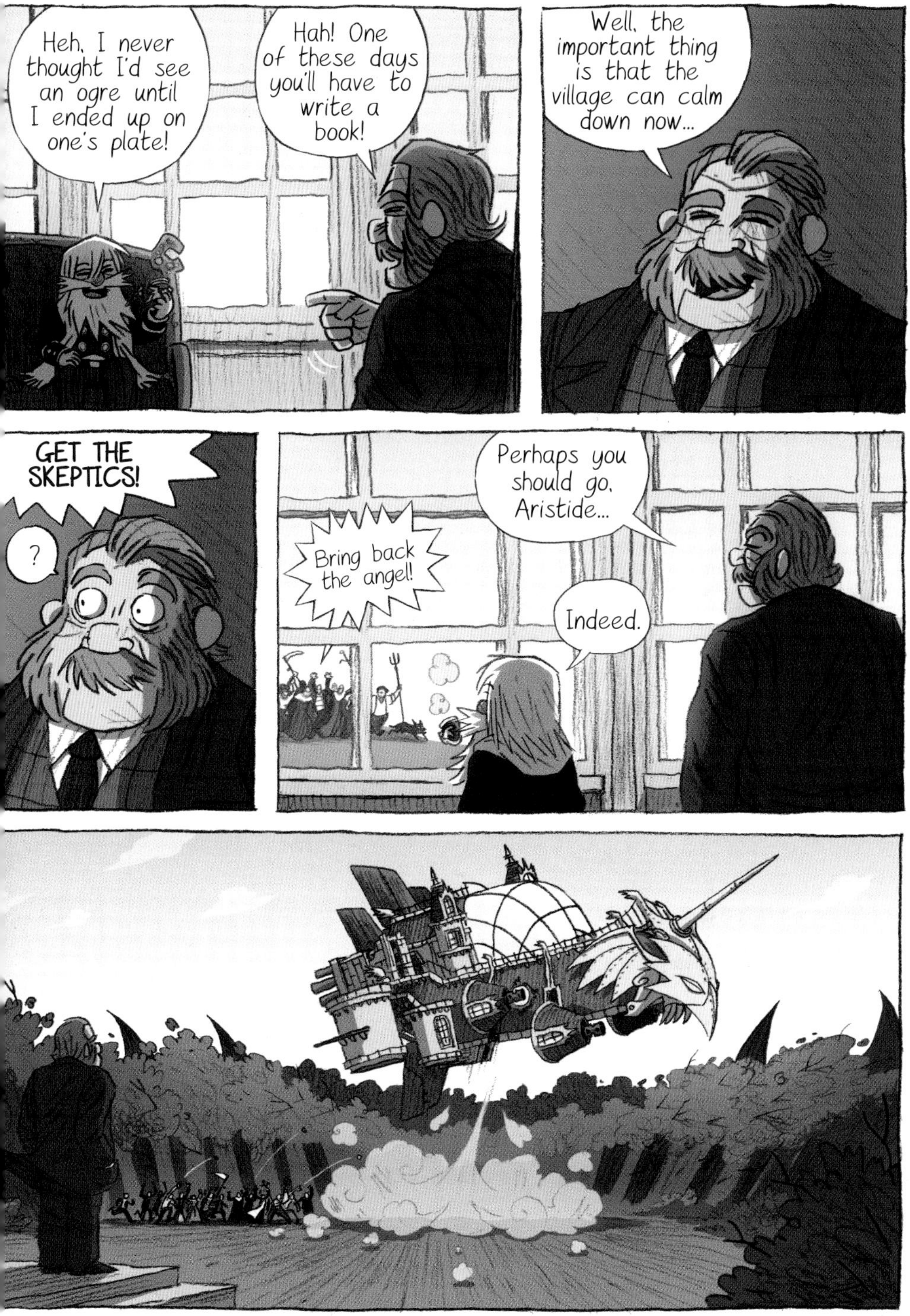
Heh, I never thought I'd see an ogre until I ended up on one's plate!
Hah! One of these days you'll have to write a book!
Well, the important thing is that the village can calm down now...
GET THE SKEPTICS!
?
Bring back the angel!
Perhaps you should go, Aristide...
Indeed.

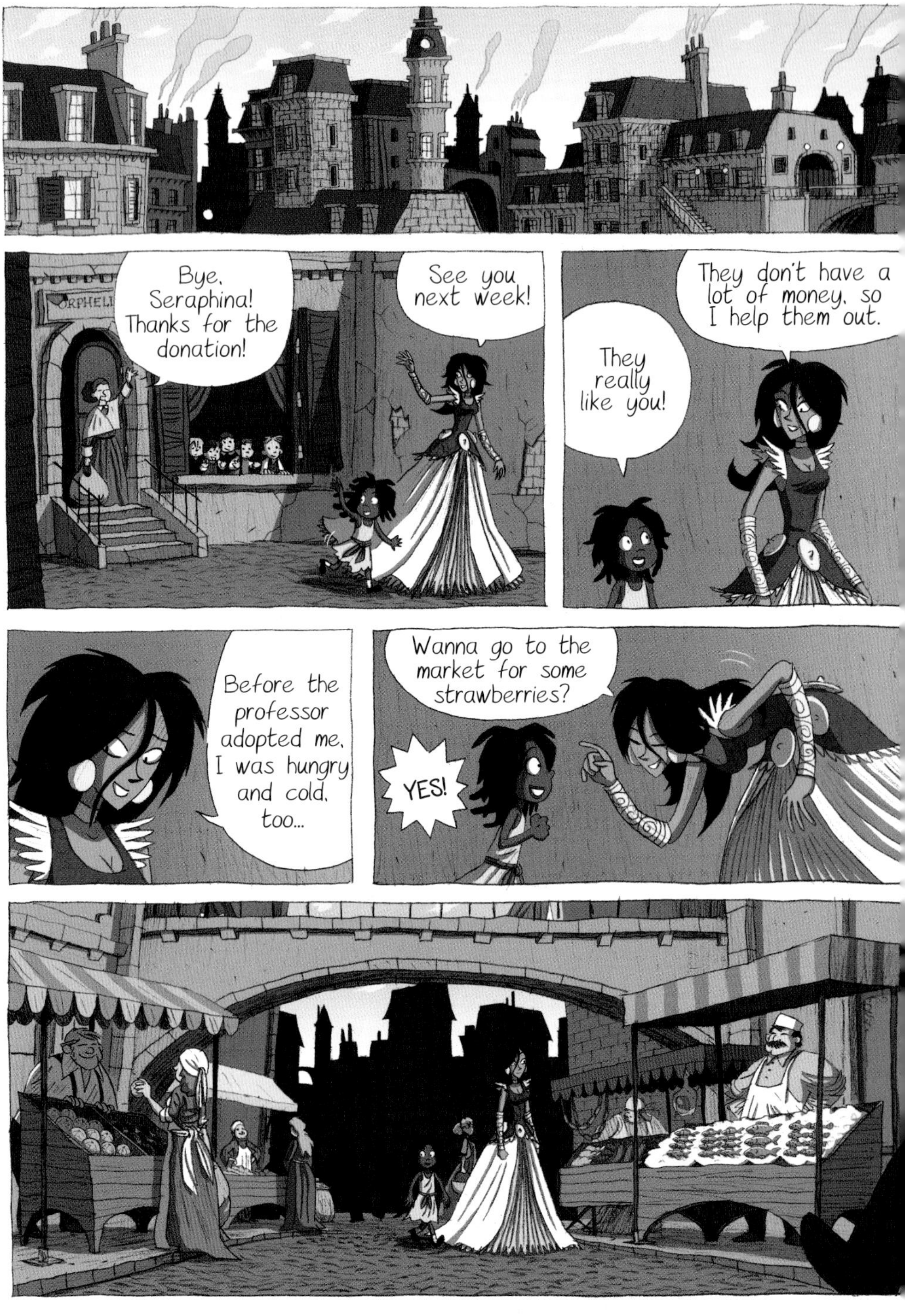
Bye, Seraphina! Thanks for the donation!
See you next week!
They don't have a lot of money, so I help them out.
They really like you!
Before the professor adopted me, I was hungry and cold, too...
Wanna go to the market for some strawberries?
YES!

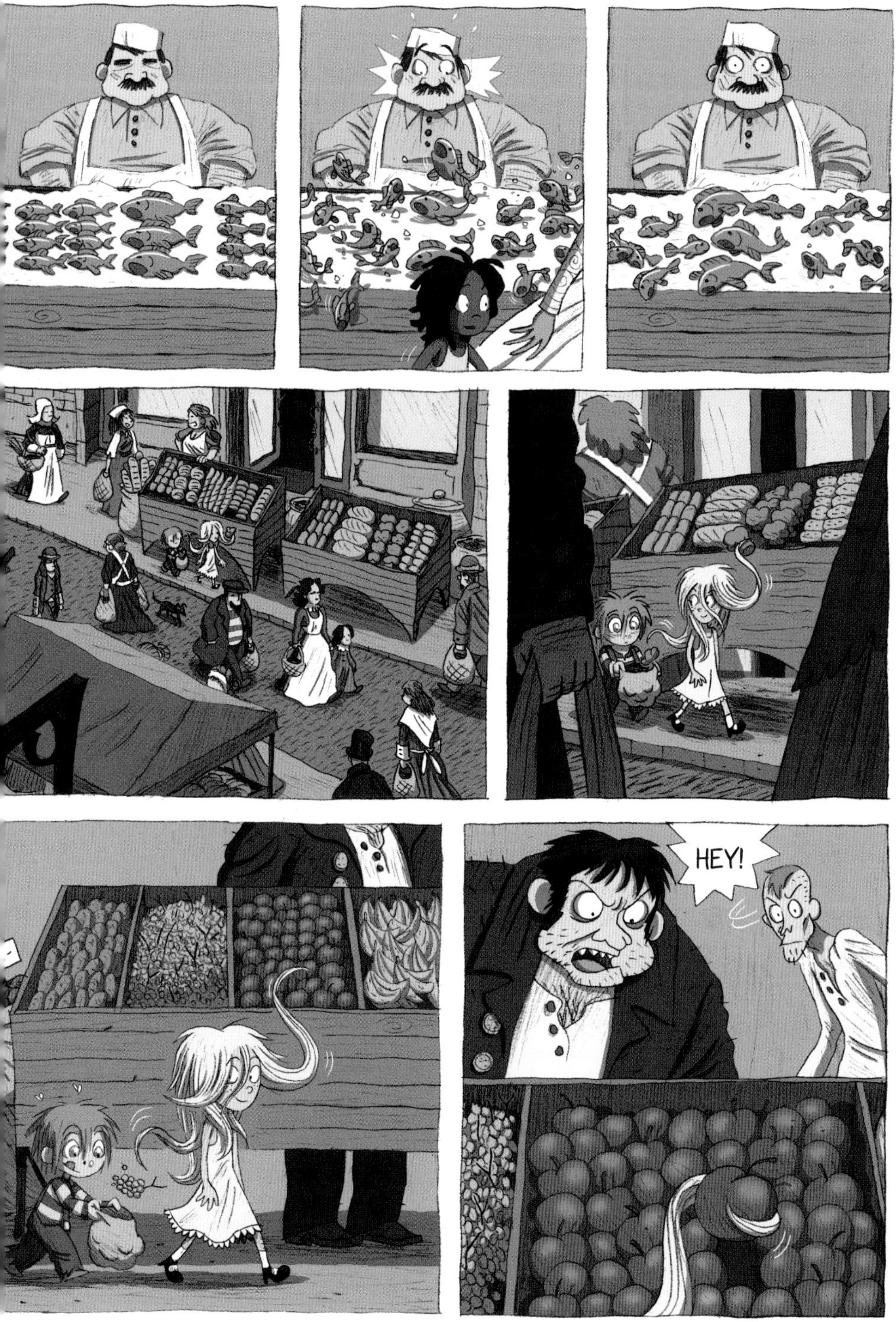
HEY!

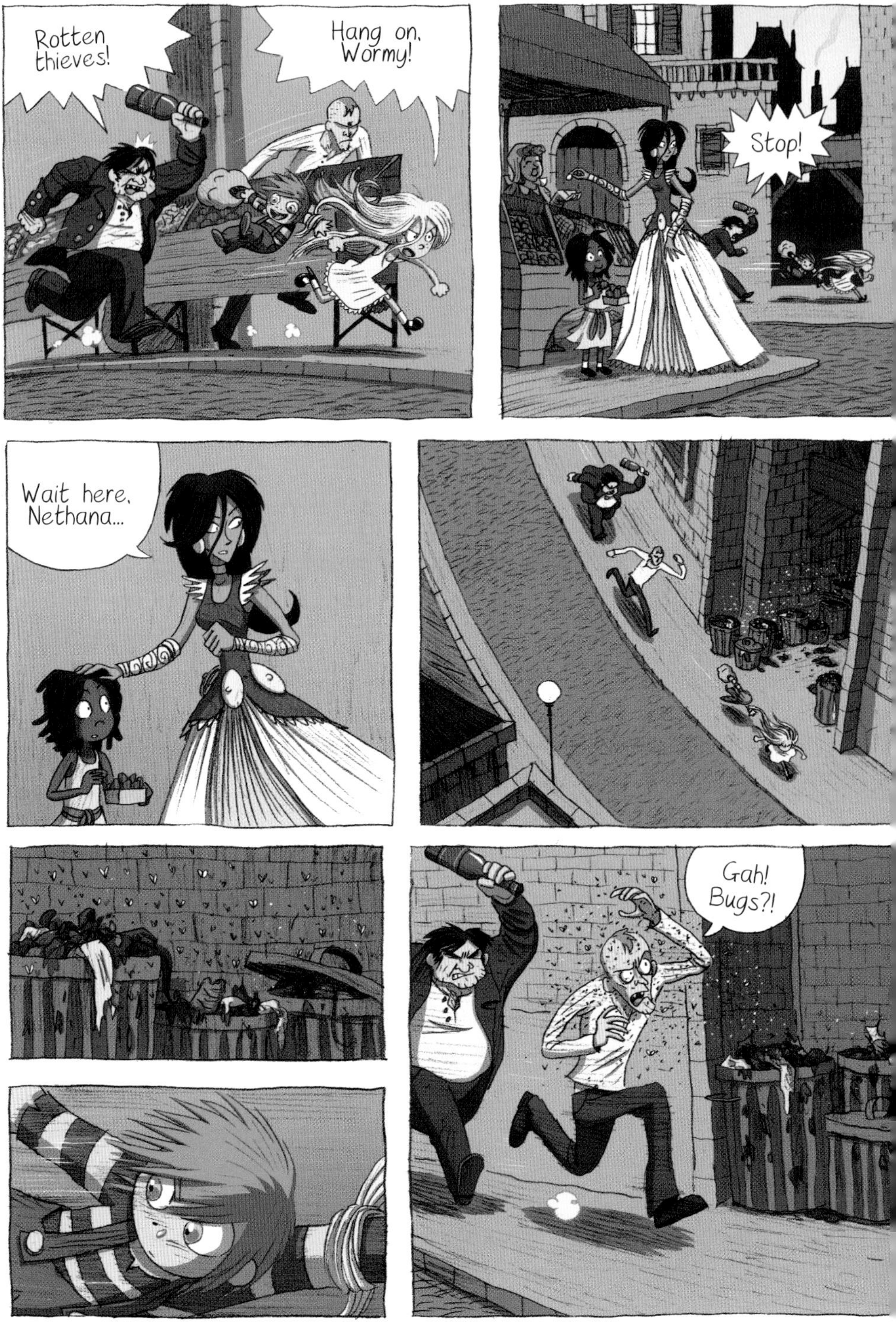
Rotten thieves!
Hang on, Wormy!
Stop!
Wait here, Nethana...
Gah! Bugs?!

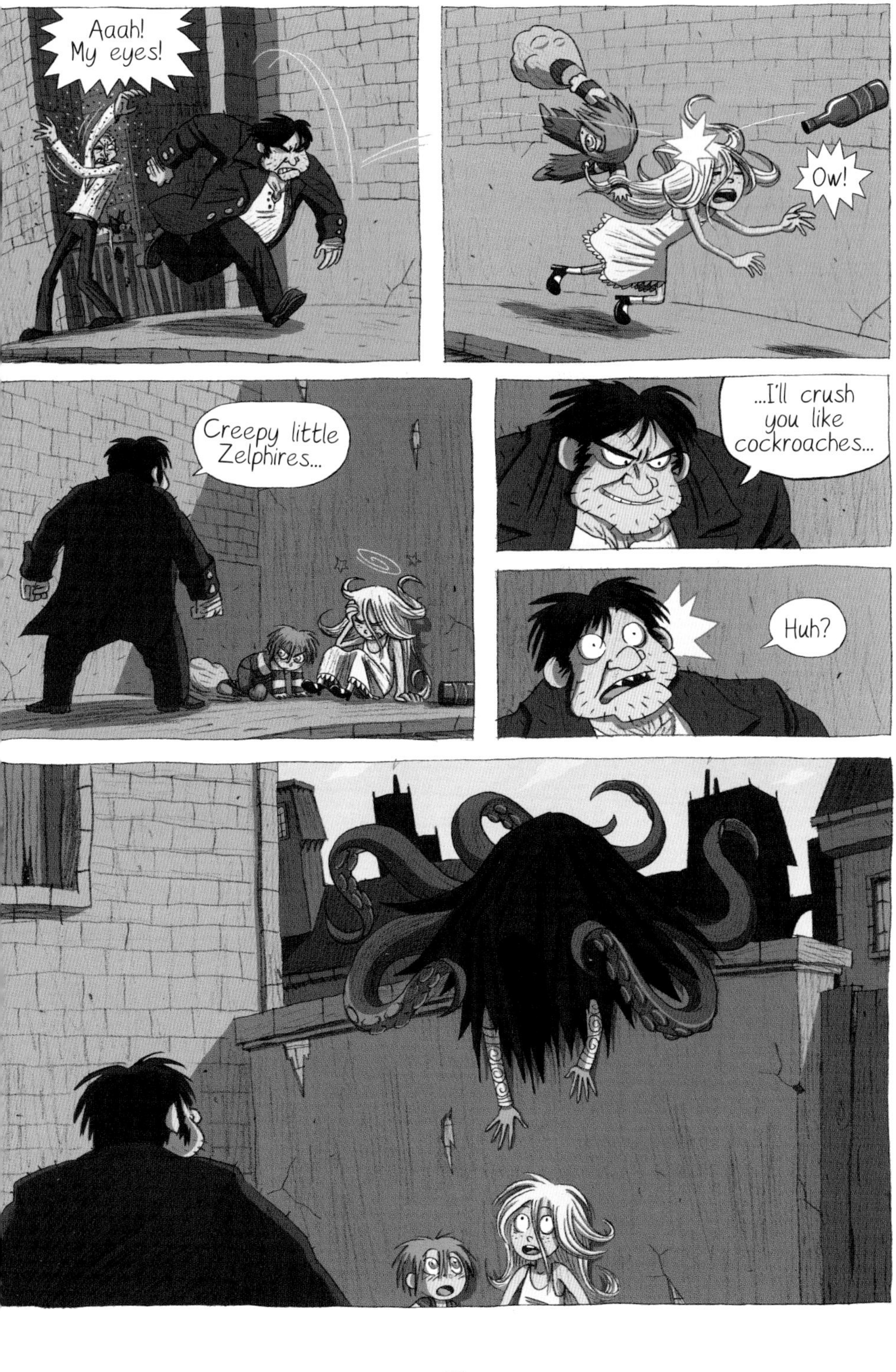
Aaah! My eyes!
Ow!
Creepy little Zelphires...
...I'll crush you like cockroaches...
Huh?

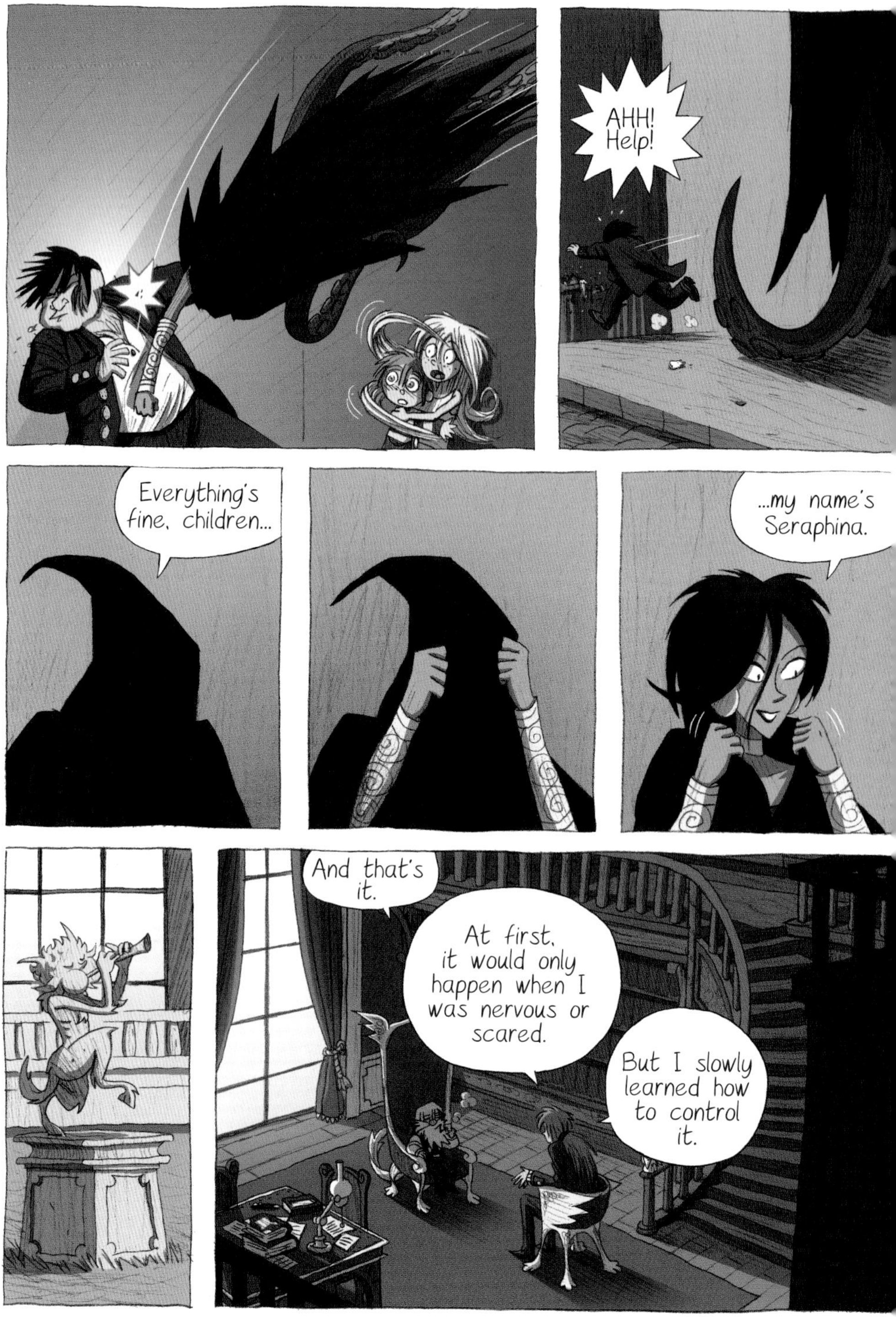
AHH! Help!
Everything's fine, children...
...my name's Seraphina.
And that's it.
At first, it would only happen when I was nervous or scared.
But I slowly learned how to control it.

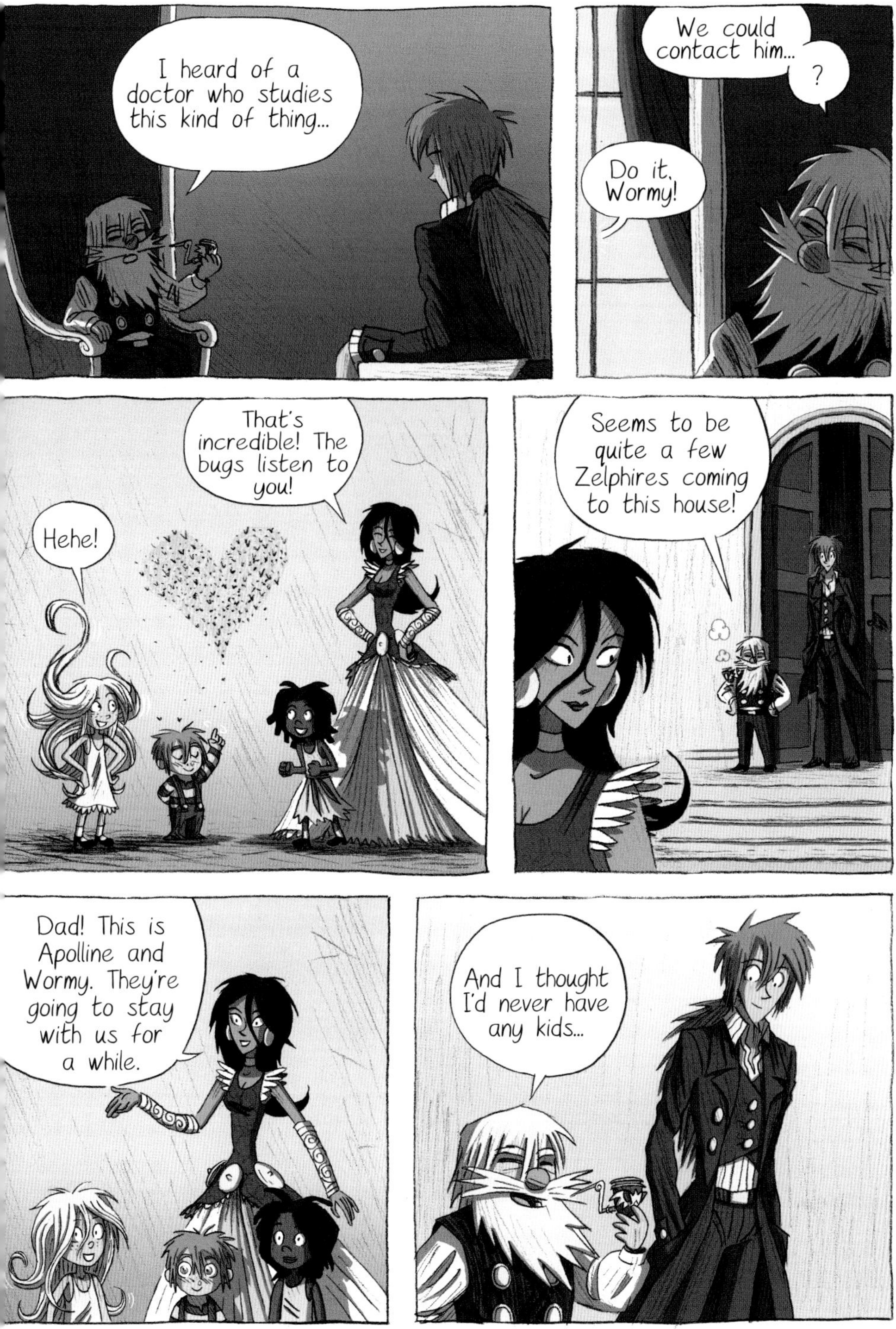
I heard of a doctor who studies this kind of thing...
We could contact him...
?
Do it, Wormy!
That's incredible! The bugs listen to you!
Hehe!
Seems to be quite a few Zelphires coming to this house!
Dad! This is Apolline and Wormy. They're going to stay with us for a while.
And I thought I'd never have any kids...

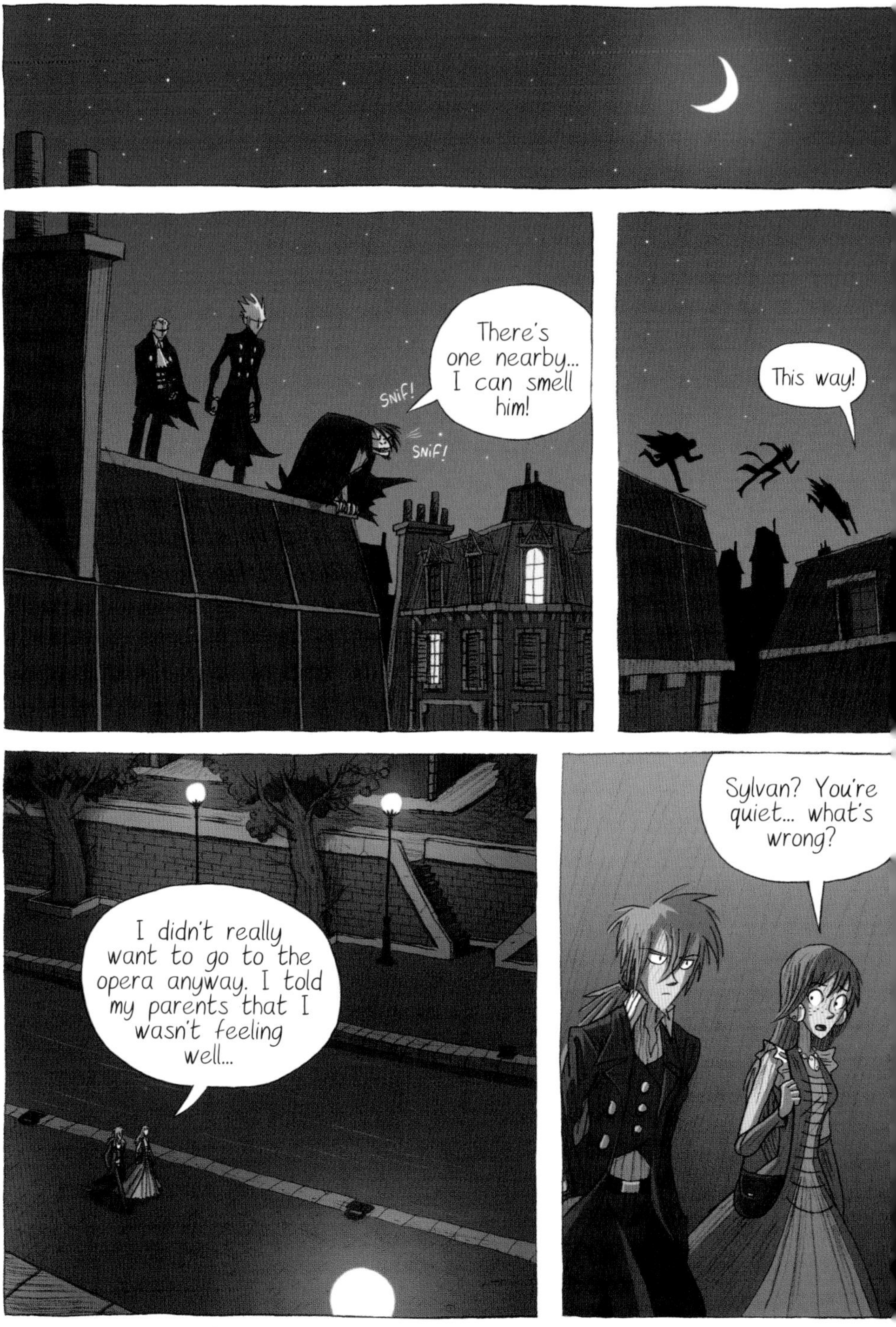
There's one nearby... I can smell him!
SNIF!
SNIF!
This way!
I didn't really want to go to the opera anyway. I told my parents that I wasn't feeling well...
Sylvan? You're quiet... what's wrong?

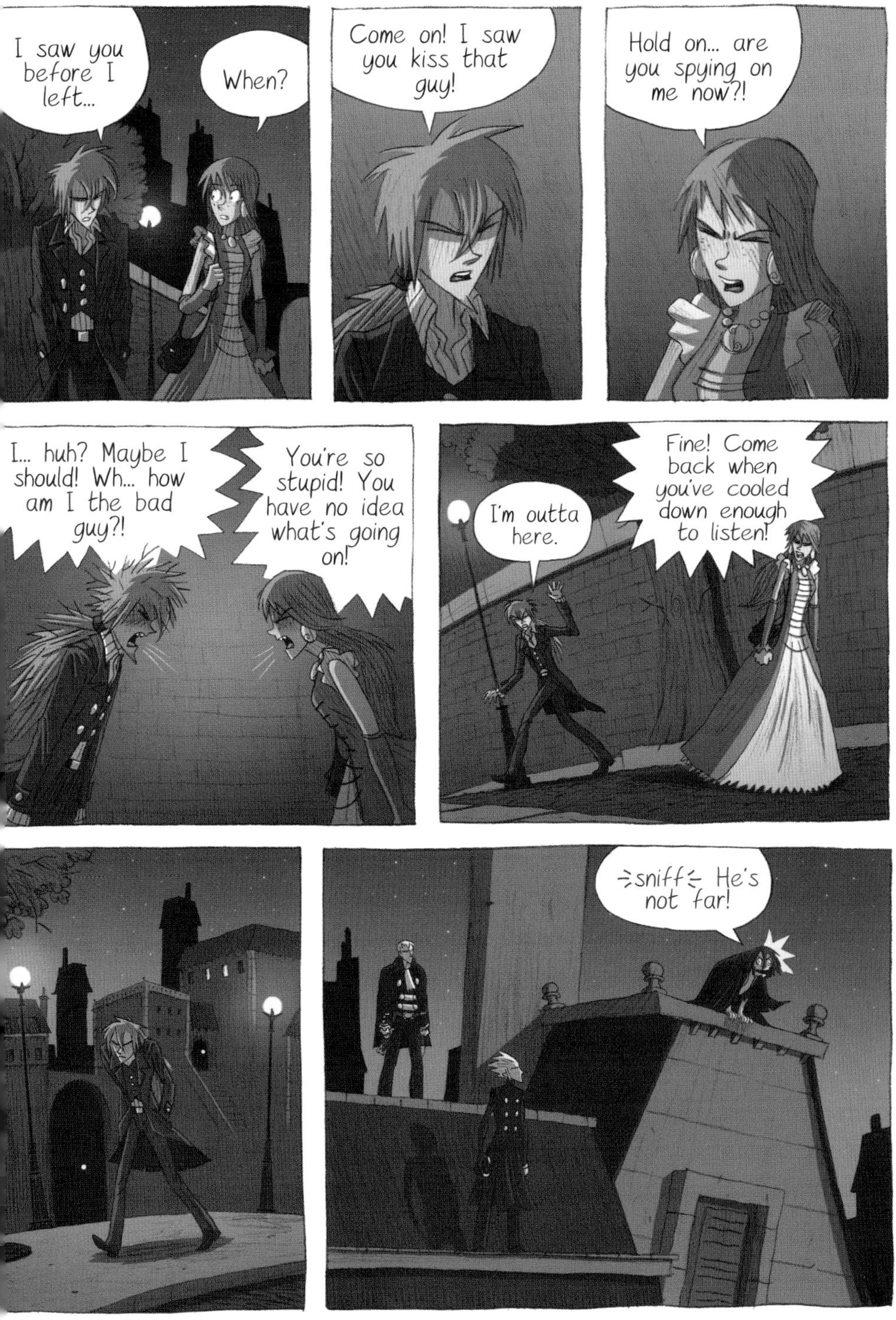
I saw you before I left...
When?
Come on! I saw you kiss that guy!
Hold on... are you spying on me now?!
I... huh? Maybe I should! Wh... how am I the bad guy?!
You're so stupid! You have no idea what's going on!
I'm outta here.
Fine! Come back when you've cooled down enough to listen!
≑sniff≑ He's not far!

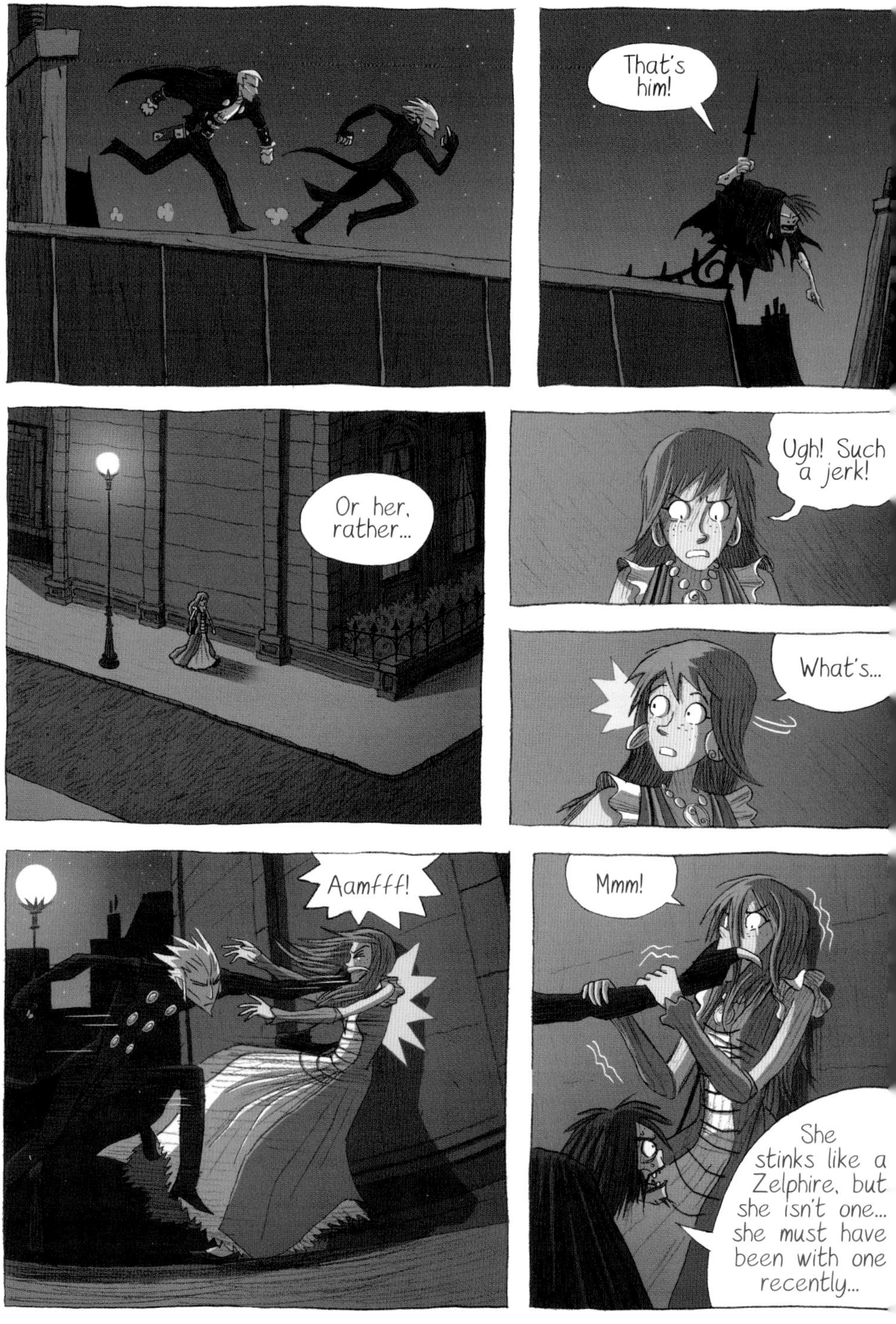
That's him!
Or her, rather...
Ugh! Such a jerk!
What's...
Aamfff!
Mmm!
She stinks like a Zelphire, but she isn't one... she must have been with one recently...

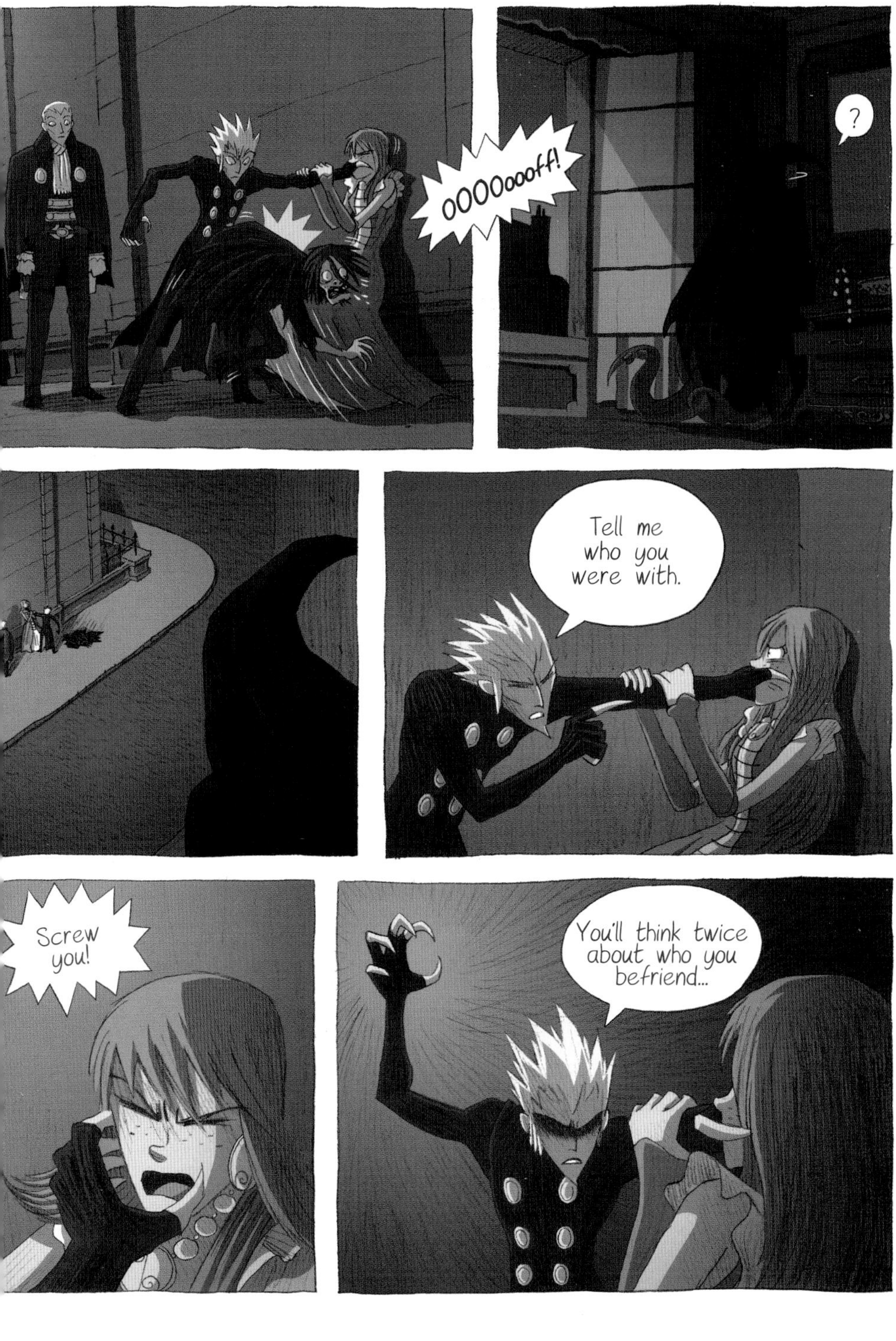
OOOOooo ff!
?
Tell me who you were with.
Screw you!
You'll think twice about who you befriend...

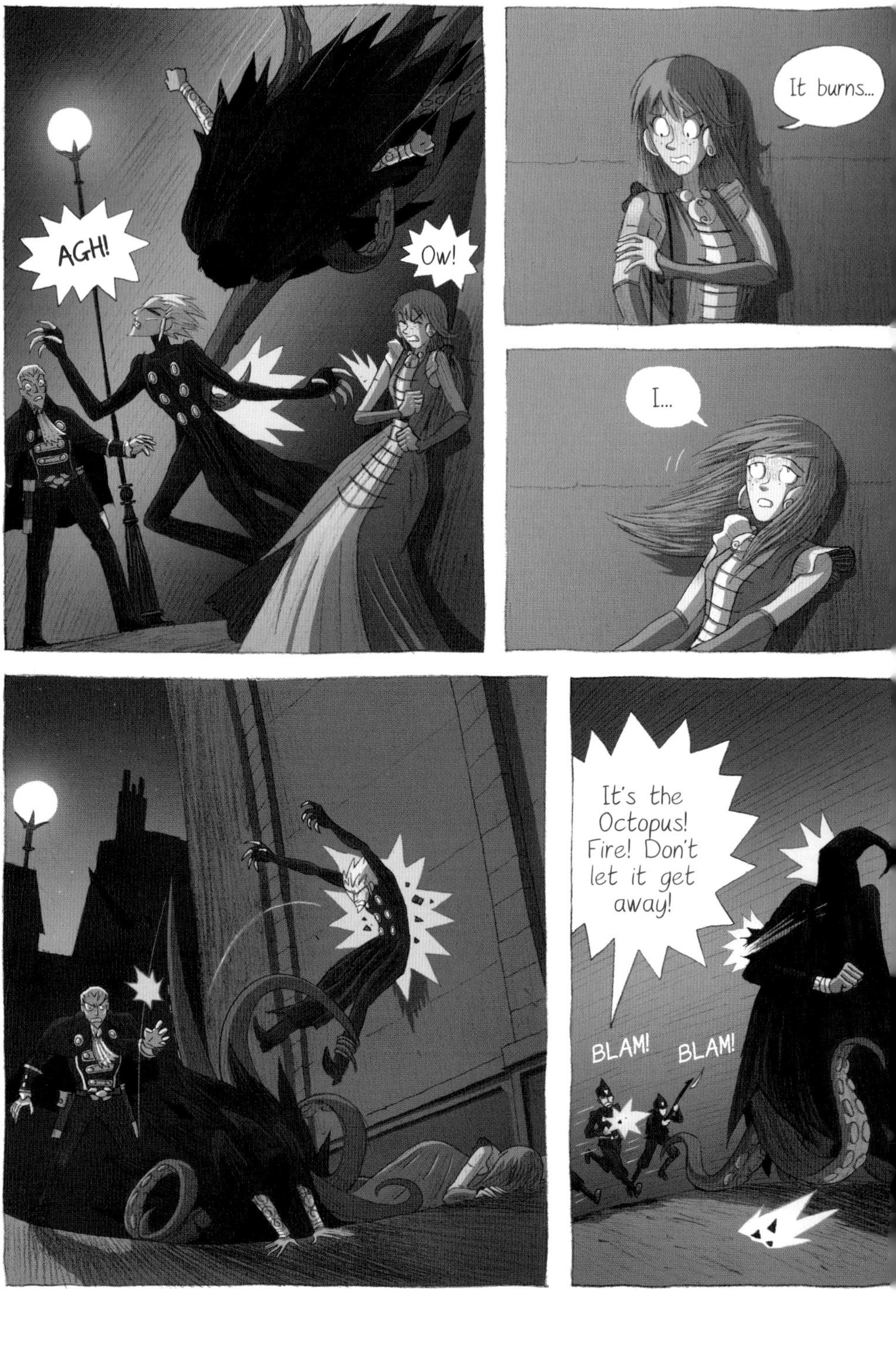
AGH!
Ow!
It burns...
I...
It's the Octopus! Fire! Don't let it get away!
BLAM!
BLAM!

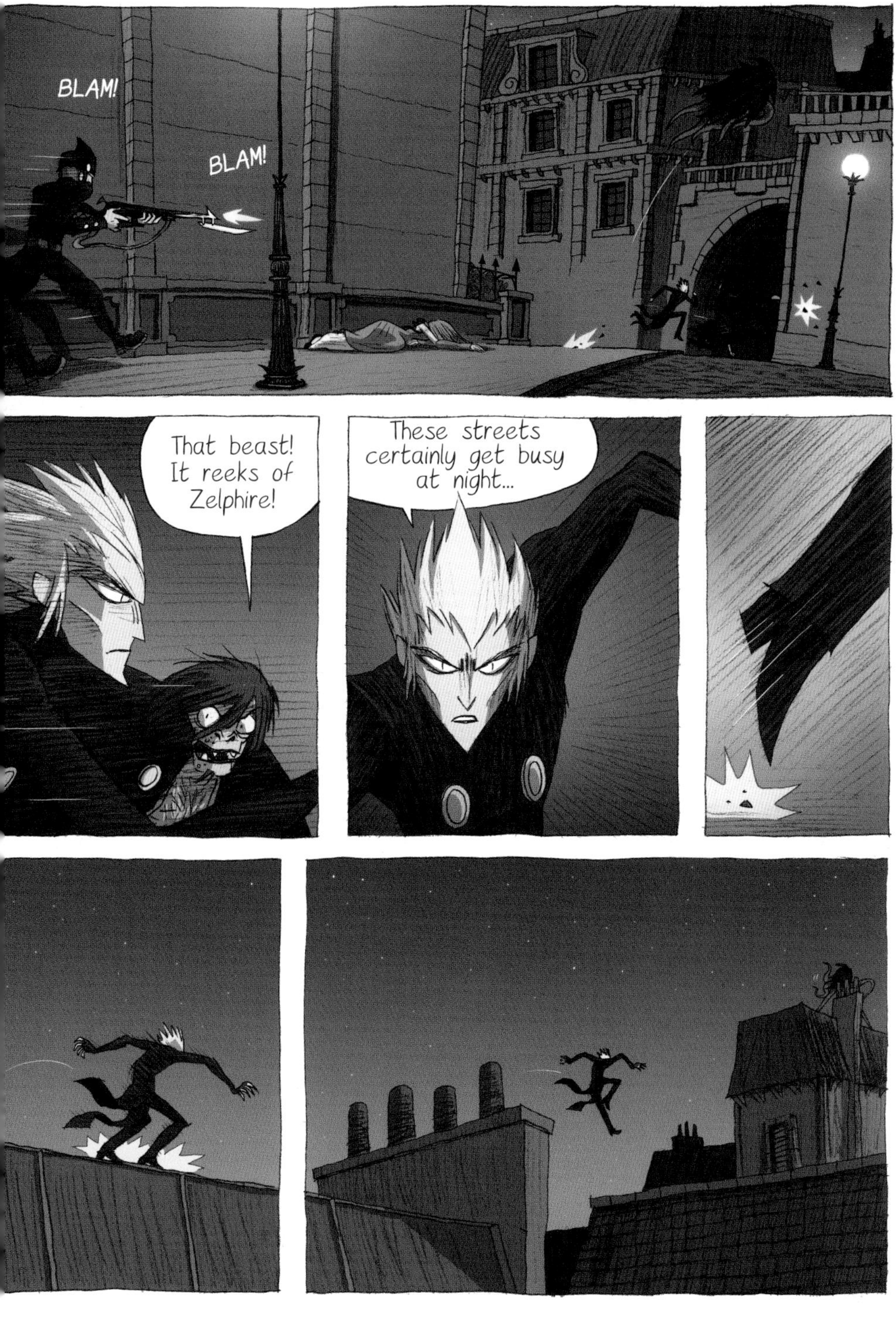
BLAM!
BLAM!
That beast! It reeks of Zelphire!
These streets certainly get busy at night...

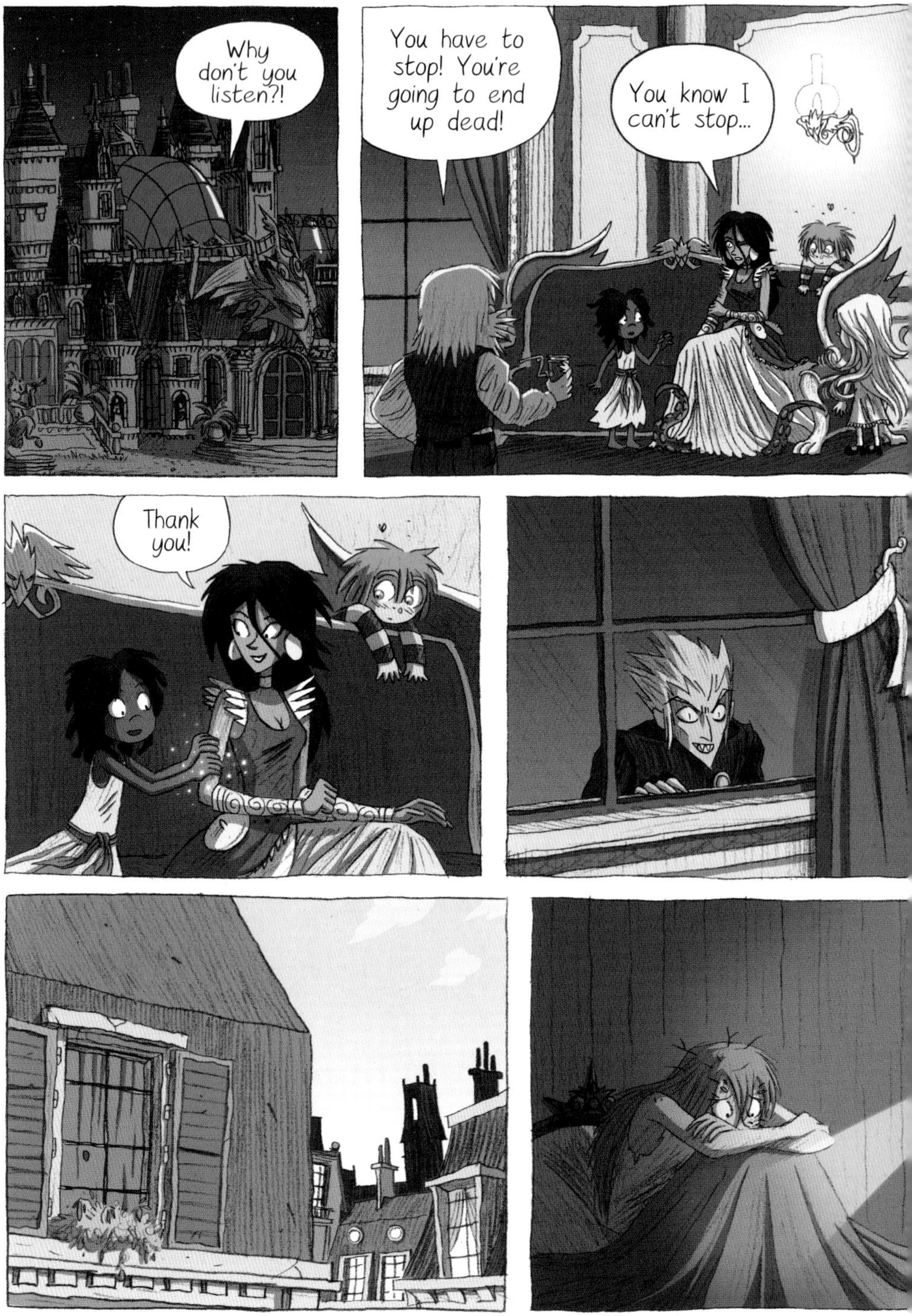
Why don't you listen?!
You have to stop! You're going to end up dead!
You know I can't stop...
Thank you!

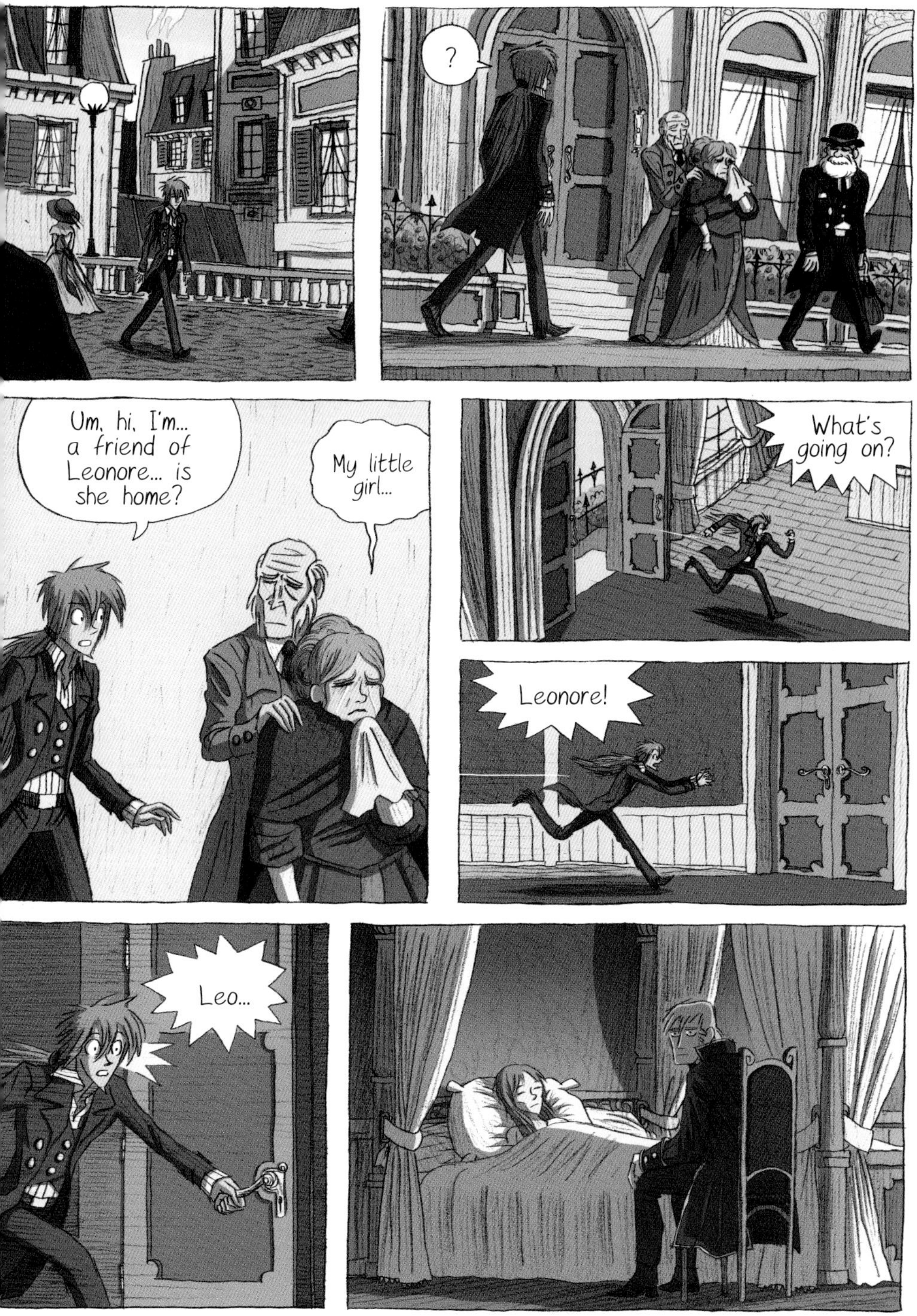
?
Um, hi, I'm... a friend of Leonore... is she home?
My little girl...
What's going on?
Leonore!
Leo...

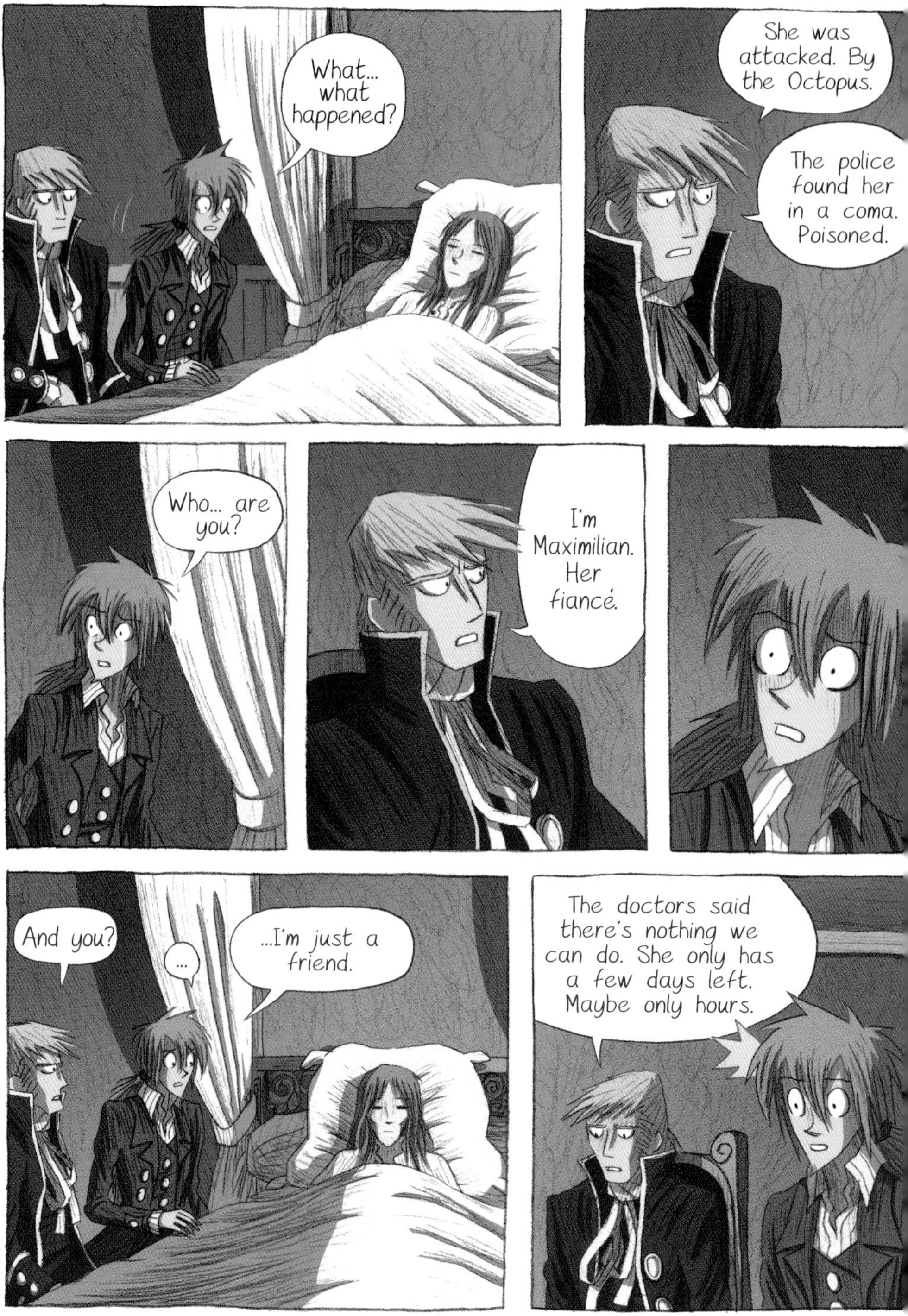
What... what happened?
She was attacked. By the Octopus.
The police found her in a coma. Poisoned.
Who... are you?
I'm Maximilian. Her fiancé.
And you?
...
...I'm just a friend.
The doctors said there's nothing we can do. She only has a few days left. Maybe only hours.

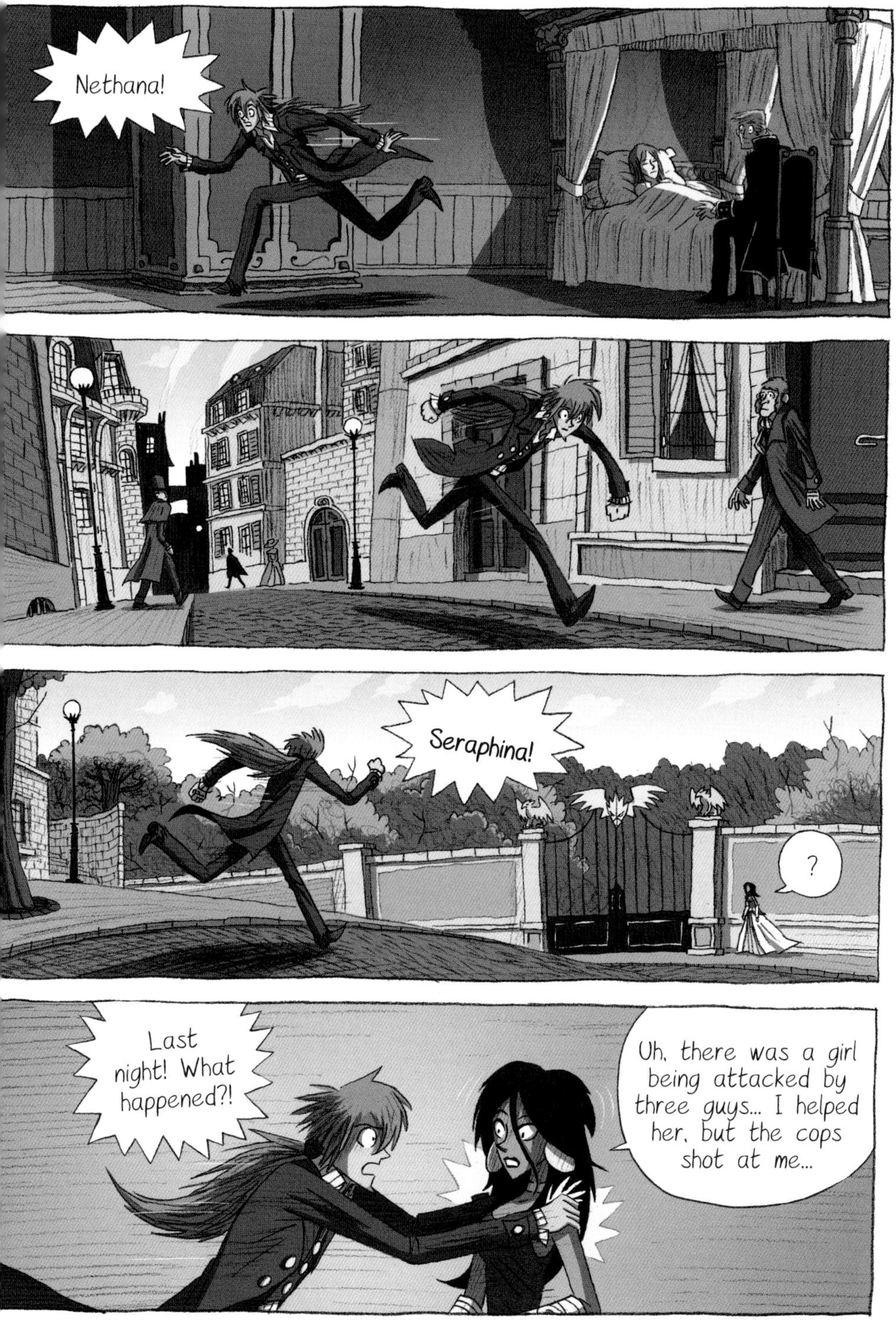
Nethana!
Seraphina!
?
Last night! What happened?!
Uh, there was a girl being attacked by three guys... I helped her, but the cops shot at me...

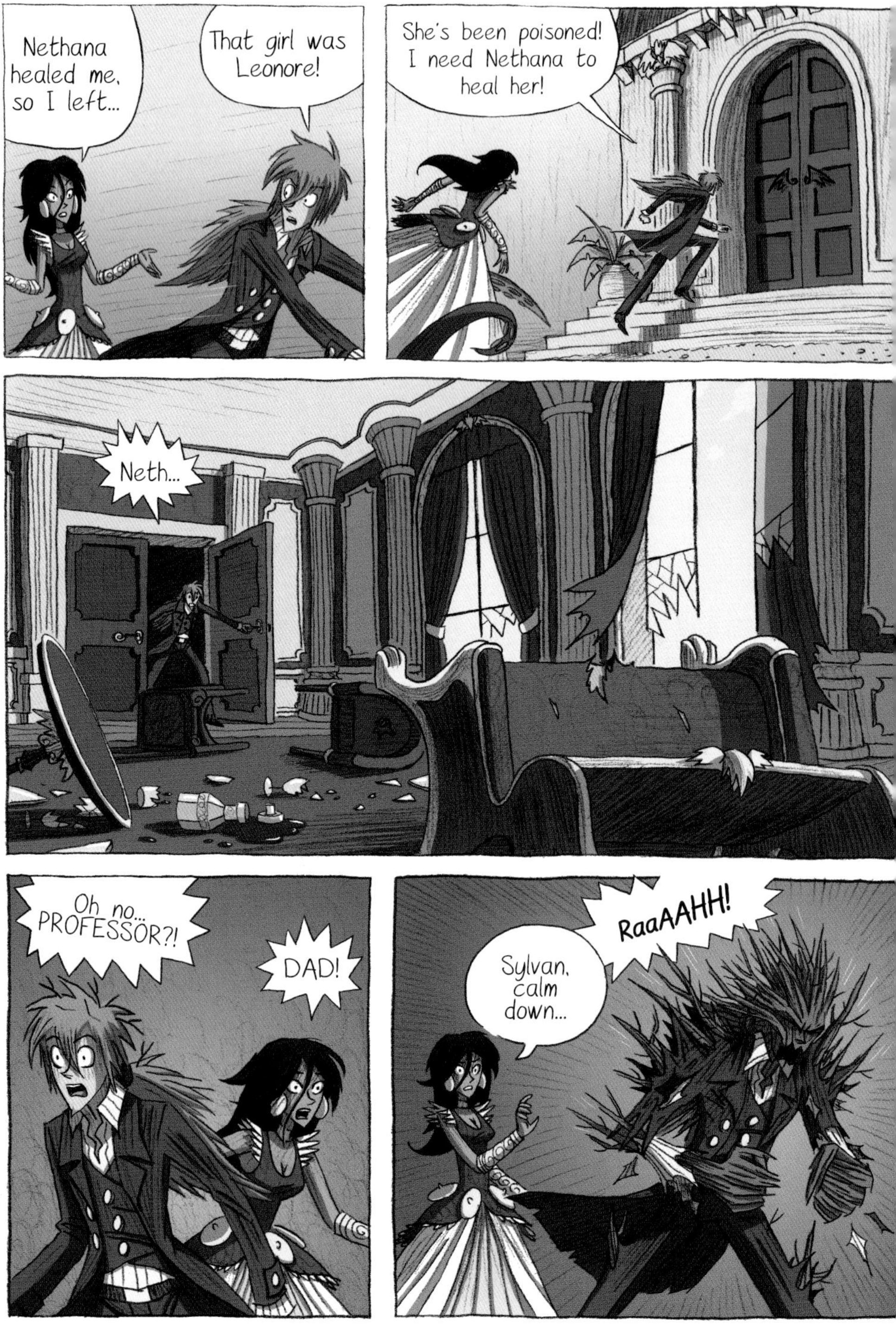
Nethana healed me, so I left...
That girl was Leonore!
She's been poisoned! I need Nethana to heal her!
Neth...
Oh no... PROFESSOR?!
DAD!
RaaAAHH!
Sylvan, calm down...

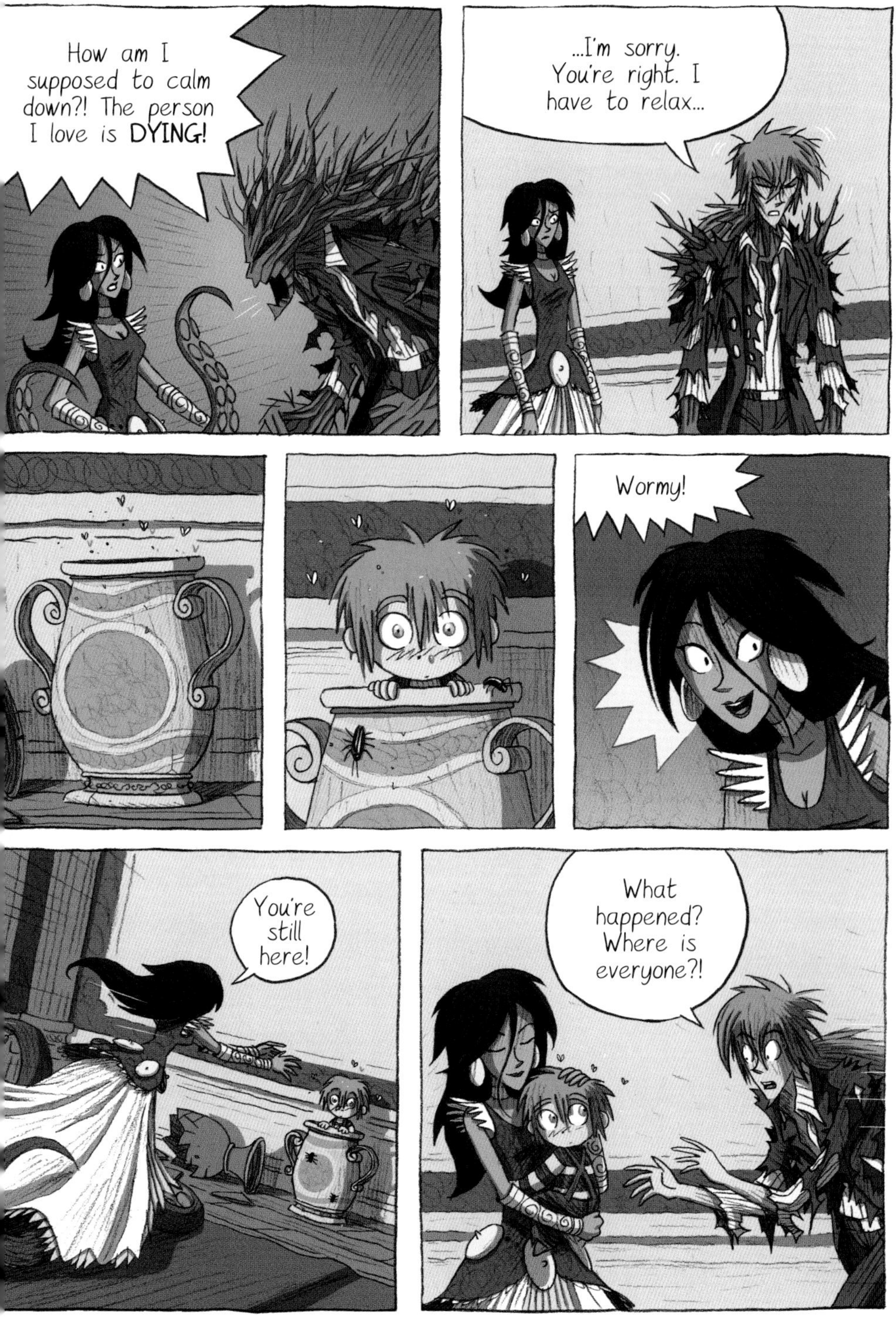
How am I supposed to calm down?! The person I love is DYING!
...I'm sorry. You're right. I have to relax...
Wormy!
You're still here!
What happened? Where is everyone?!

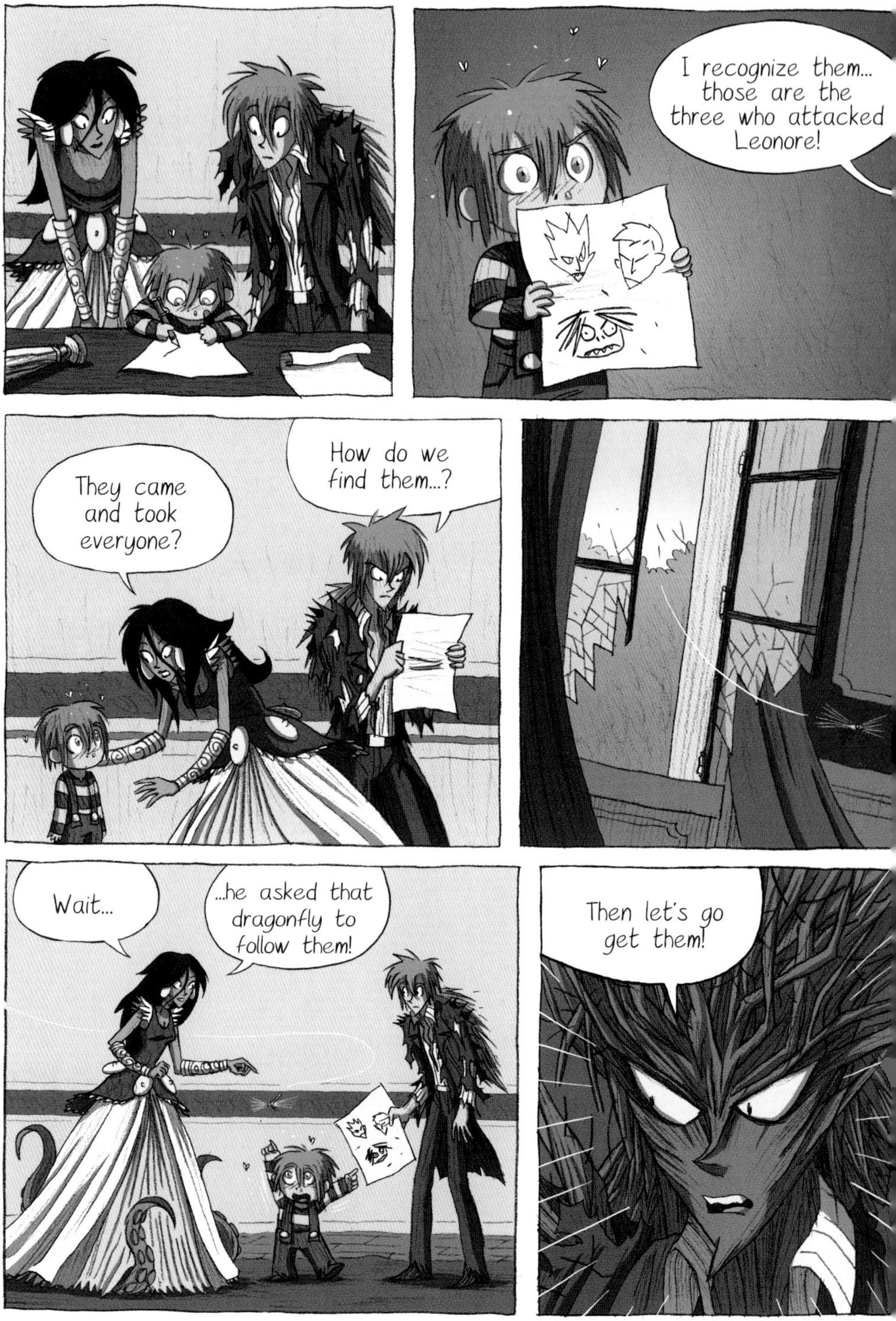
I recognize them... those are the three who attacked Leonore!
They came and took everyone?
How do we find them...?
Wait...
...he asked that dragonfly to follow them!
Then let's go get them!

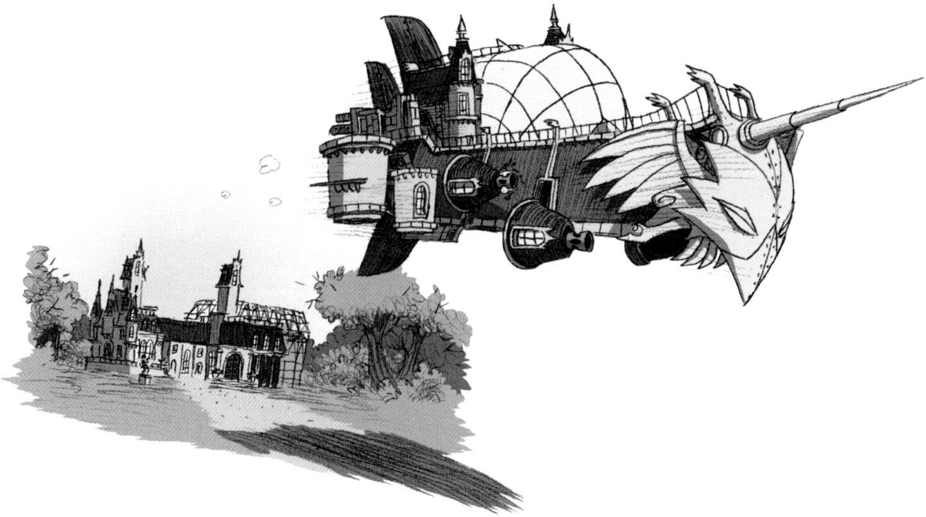

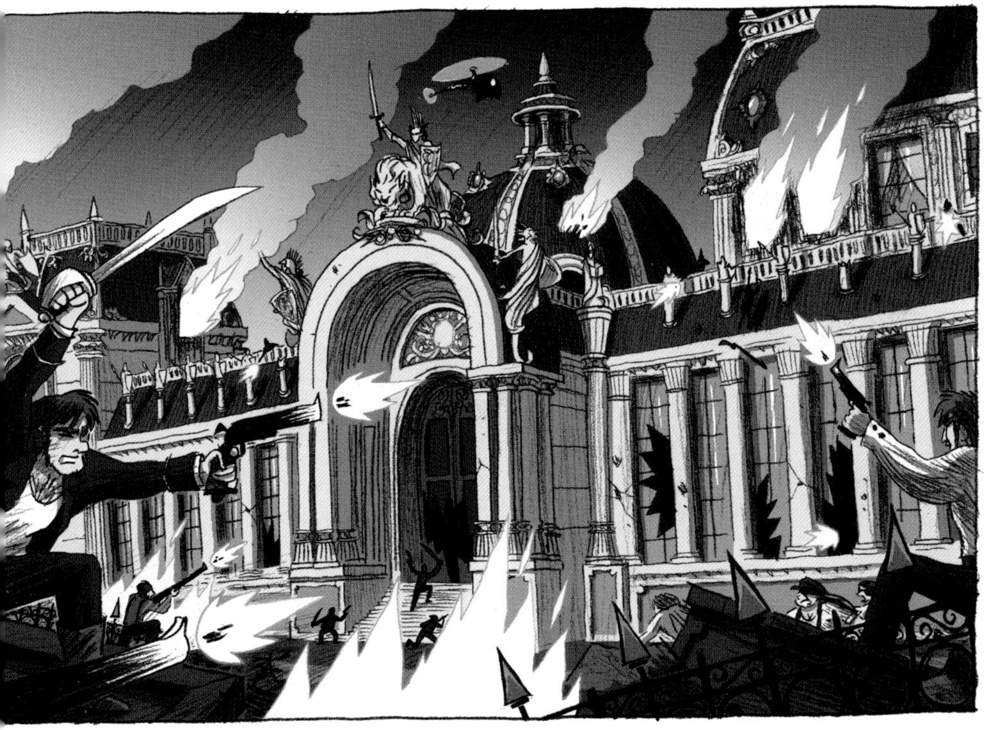

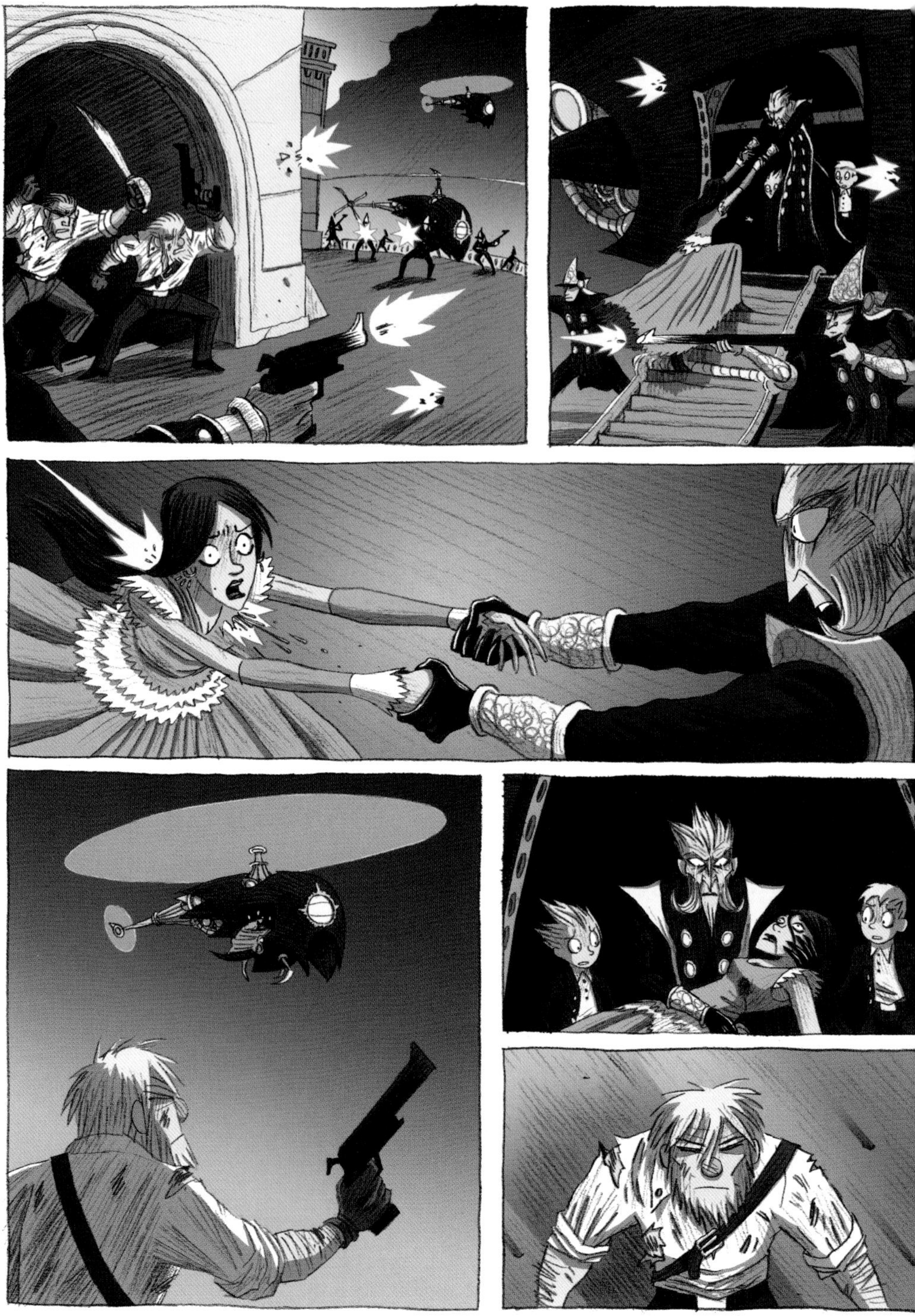

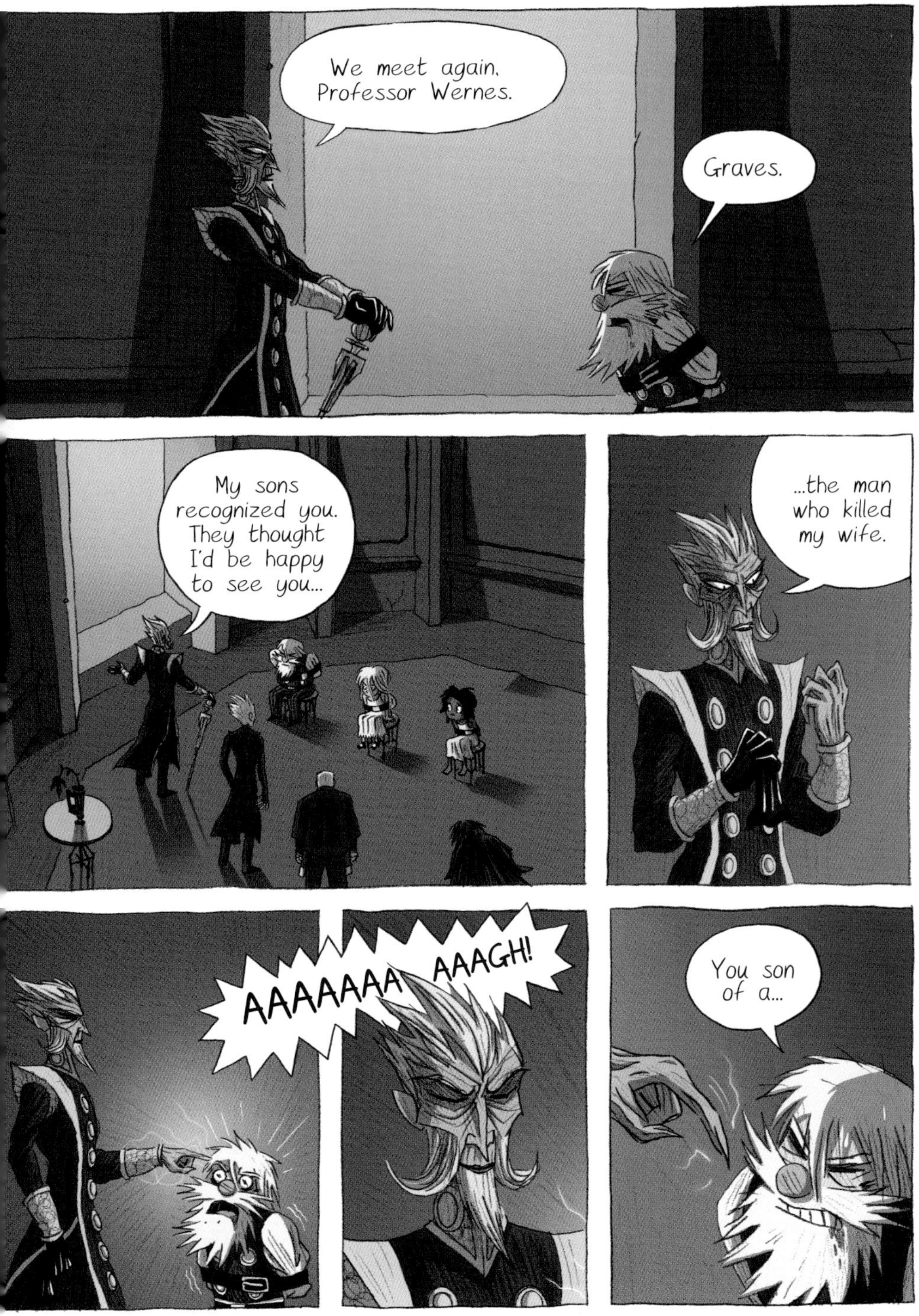
We meet again, Professor Wernes.
Graves.
My sons recognized you. They thought I'd be happy to see you...
...the man who killed my wife.
AAAAAAA AAAGH!
You son of a...

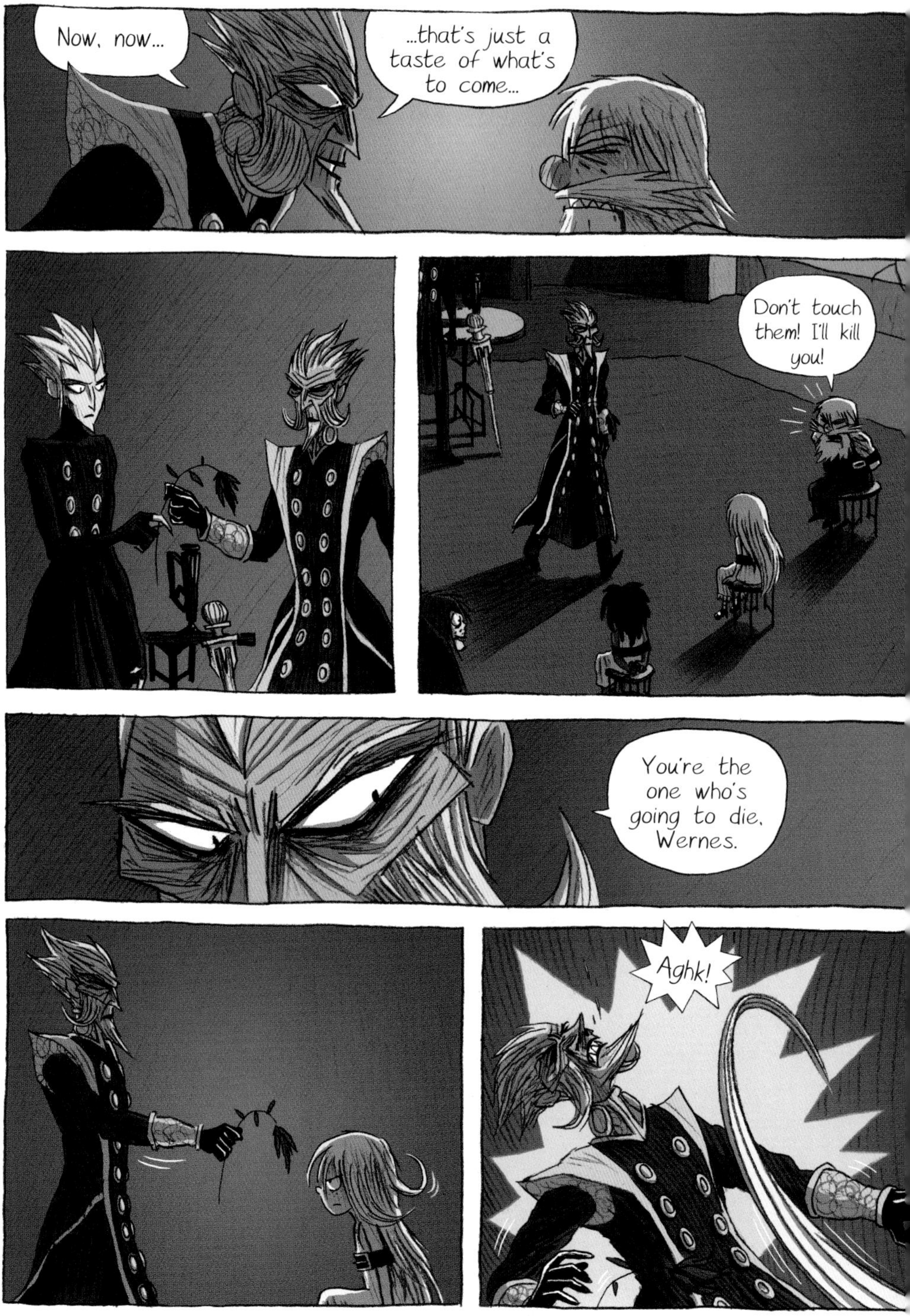
Now, now...
...that's just a taste of what's to come...
Don't touch them! I'll kill you!
You're the one who's going to die, Wernes.
Aghk!

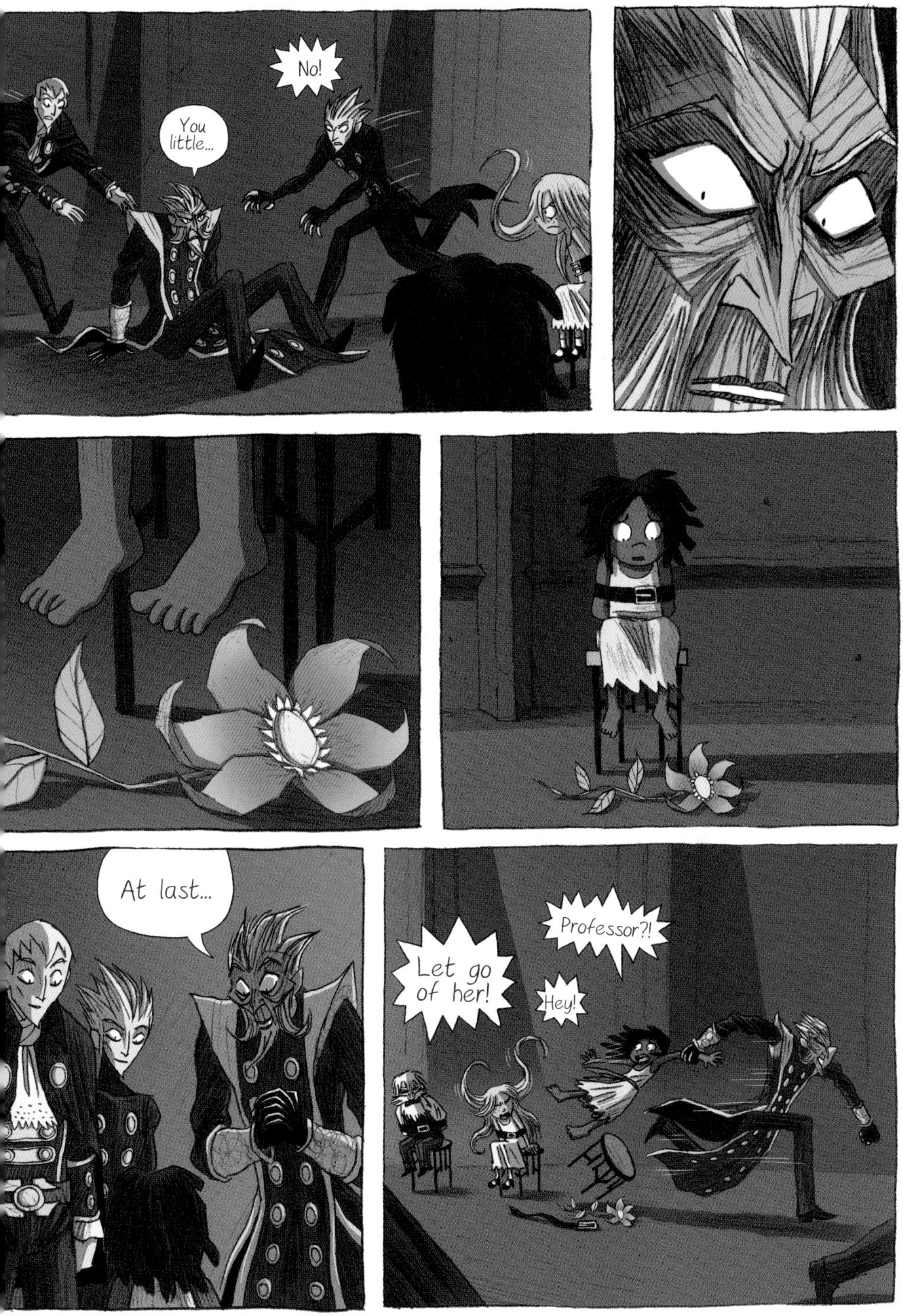
No!
You little...
At last...
Professor?!
Let go of her!
Hey!

All this time, I knew...

...that if I could take a life, there must be a Zelphire somewhere who could give it...

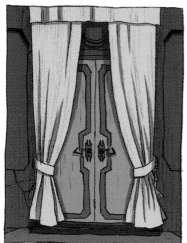

Behave yourself, girl. You're about to meet the person I hold most dear.

Enter.

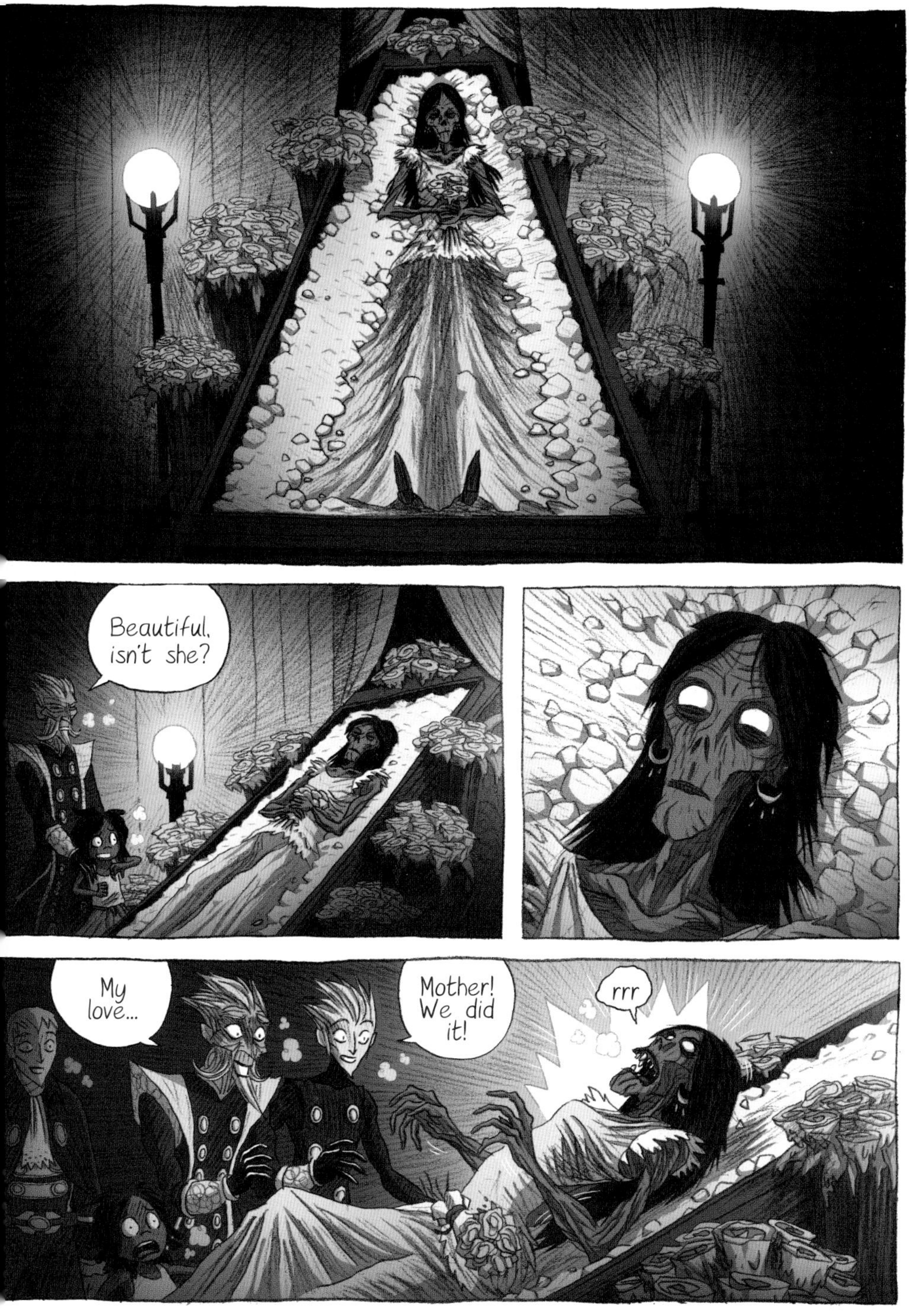
Beautiful, isn't she?
My love...
Mother! We did it!
rrr

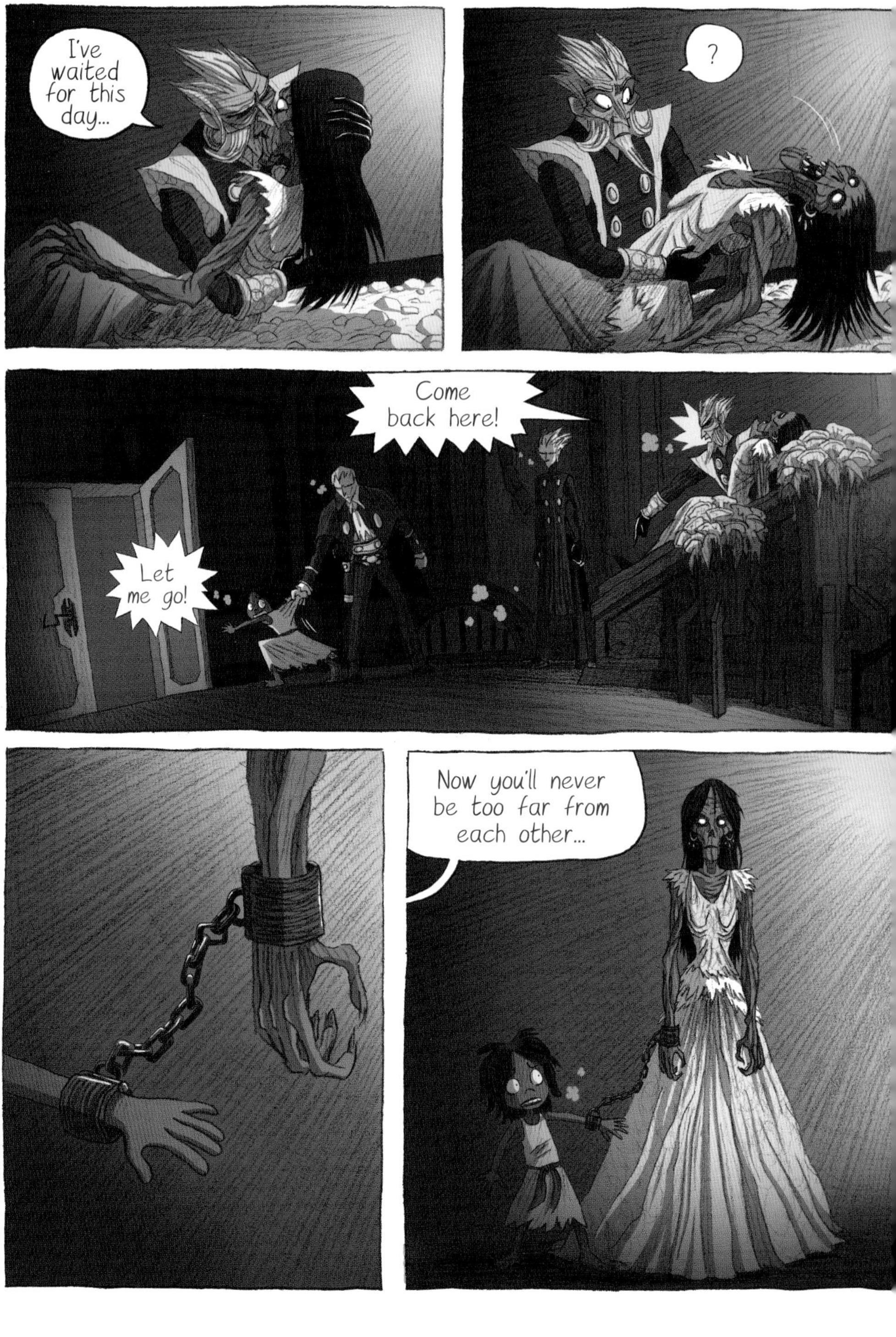
I've waited for this day...
?
Come back here!
Let me go!
Now you'll never be too far from each other...

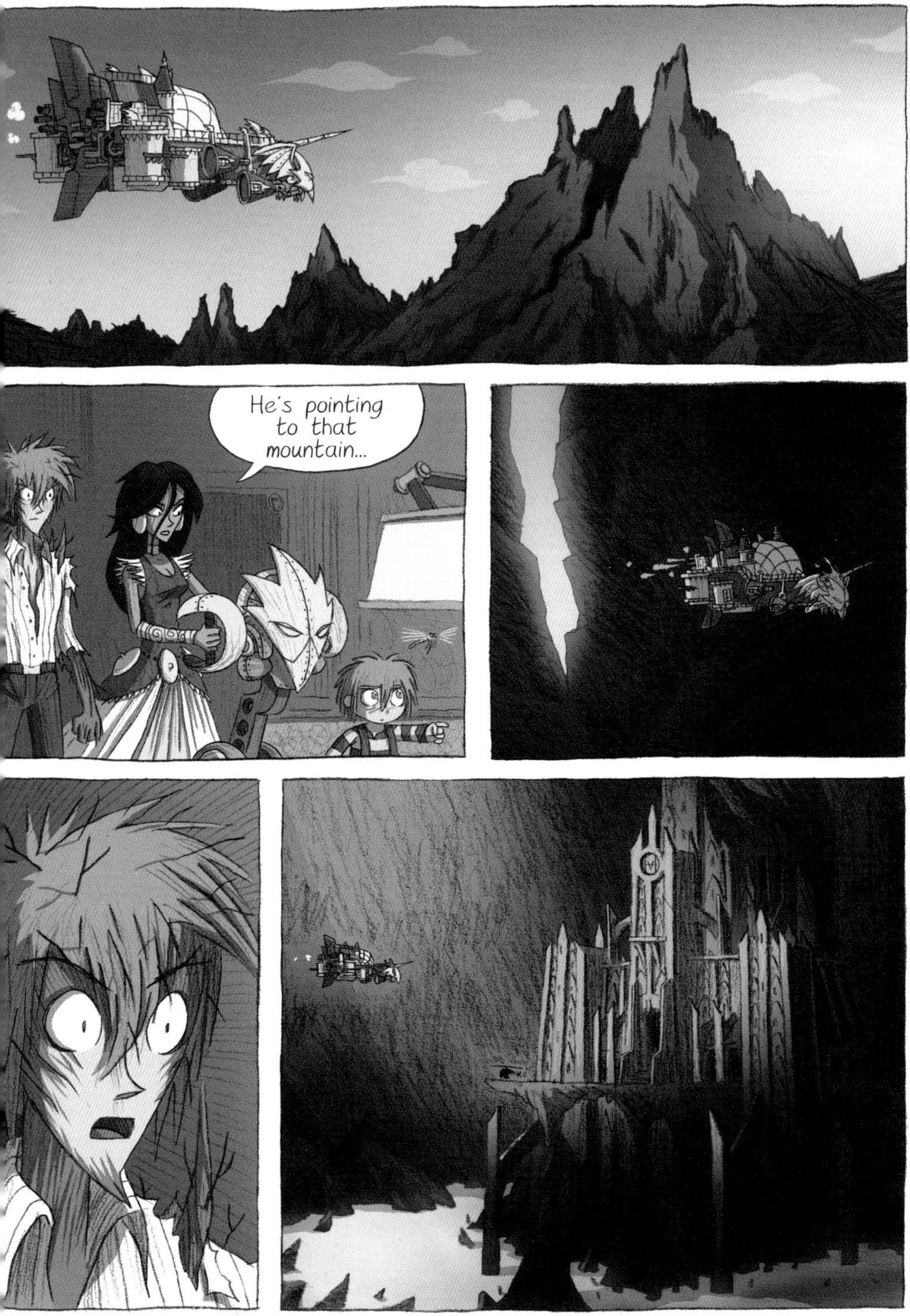
He's pointing to that mountain...

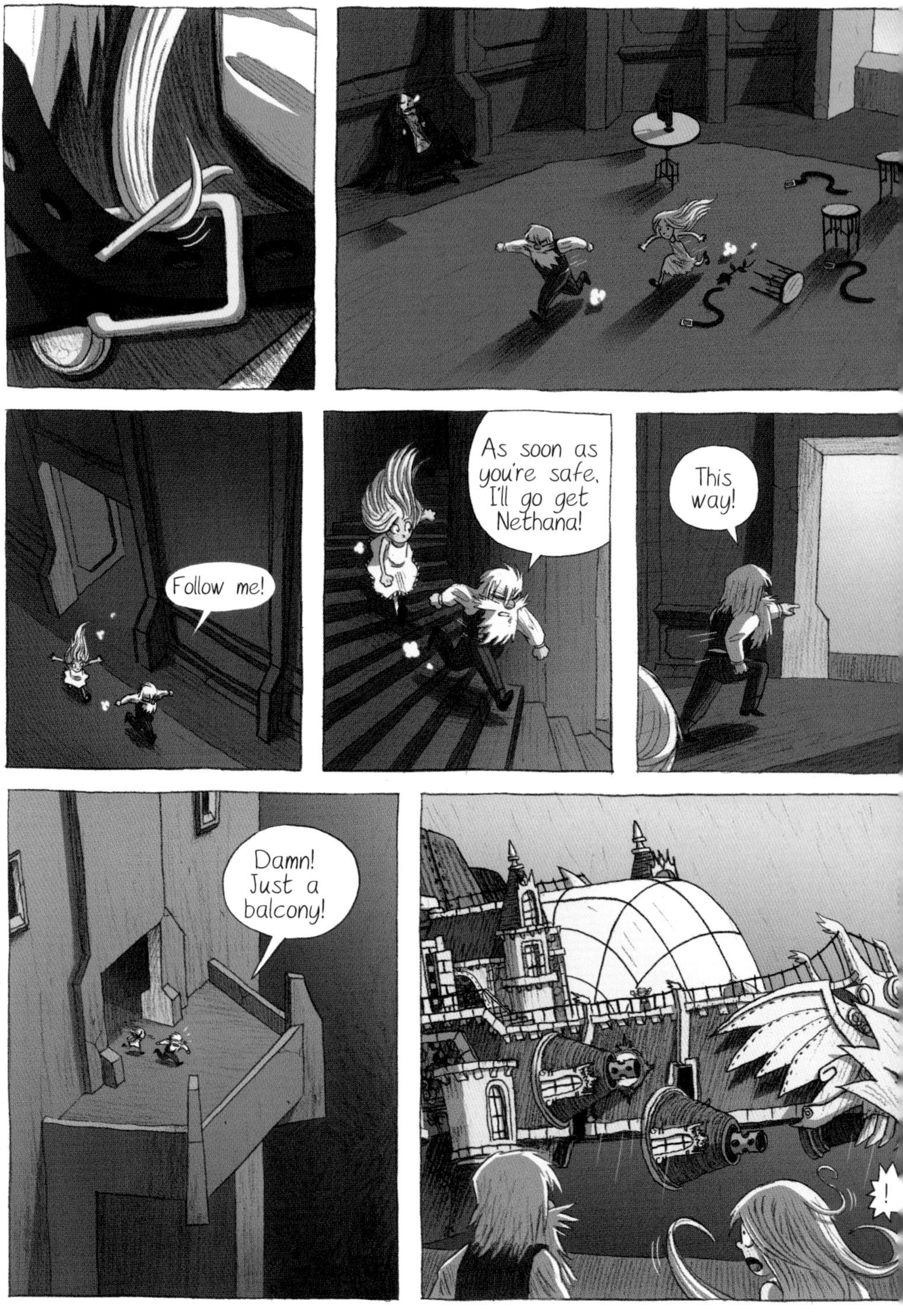
Follow me!
As soon as you're safe, I'll go get Nethana!
This way!
Damn! Just a balcony!
!

I'll get close enough for them to jump!

BLAM!

Hahaha!

What? No goodbye?

BLAM!

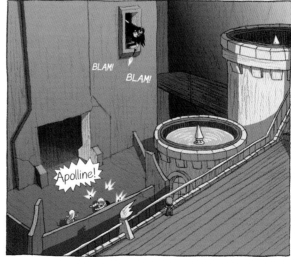

BLAM!

BLAM!

Apolline!

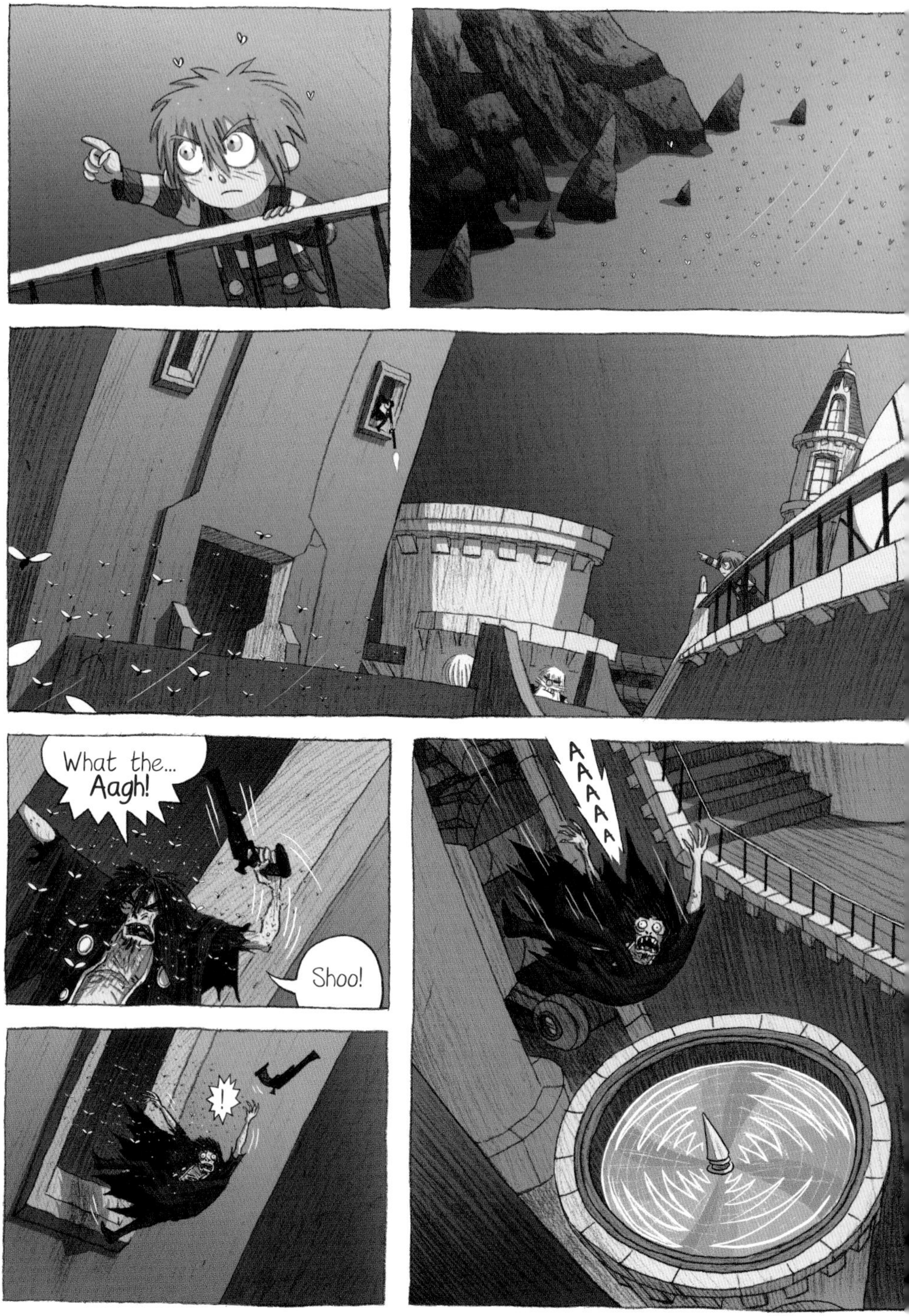
What the... Aagh!
Shoo!
!
AAAAA

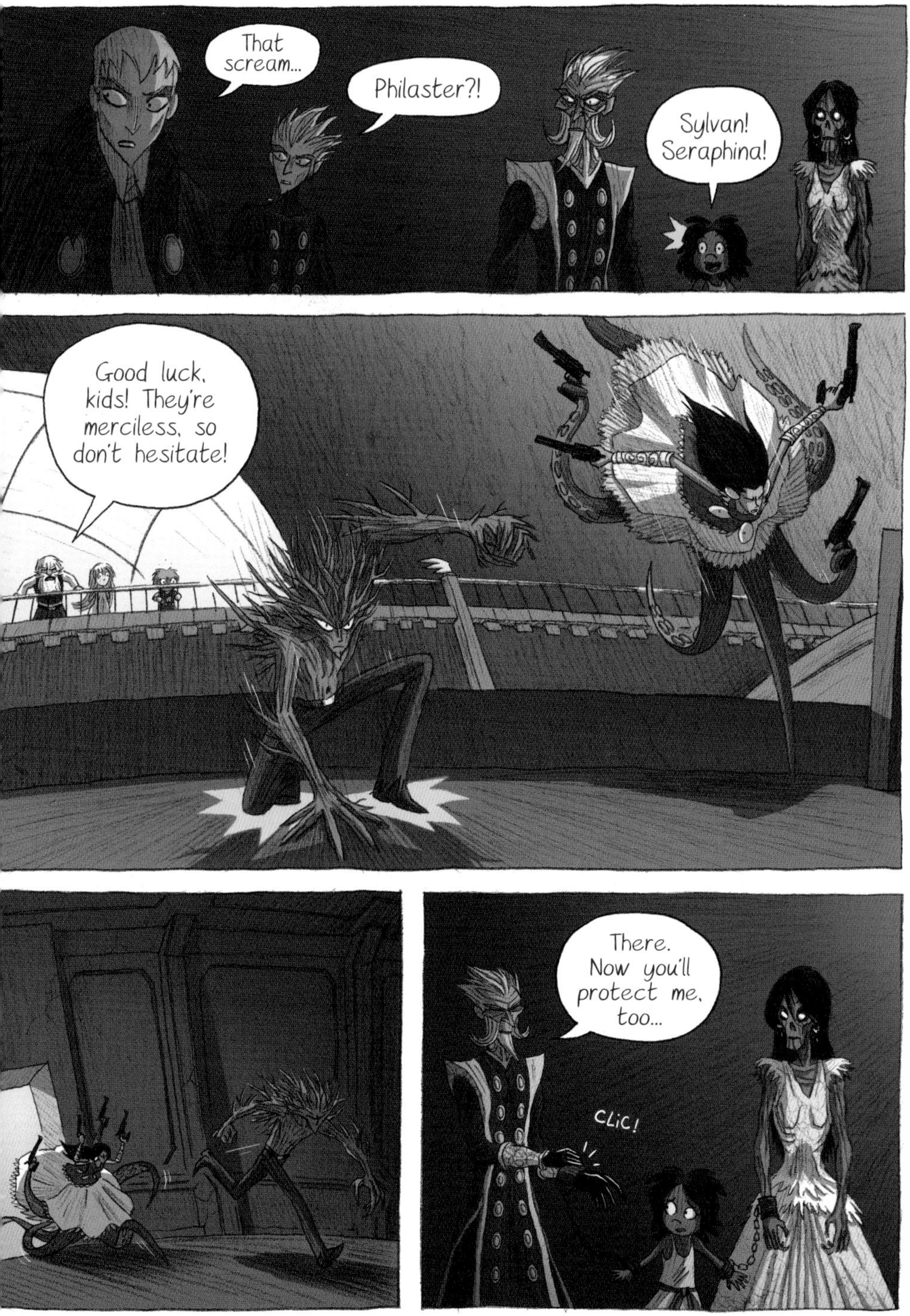
That scream...
Philaster?!
Sylvan! Seraphina!
Good luck, kids! They're merciless, so don't hesitate!
There. Now you'll protect me, too...
CLIC!

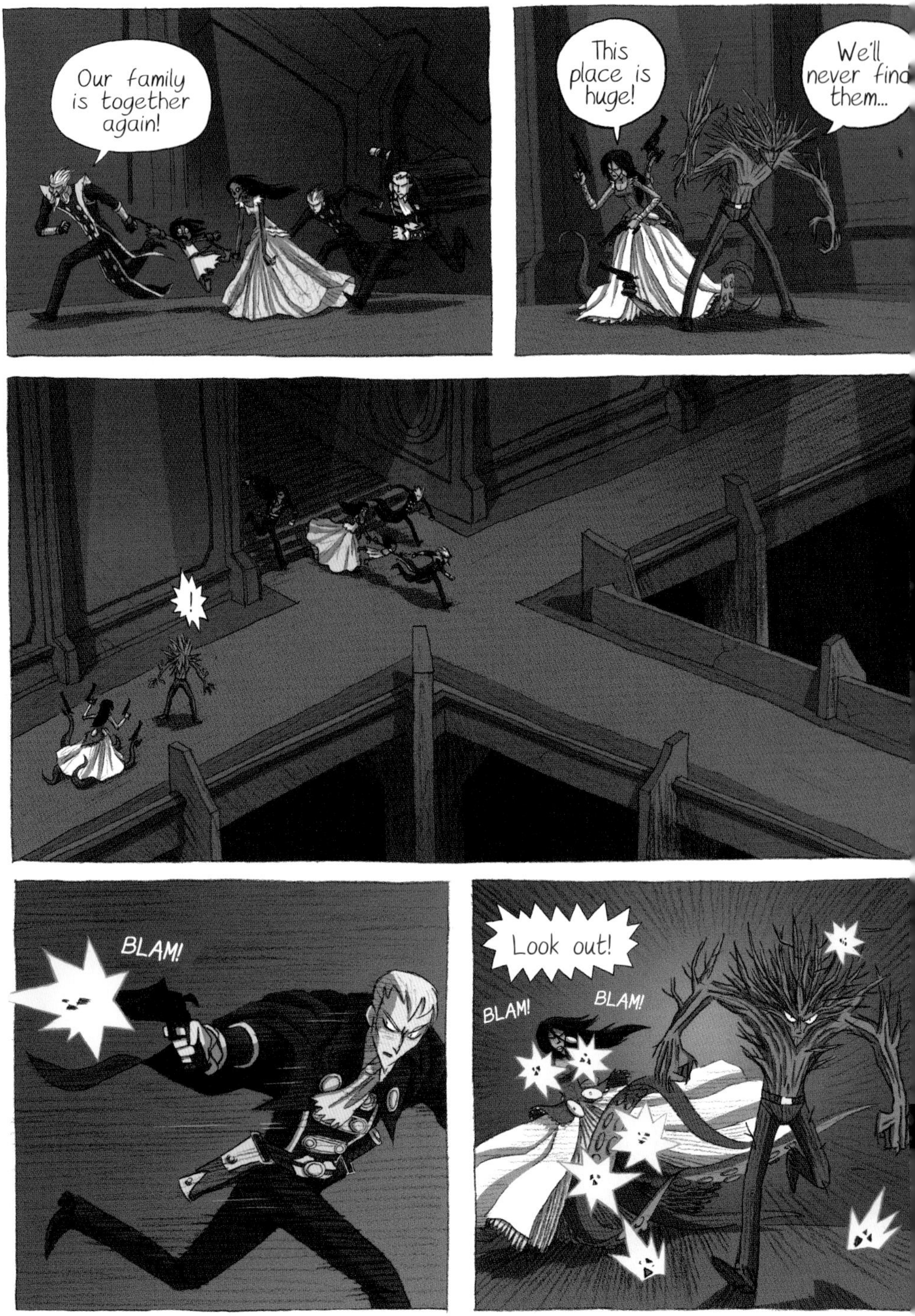
Our family is together again!
This place is huge!
We'll never find them...
!
BLAM!
Look out!
BLAM!
BLAM!

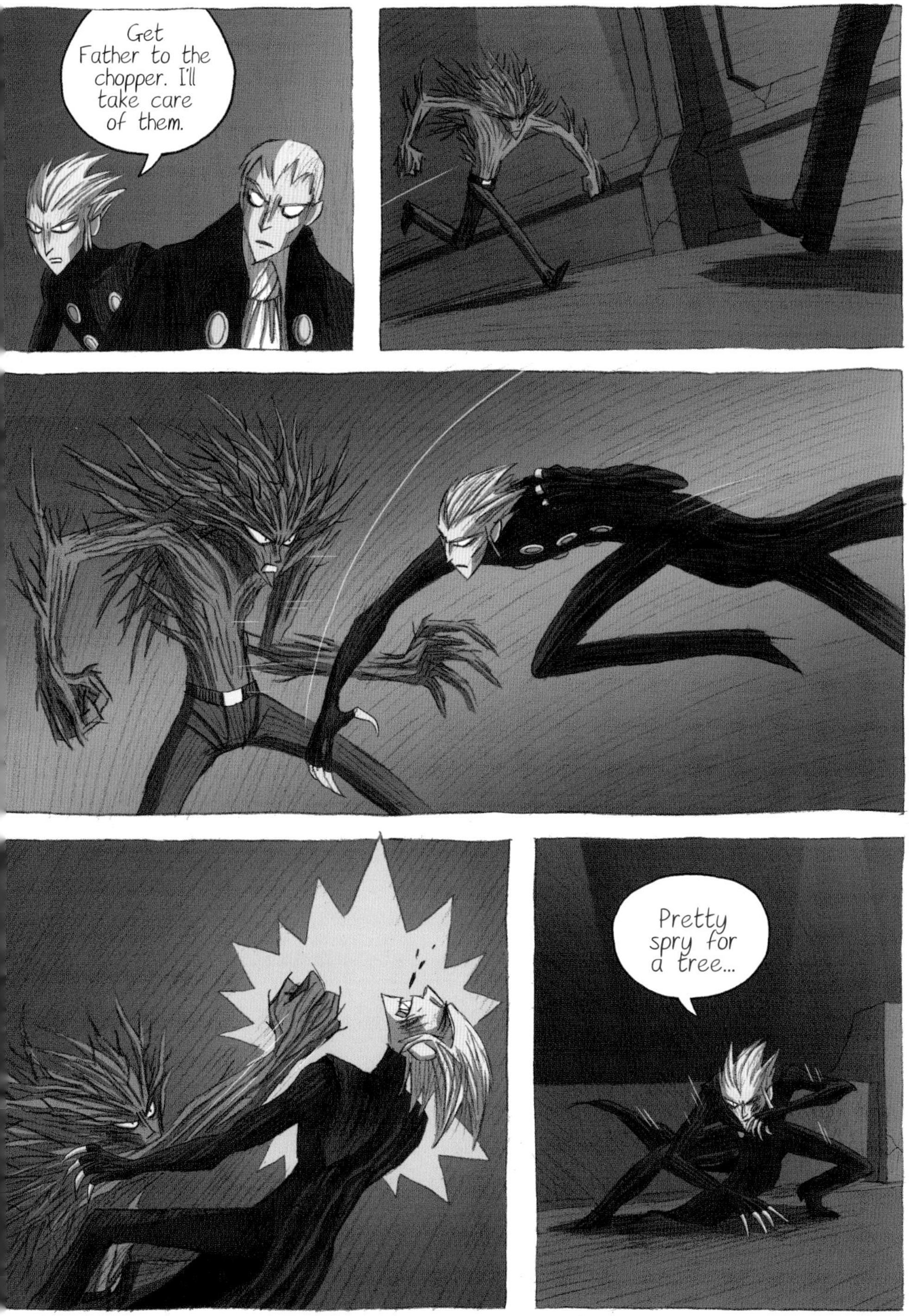
Get Father to the chopper. I'll take care of them.
Pretty spry for a tree...

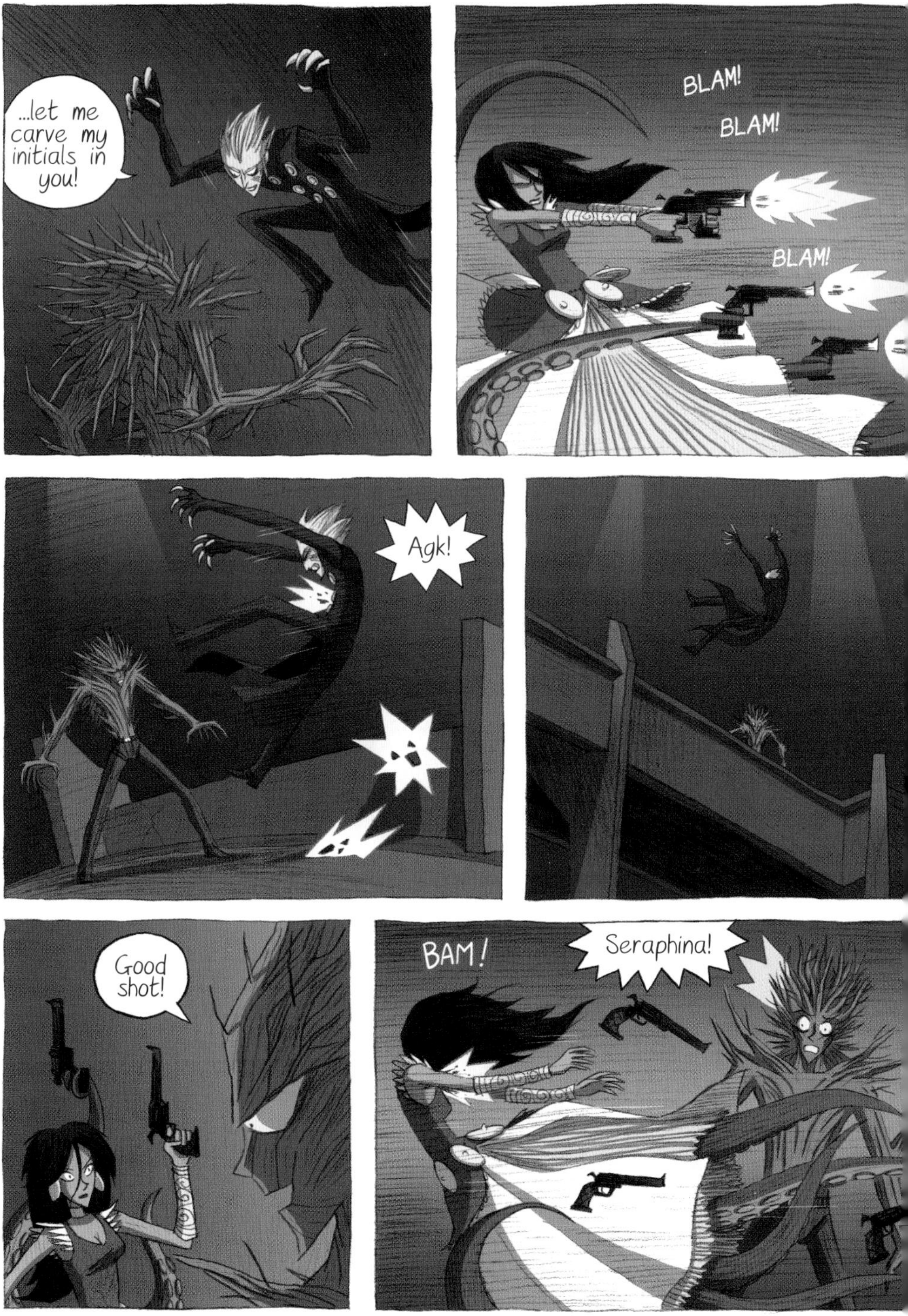
...let me carve my initials in you!
BLAM!
BLAM!
BLAM!
Agk!
Good shot!
BAM!
Seraphina!

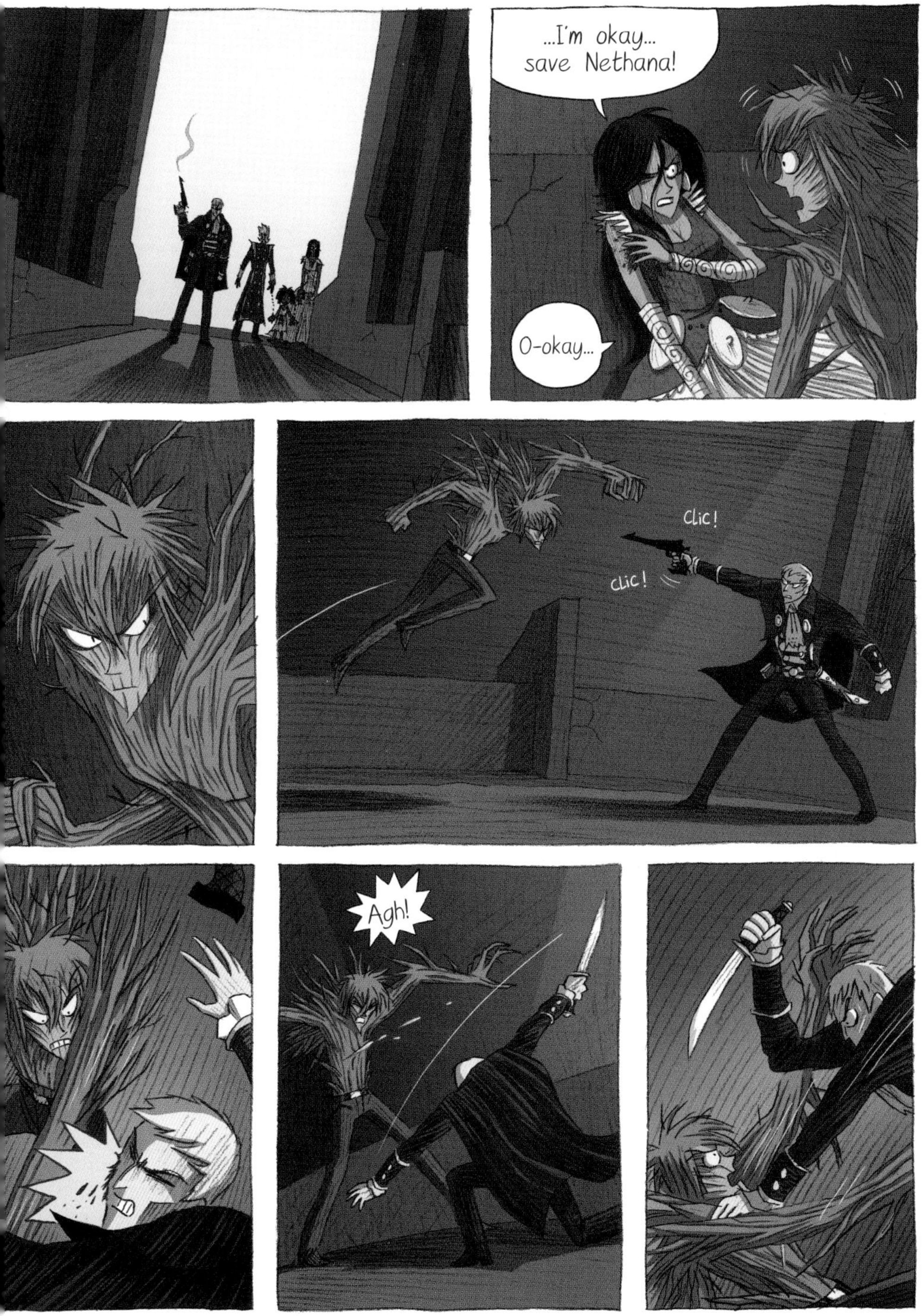
...I'm okay...
save Nethana!
O-okay...
Clic!
Clic!
Agh!

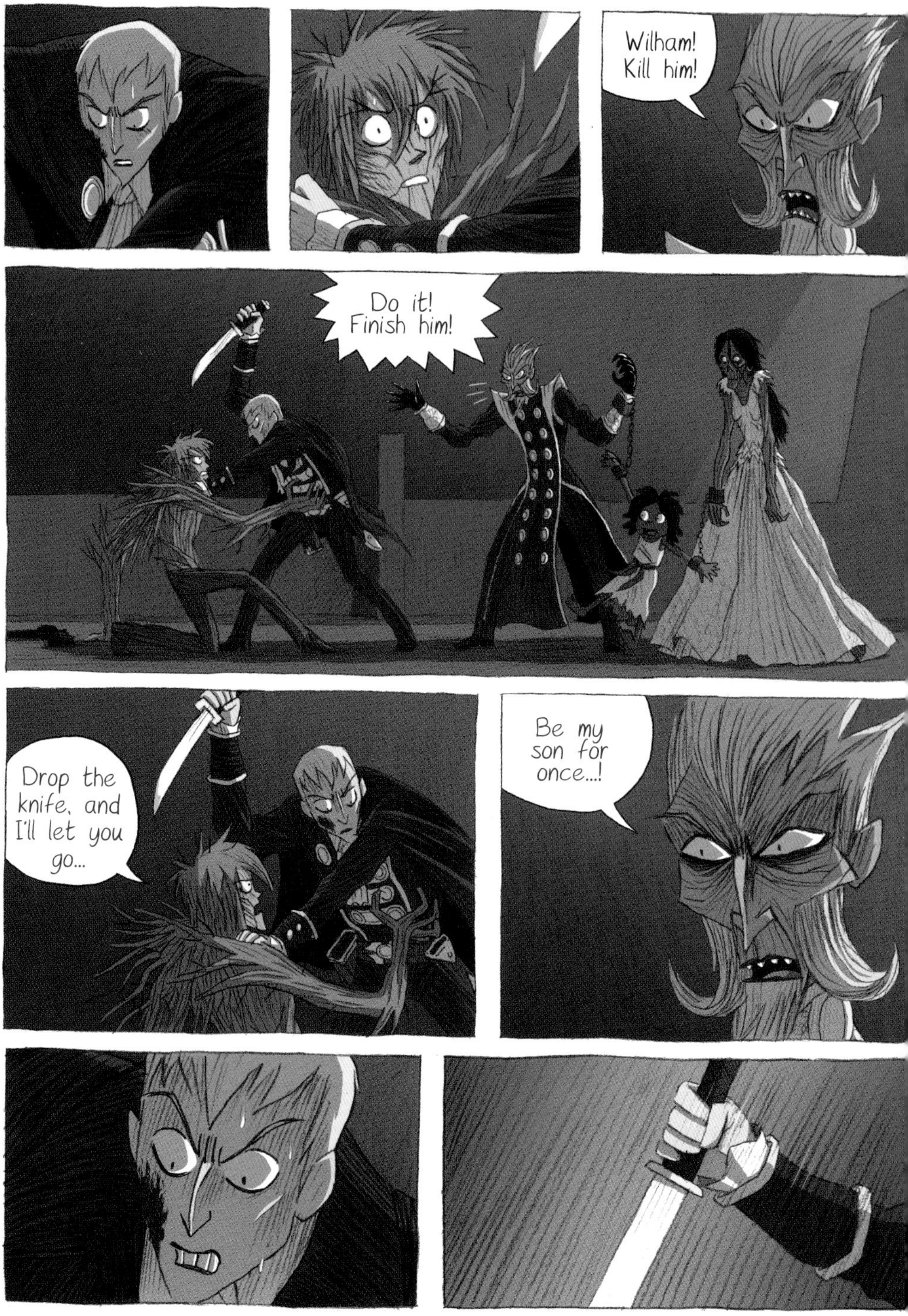
Wilham! Kill him!
Do it! Finish him!
Drop the knife, and I'll let you go...
Be my son for once...!

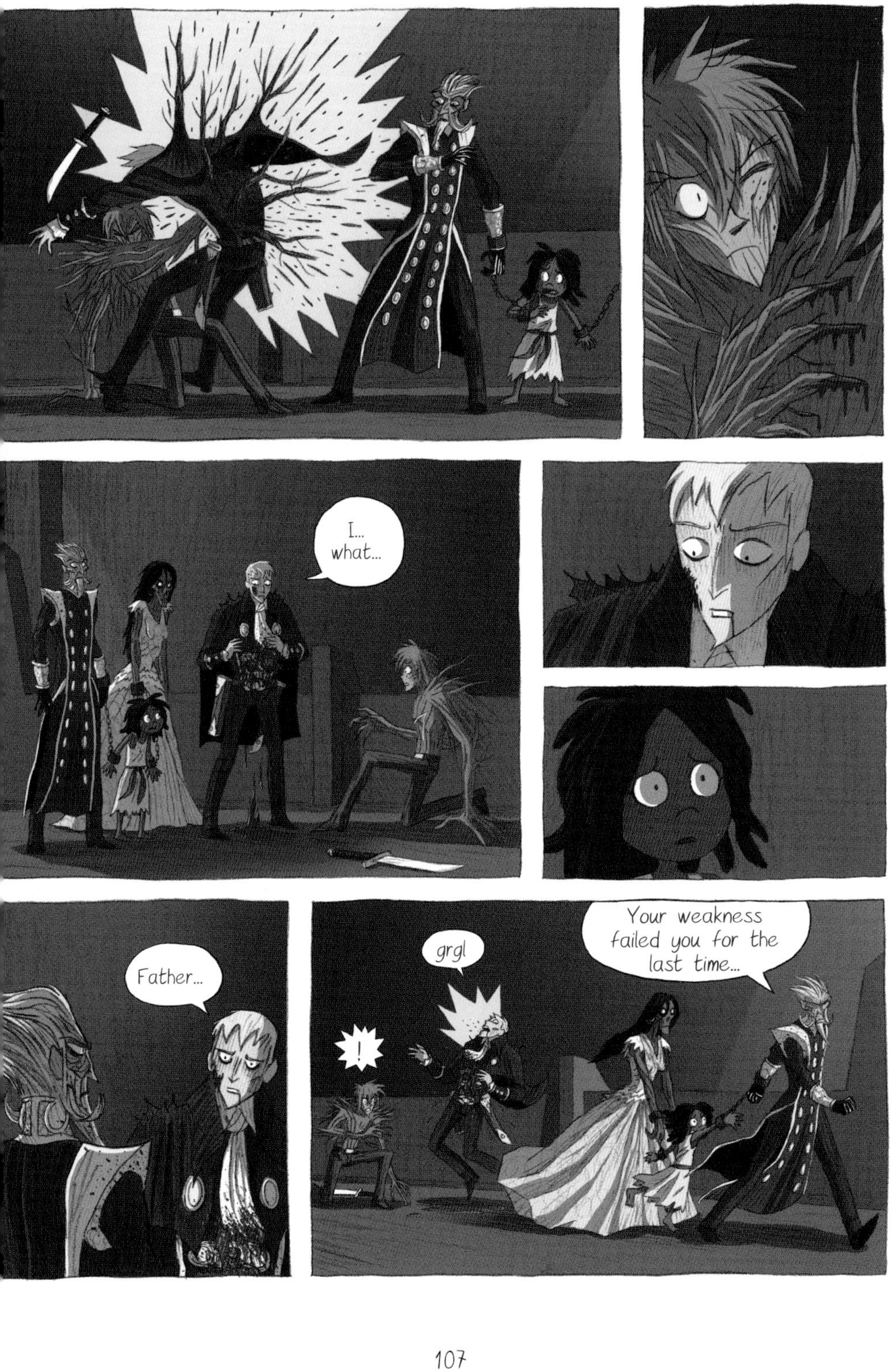
I... what...
Father...
!
grgl
Your weakness failed you for the last time...

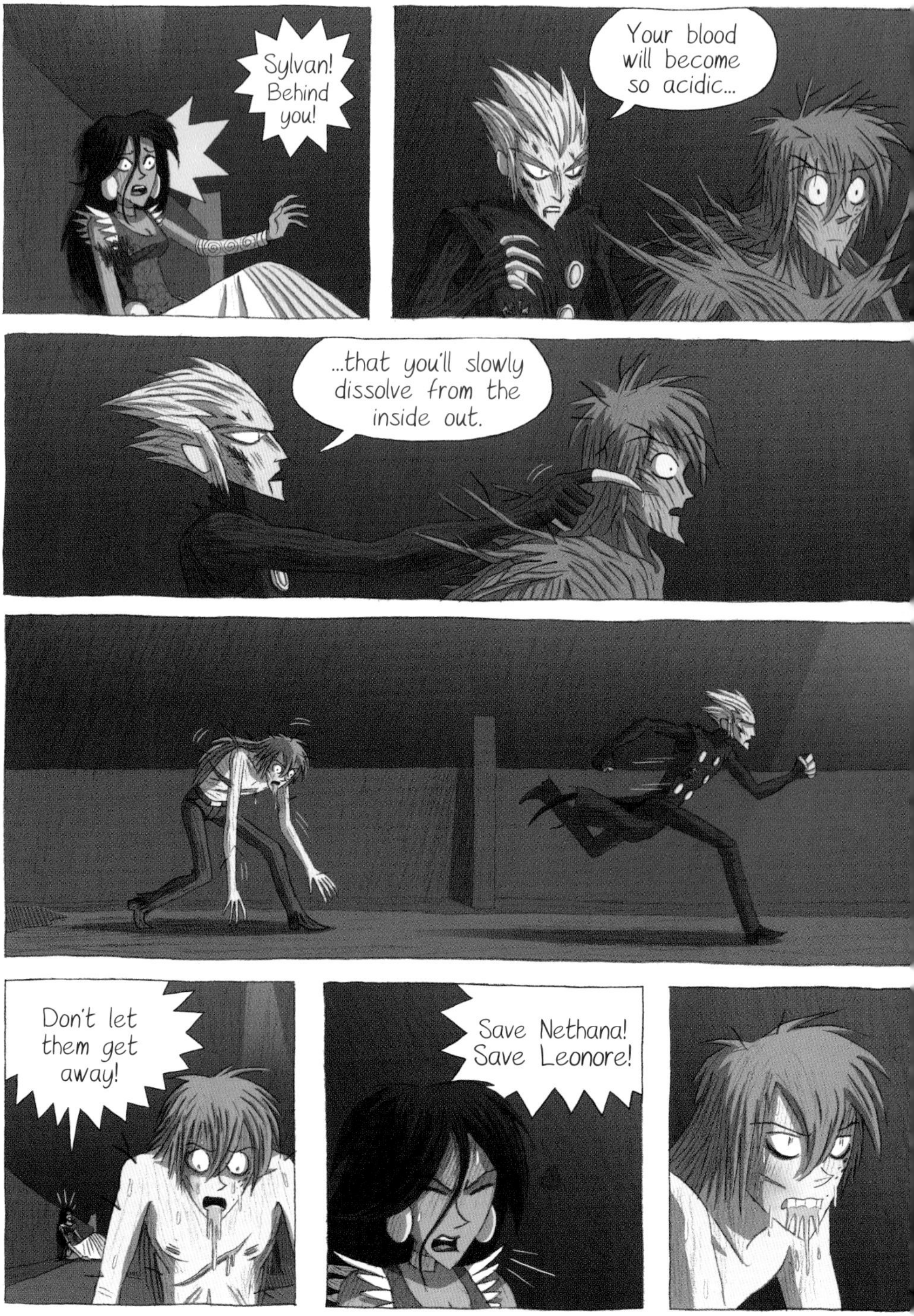
Sylvan! Behind you!
Your blood will become so acidic...
...that you'll slowly dissolve from the inside out.
Don't let them get away!
Save Nethana! Save Leonore!

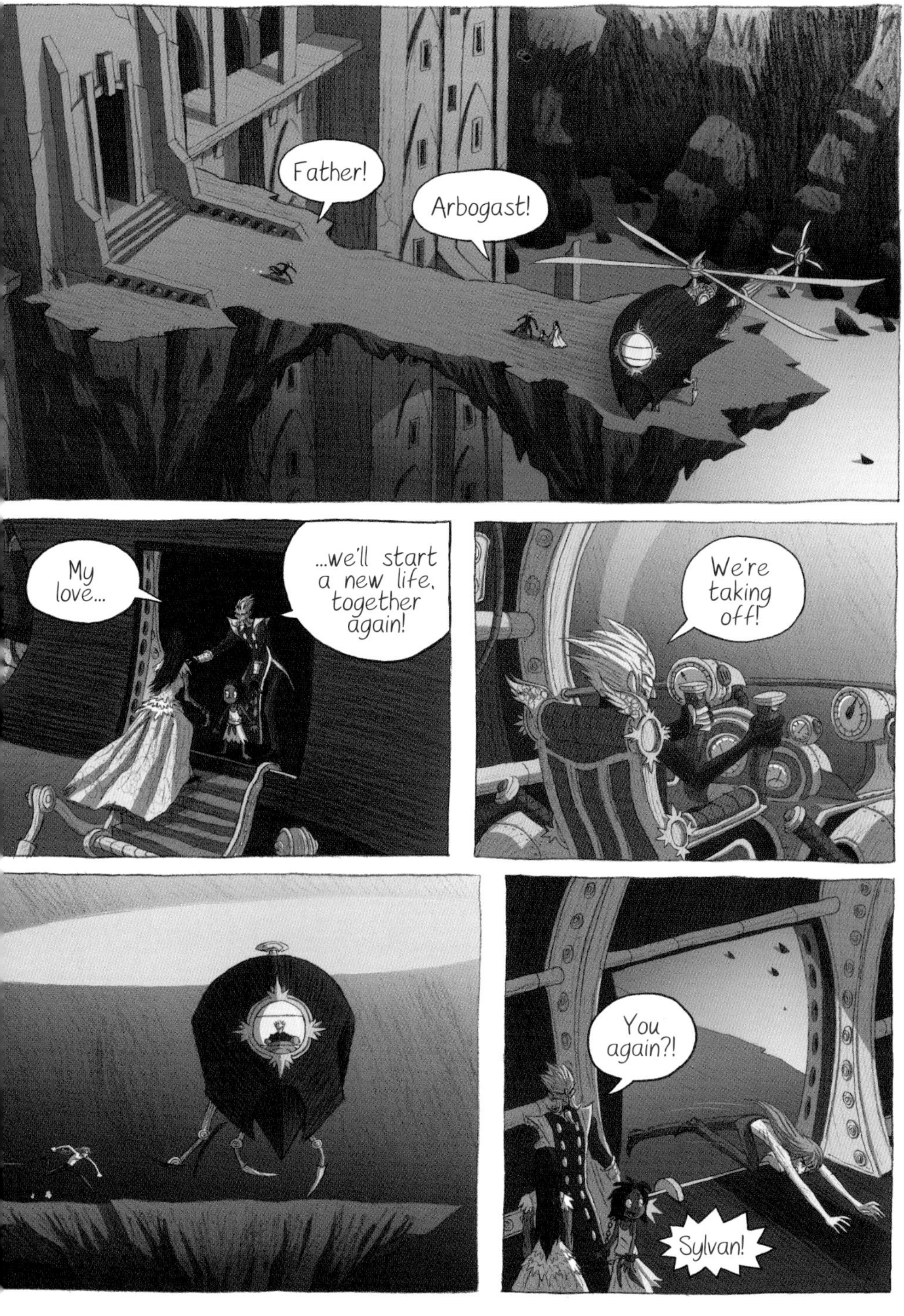
Father!
Arbogast!
My love...
...we'll start a new life, together again!
We're taking off!
You again?!
Sylvan!

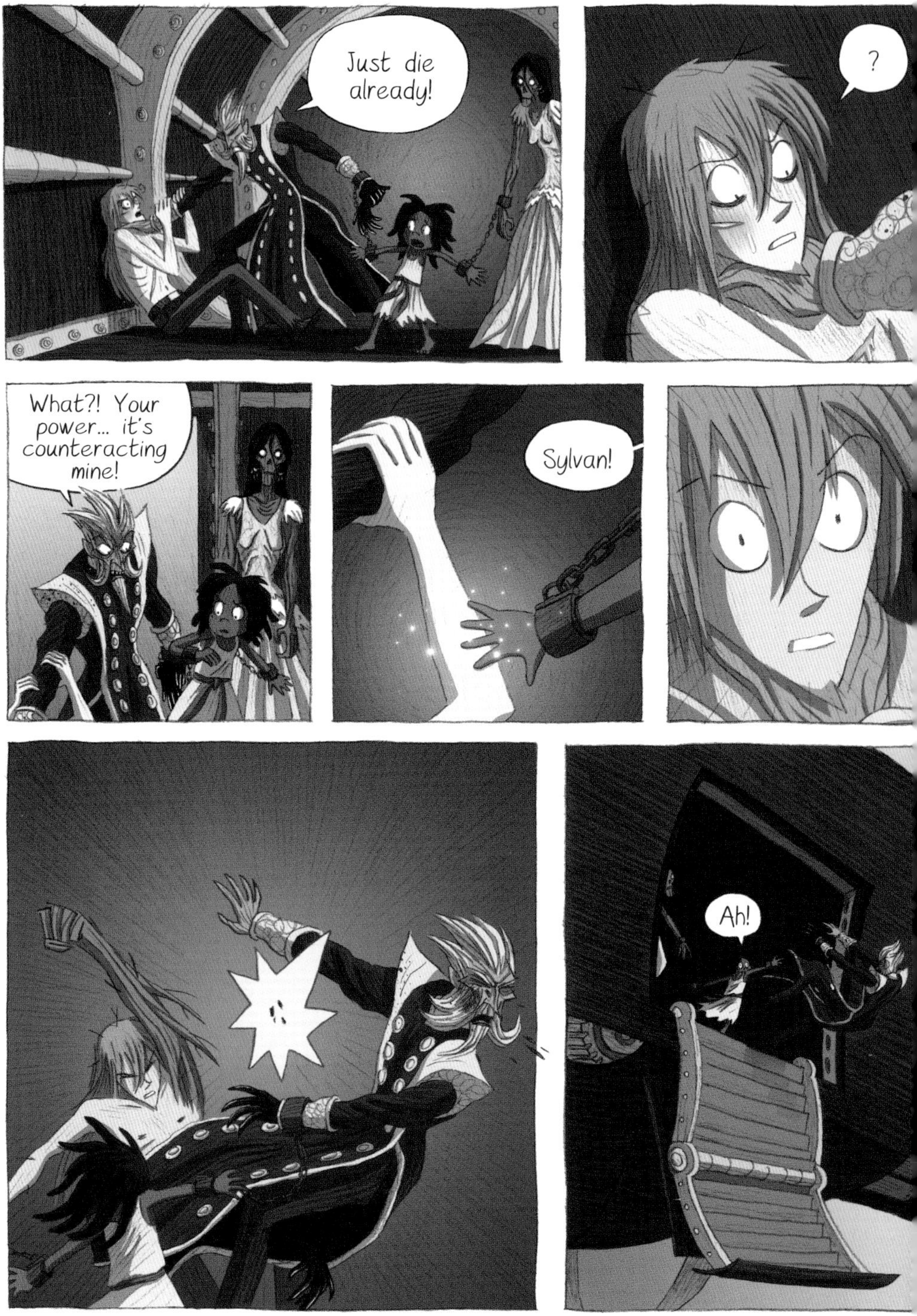
Just die already!
?
What?! Your power... it's counteracting mine!
Sylvan!
Ah!

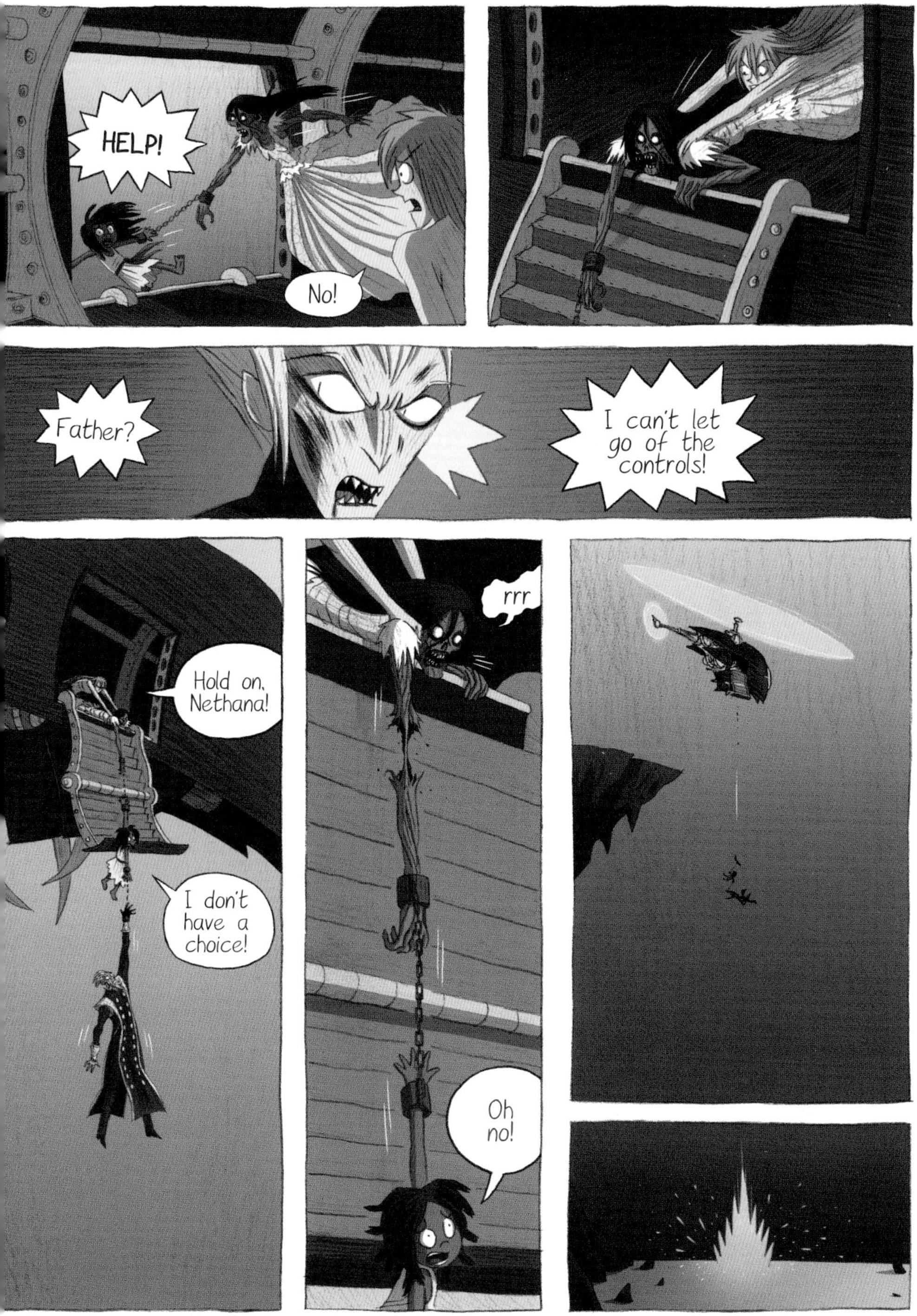
HELP!
No!
Father?
I can't let go of the controls!
Hold on, Nethana!
I don't have a choice!
rrr
Oh no!

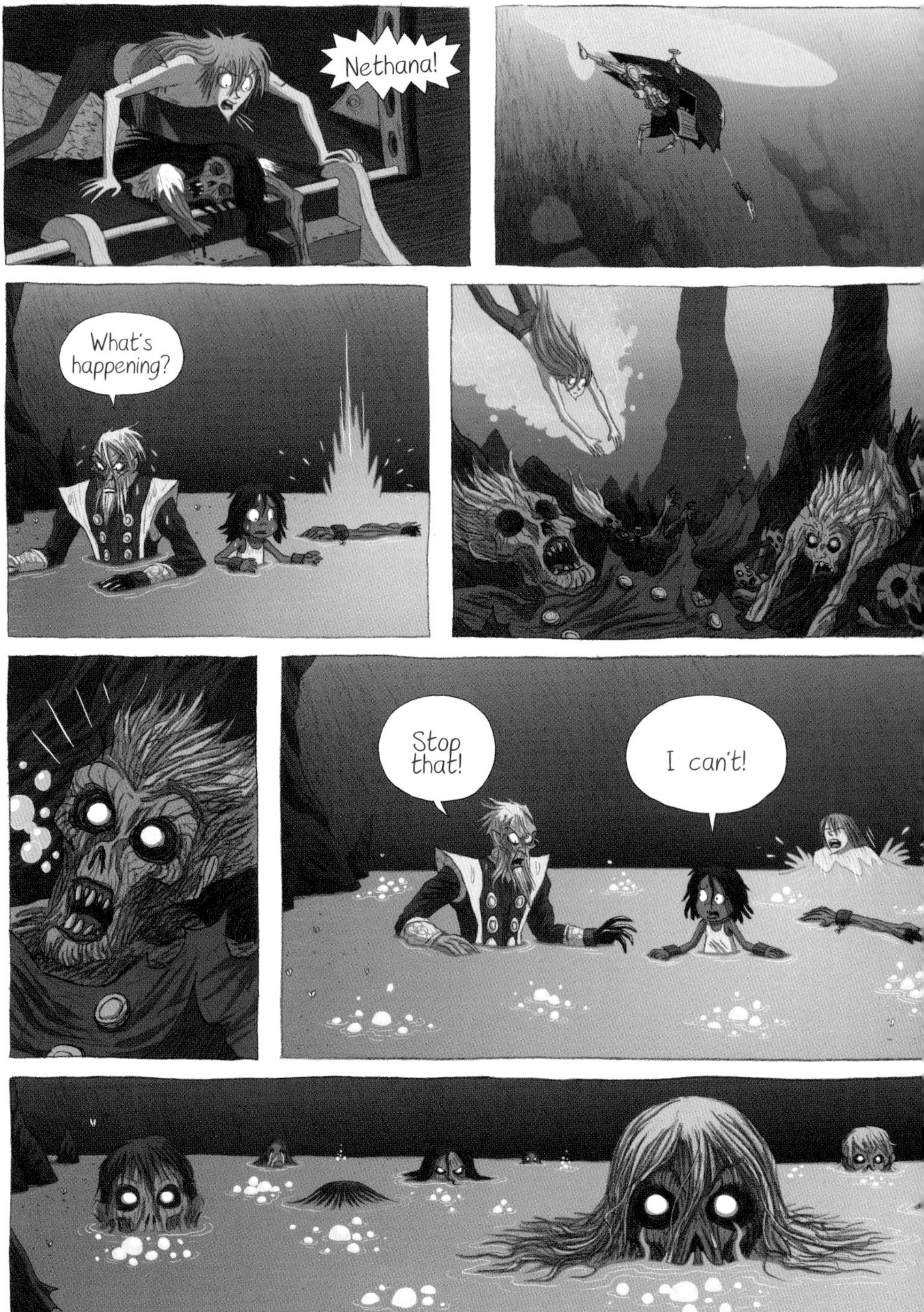
Nethana!
What's happening?
Stop that!
I can't!

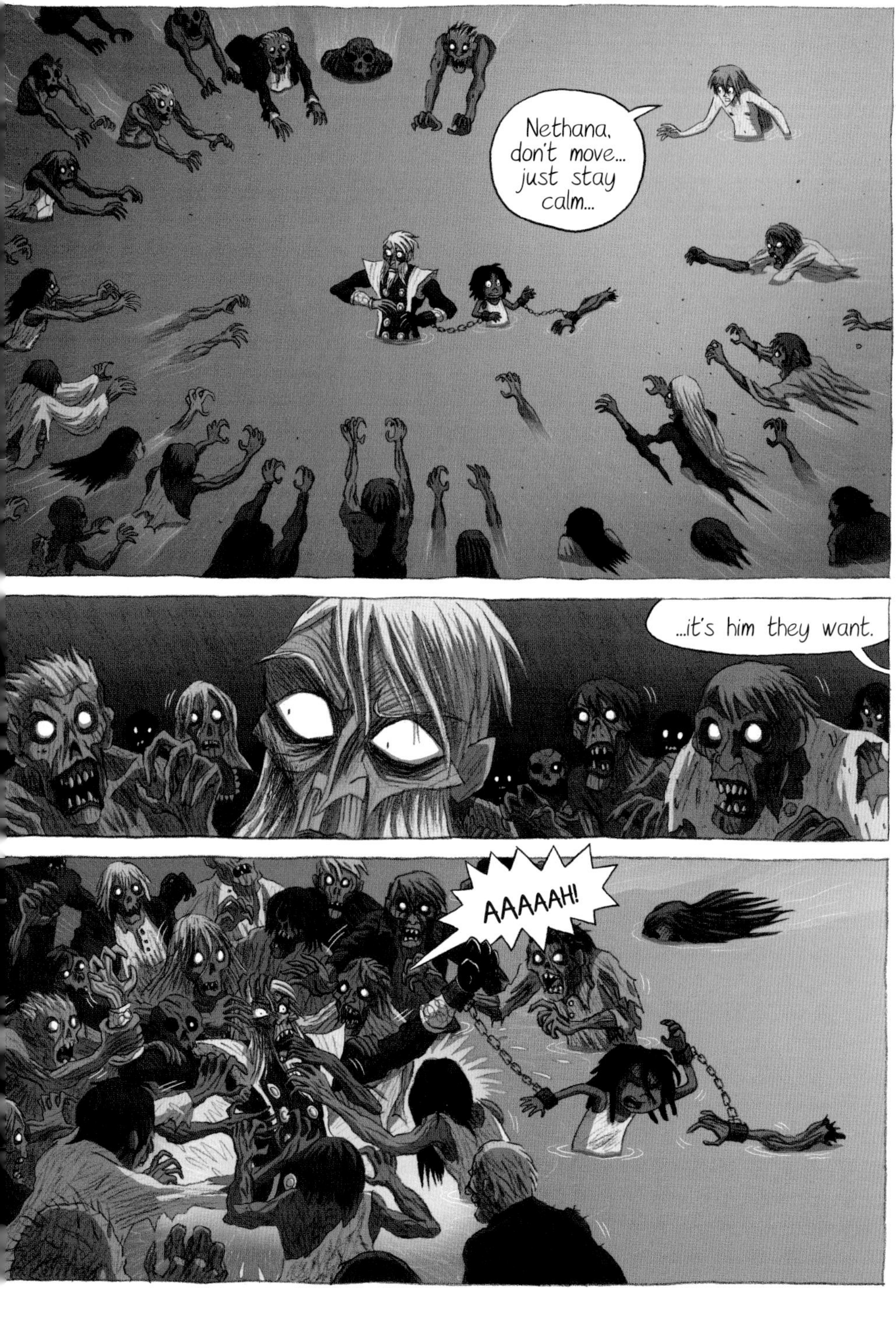
Nethana, don't move... just stay calm...
...it's him they want.
AAAAAH!

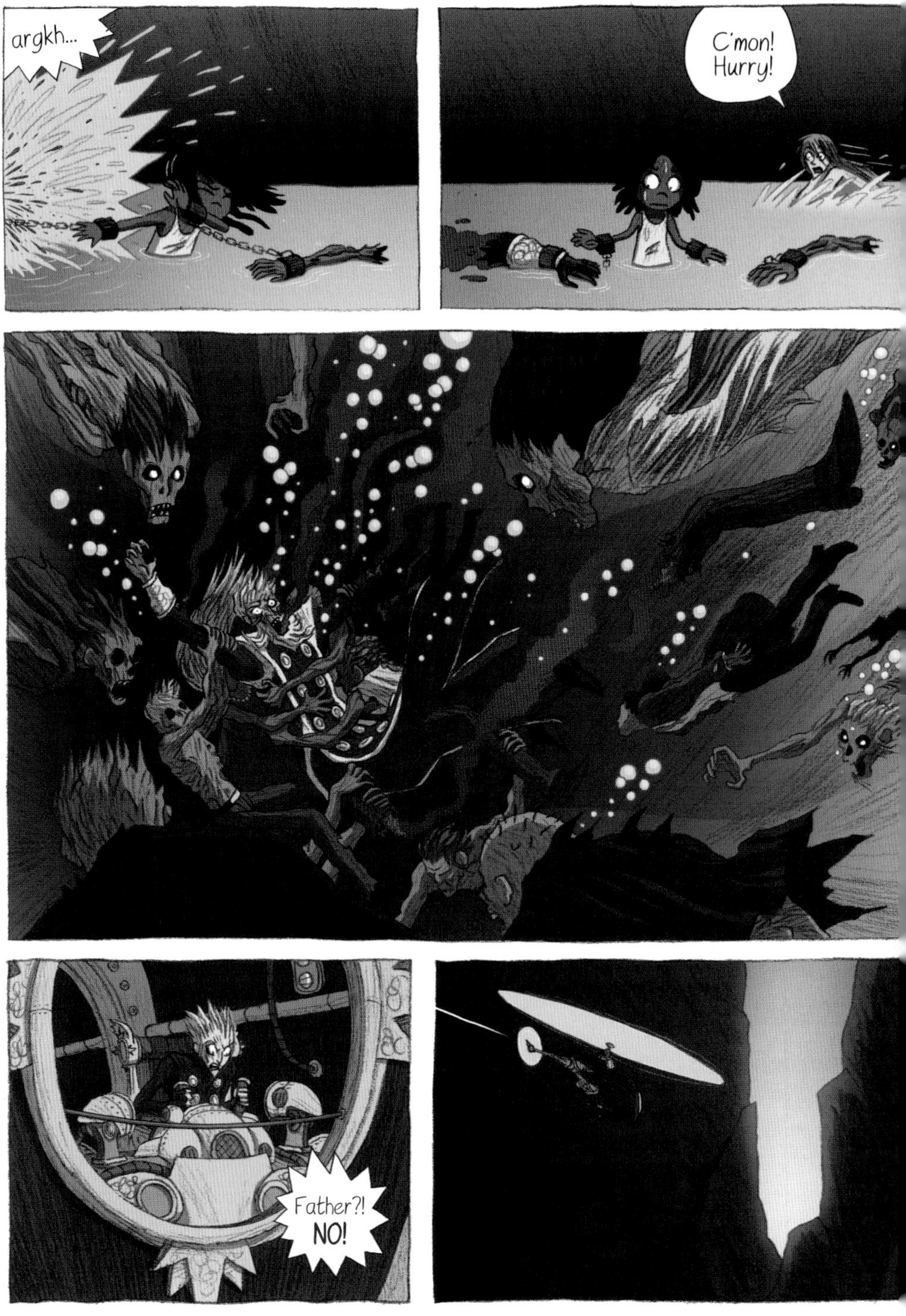
argkh...
C'mon! Hurry!
Father?! NO!

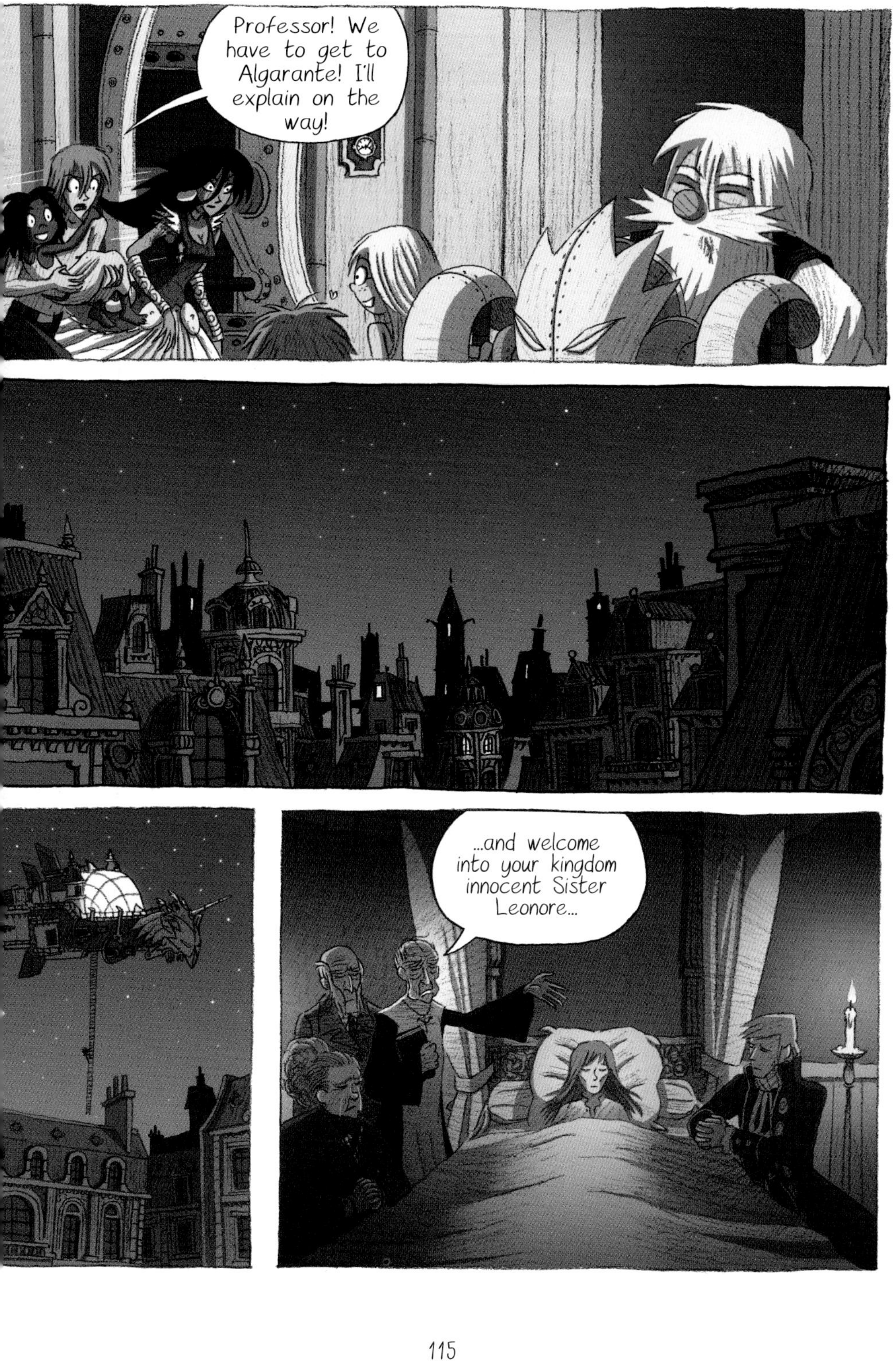
Professor! We have to get to Algarante! I'll explain on the way!
...and welcome into your kingdom innocent Sister Leonore...

Oh, God! What horror is this?!

Leave, monster, or I'll...

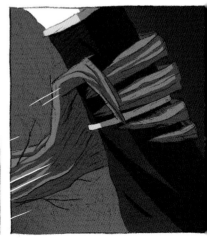

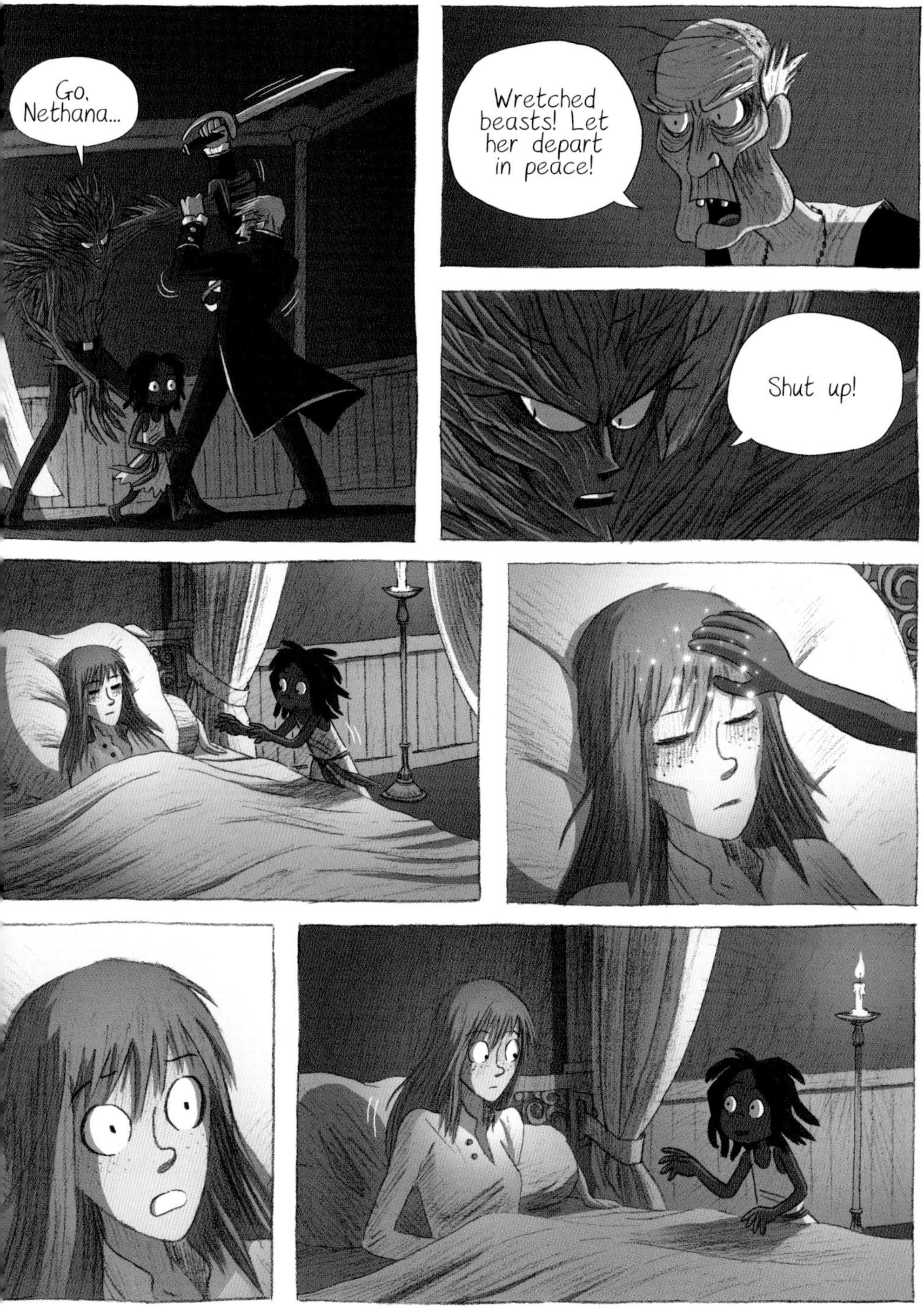
Go, Nethana...
Wretched beasts! Let her depart in peace!
Shut up!

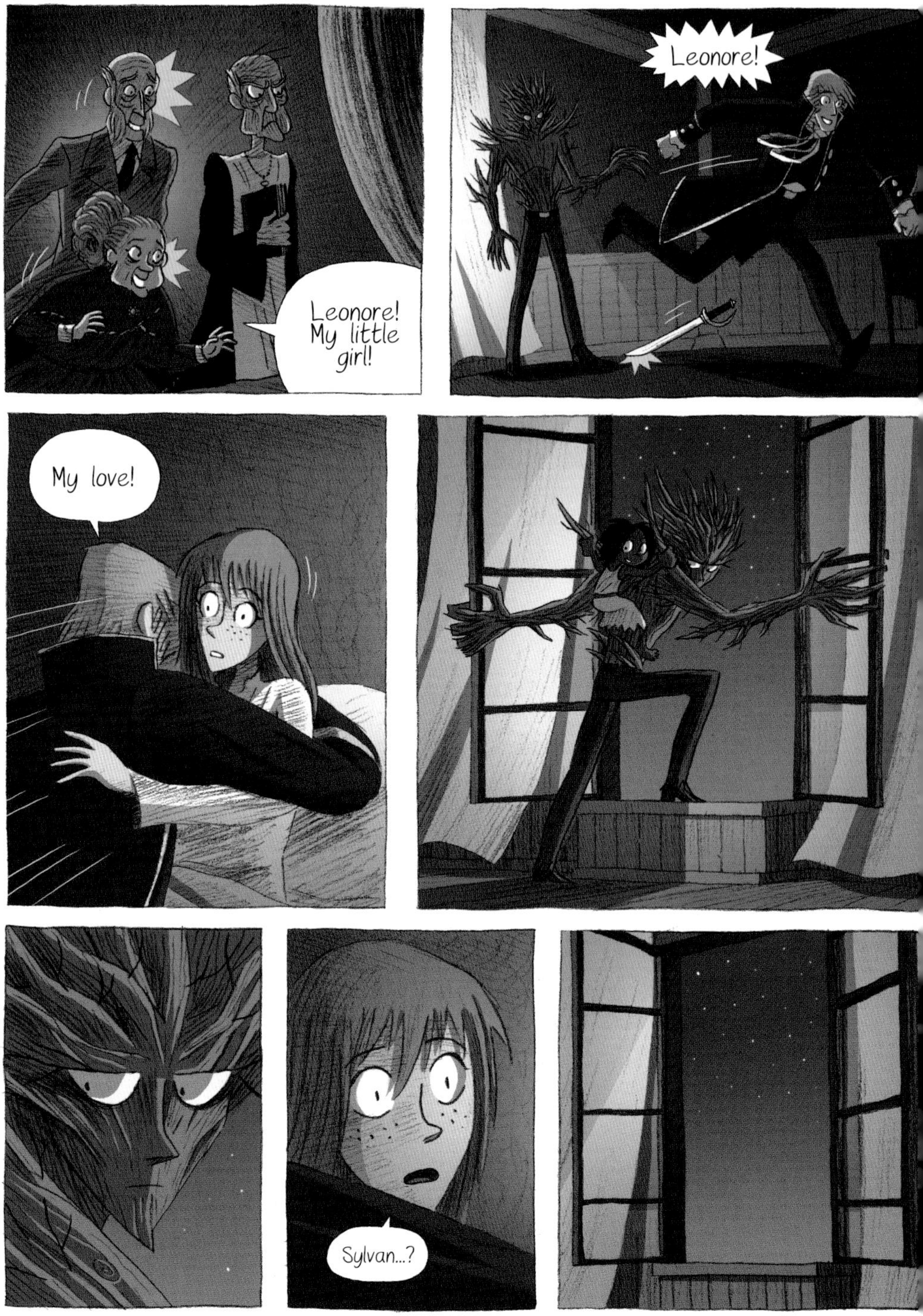
Leonore! My little girl!
Leonore!
My love!
Sylvan...?

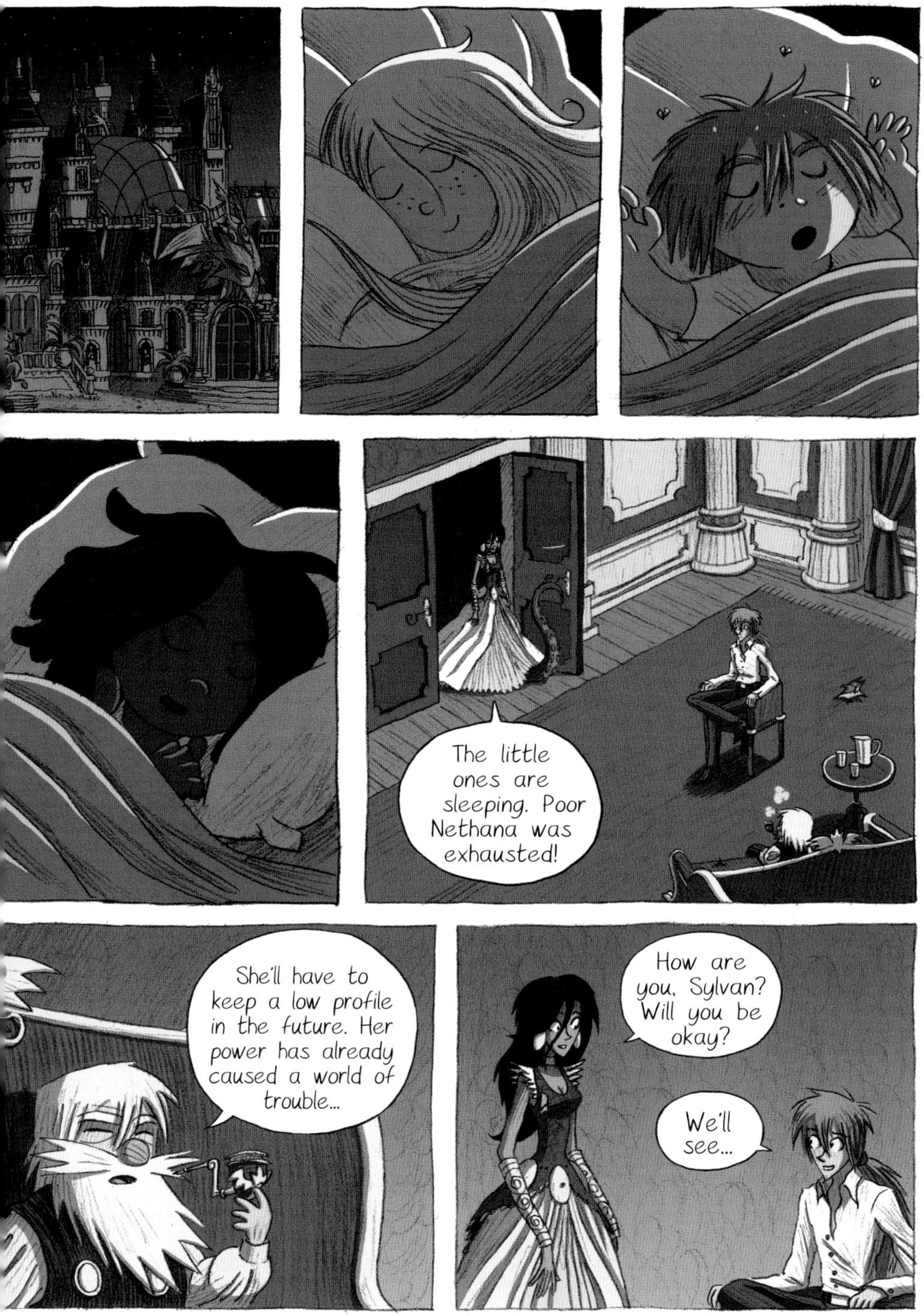
The little ones are sleeping. Poor Nethana was exhausted!
She'll have to keep a low profile in the future. Her power has already caused a world of trouble...
How are you, Sylvan? Will you be okay?
We'll see...

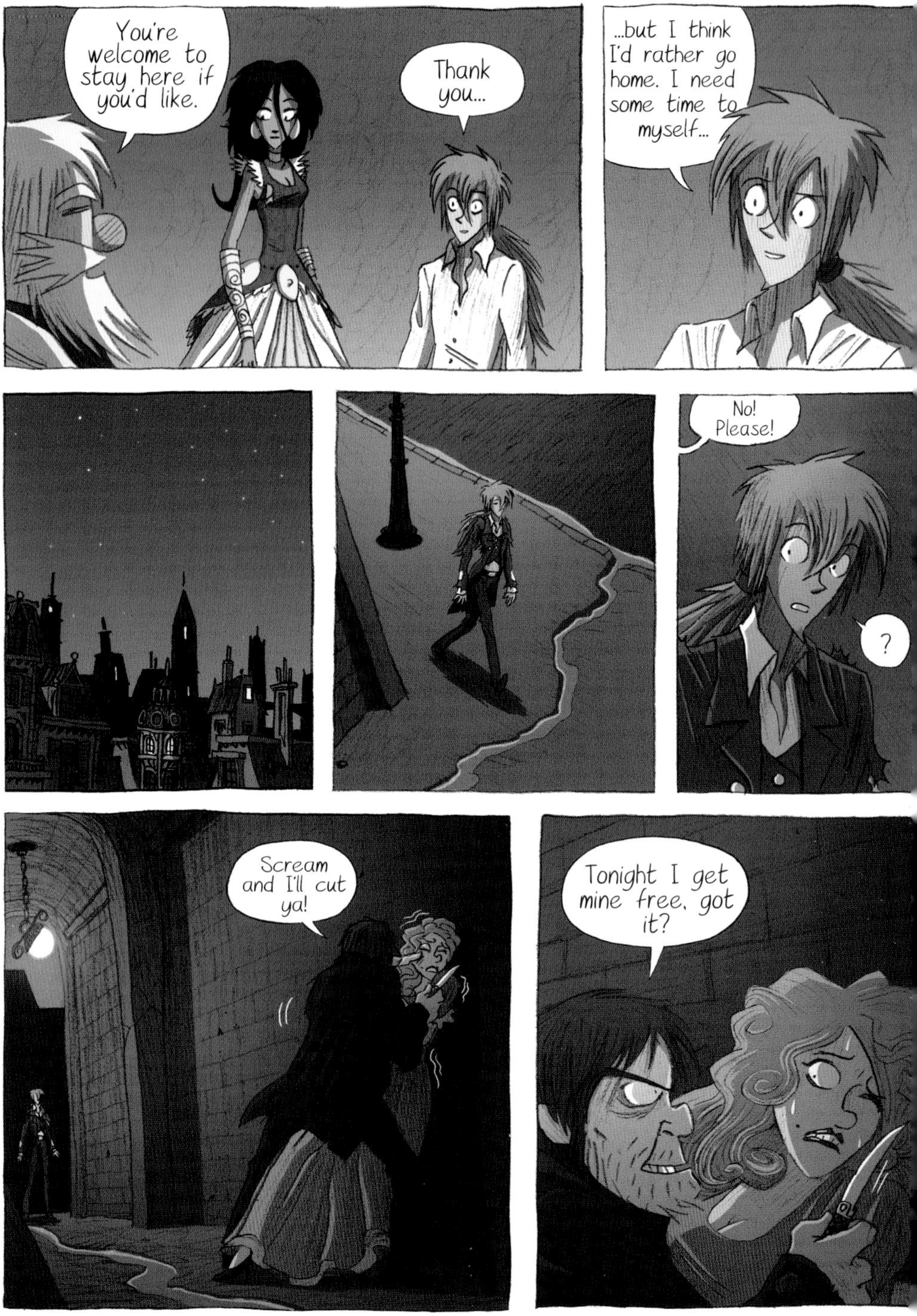
You're welcome to stay here if you'd like.
Thank you...
...but I think I'd rather go home. I need some time to myself...
No! Please!
?
Scream and I'll cut ya!
Tonight I get mine free, got it?

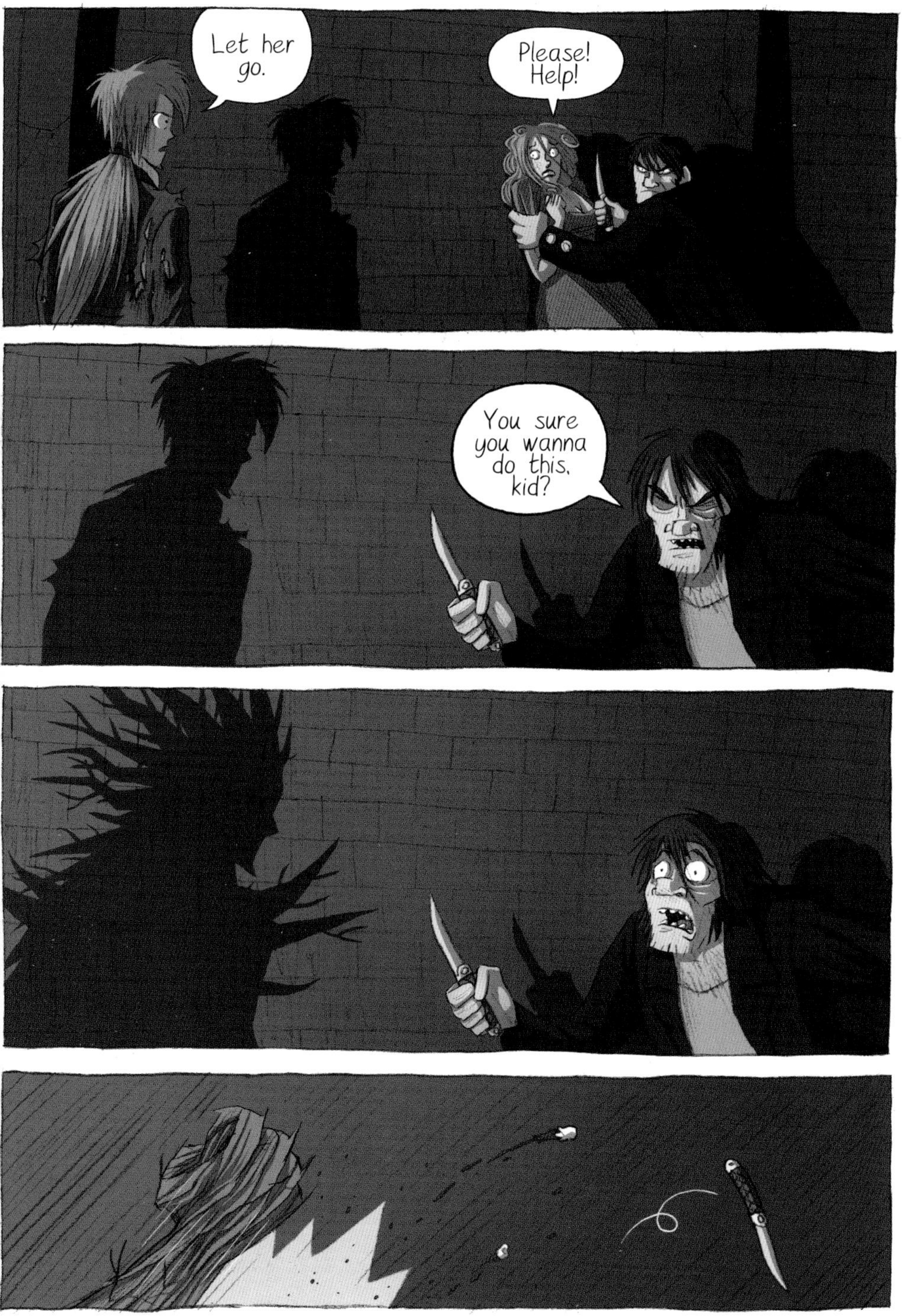
Let her go.
Please! Help!
You sure you wanna do this, kid?

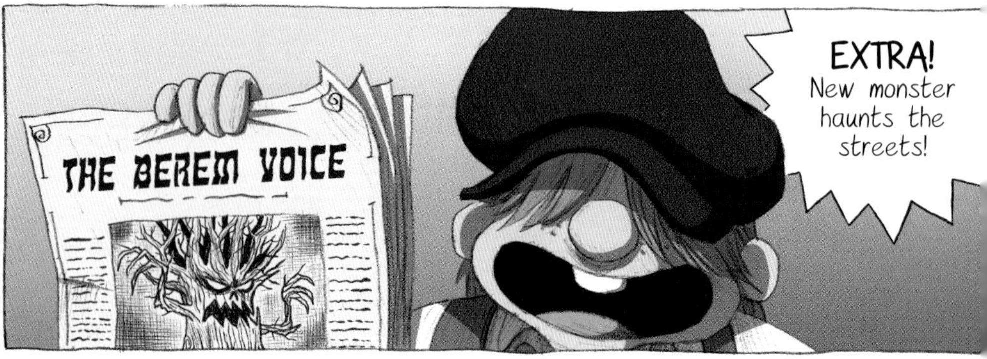
THE BEREM VOICE
EXTRA! New monster haunts the streets!

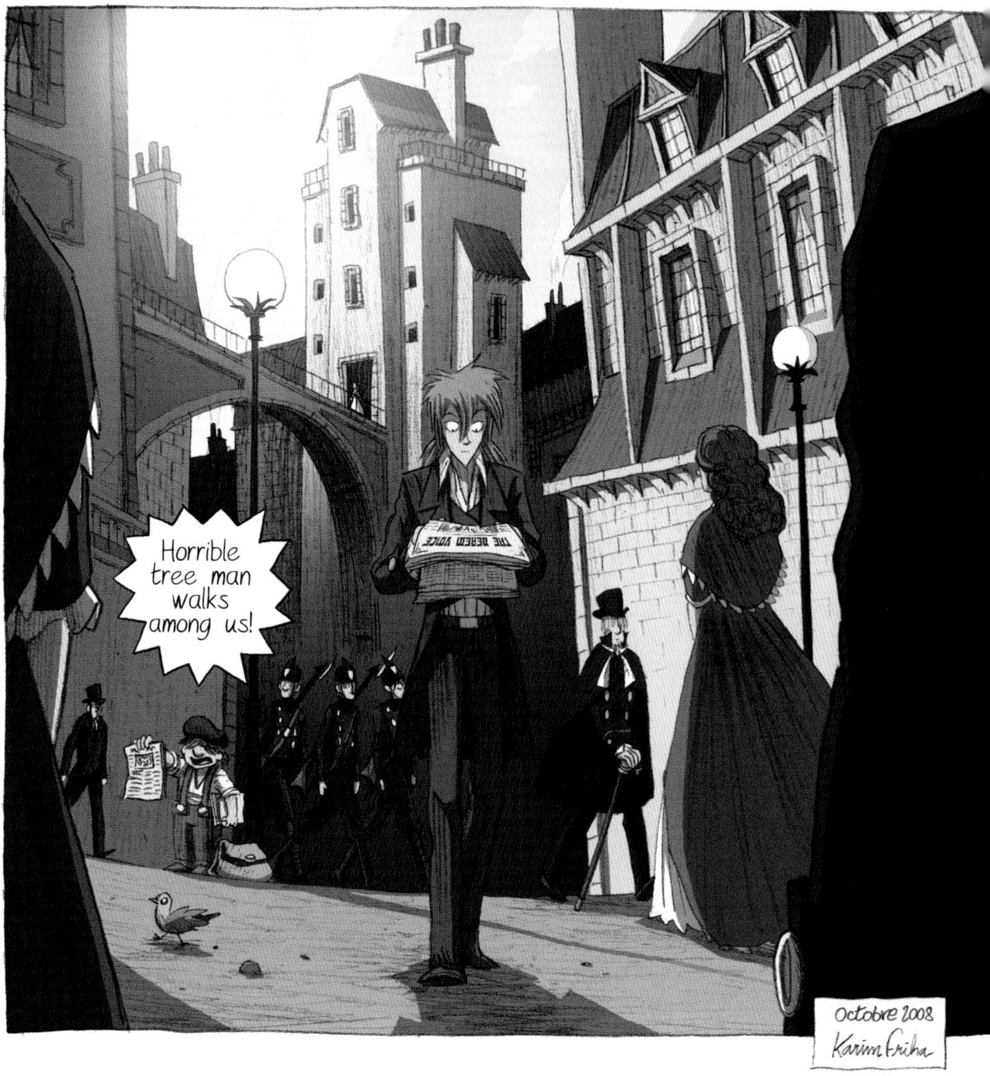
THE BEREM VOICE
Horrible tree man walks among us!
Octobre 2008
Karim Friha

Wernes versus the ogre

Wernes versus the sea serpent of the Sira Quon-ra Archipelago

Wernes, by Munet

ABOUT THE AUTHOR

 Karim Friha was born in Maisons-Laffitte, France, in 1980. As a child, he took a liking to comics with the Franco-Belgian classics, most notably *Asterix* and *Gaston Lagaffe*. After receiving his bachelors degree in science, he studied math but ended up drawing far more than anything else, enjoying the history of art more than trigonometry. While he became passionate about the artistic period of the eighteenth and nineteenth centuries, particularly the works of Voltaire and Victor Hugo, that didn't keep him from enjoying *The Simpsons*, *Calvin and Hobbes*, the works of Tim Burton, *Batman*, and a whole host of other superhero stories. Eventually, his art allowed him to work on kids' magazines and several animated films. *Rise of the Zelphire* is his first graphic novel series, showcasing his great talent for both storytelling and sequential art. It was an official selection of the 2010 Angoulême International Comics Festival and has been translated into several languages since.